Brides of the Roaring Twenties

Finding husbands in Hollywood!

Helen and Shirley are looking for a fresh start, and the bright lights of Hollywood beckon.

They thought they'd left scandal behind them, but find plenty more adventure awaits them among the speakeasies, starlets and the silver screen.

What they need are two handsome Hollywood bachelors to guide them through this dazzling new world—and down the aisle?

Read Helen's story in

Baby on His Hollywood Doorstep

And look out for Shirley's story

Coming soon!

D1366673

Author Note

When given the option, I regularly choose books over movies; however, there truly is nothing like becoming engrossed in a movie while digging into a big container of warm buttered popcorn. It's a pastime that formed solid roots during the 1920s and is still going strong today. The Roaring Twenties was a fascinating time for America and a time of great change around the world. Economies were thriving, cities were booming and industries were blossoming—including the movie industry. Americans had more leisure time than ever before and quickly fell in love with going to the movies. Stars of black-and-white films became household names as theaters popped up across the nation. By the end of the decade, movies had sound, color and even an array of special effects—not as we know them today, but each was a huge advance in its own right.

The movie industry gave us something else—a place for young couples to go on dates. That's where I went on my first date. Not with my hubby. He took me horseback riding. Stole my heart right then and there.

In this story, Jack and Helen don't go to the movies on their first date, either. Jack is the owner of Star's Studio, and he has put his heart, soul and pocketbook into making his next movie. And Helen, well, she's the woman who drops a baby off on his doorstep.

I hope you enjoy their story, and their trials and errors as they journey to their happily-ever-after.

LAURI ROBINSON

—

Baby on His Hollywood Doorstep

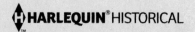

HARLEQUIN® HISTORICAL

Recycling programs
for this product may
not exist in your area.

ISBN-13: 978-1-335-63512-9

Baby on His Hollywood Doorstep

Copyright © 2019 by Lauri Robinson

Printed in U.S.A.

A lover of fairy tales and cowboy boots, **Lauri Robinson** can't imagine a better profession than penning happily-ever-after stories about men and women who pull on a pair of boots before riding off into the sunset...or kick them off for other reasons. Lauri and her husband raised three sons in their rural Minnesota home and are now getting their just rewards by spoiling their grandchildren.

Visit her at laurirobinson.blogspot.com, Facebook.com/lauri.robinson1 or Twitter.com/laurir.

Books by Lauri Robinson

Harlequin Historical

Western Spring Weddings
"When a Cowboy Says I Do"
Her Cheyenne Warrior
Unwrapping the Rancher's Secret
The Cowboy's Orphan Bride
Western Christmas Brides
"A Bride and Baby for Christmas"
Married to Claim the Rancher's Heir
Diary of a War Bride

Oak Grove

Mail-Order Brides of Oak Grove
"Surprise Bride for the Cowboy"
Winning the Mail-Order Bride
In the Sheriff's Protection

Brides of the Roaring Twenties

Baby on His Hollywood Doorstep

Visit the Author Profile page
at Harlequin.com for more titles.

To my only sister, Cheri. An amazing woman.

Prologue

Chicago, Illinois, 1925

She'd done it!

Helen Hathaway pinched the clasp on her purse, making sure it was securely closed. It was only a piece of paper, but that secretarial course certificate meant far more to her. It was her future.

She already had a job!

Would start tomorrow.

The happiness of her accomplishment was overshadowed by worry of what her father would say about it all. She pressed a hand to her churning stomach while glancing at the back of his head in front of her. He was driving, her brother sitting next to him. The two of them were laughing about something. She hadn't heard what. Hadn't been paying attention.

Her mind was on that certificate in her purse.

She glanced at her mother, sitting next to her in the backseat. Mother was the only one who knew she'd taken the secretarial course. Who knew she wanted a job outside of the family business. One that would eventually get her out of Chicago.

Far. Far away.

A hint of guilt tickled Helen's stomach. Not even Mother knew how far away she wanted to get.

Offering her one of her secretive smiles, Mother nodded. "Ray," she said while smoothing the cuff of the pink glove on her wrist. "Helen has something to celebrate tonight, too."

"She does?" Father answered.

A ripple of excitement shot through Helen at the sound of enthusiasm in his voice. She bit back a smile, but it was to no avail. She couldn't keep it hidden.

Mother nodded again, and glanced toward the front seat.

"Yes," Helen said. "I got a job today."

"A job?" Junior, her brother twisted and lifted a dark brow as he looked at her over the seat. "Doing what?"

He was only three years older than her, had just turned twenty last month, but acted far older and far more superior. As most of the men she knew did.

She lifted her head and looked him in the eye. "Typing."

He rolled his eyes. "Typing what? Where?"

"Helen completed a secretarial course, and today Mr. Stamper offered her a job at the laundry," Mother said, giving Junior an eye that told him to keep any comments to himself. "It's only a couple blocks away from the house, and will be something to keep her busy."

The smile tried to slip off Helen's face, but she wouldn't let it. Not while Junior was still looking at her. This job would do more than keep her busy, she'd show him. Show all of them.

Junior snorted, and then turned around as father pulled the car into the lot near the restaurant. It was her uncle's birthday. A big celebration. It was the first one like this that she'd been allowed to attend. She wasn't overly excited about that. The less she had to do with the family, the more she liked it, but she was excited about her new dress. White with green stripes. The weather was warm, so she wasn't wearing a jacket, but did have on a pair of pristine white gloves and matching shoes. Mother had helped her pick out the outfit and she would wear it again tomorrow, to her first day of work.

That's what she was really excited for.

Father kissed her cheek as she climbed out of the car. "You want to work at the laundry?" he asked.

Fearful that he'd deny her this, she nodded. "Yes, I do. Very much."

He smiled and nodded. "All right, then."

Happiness fully engulfed her. She wrapped her arms around him. "Thank you. Thank you."

He gave her a tight squeeze and then let her go to take ahold of Mother's arm. Junior walked beside her as they all headed toward the restaurant. Junior gave her a questioning look, but she kept her eyes forward. It wasn't that she didn't love her parents and her brother, she just didn't like who they were. Who she was. Now that she fully understood. The truth hadn't shocked her, she'd always known they were different, that her father and brother didn't have normal jobs.

They were part of the Outfit. All of them. Her parents. Junior. Her. They were one of many families who lived two lives. An outside one, and an inside one.

The noise inside the restaurant filtered out as Father opened the door and Junior held it as they all stepped inside. It was wall-to-wall people. Her uncle Vinnie, a formidable figure, stood on the far side of the room, surrounded by others, and waved at them as they entered.

Mother took ahold of her arm. "Let's go to the powder room while the men get a drink."

Helen caught glimpses of people she'd known her entire life, cousins, aunts and uncles as she followed her mother around tables and chairs toward the hallway at the back of the building. Most of them weren't blood relatives, but were referred to as *family* because they were all part of the Outfit. Helen wondered if any of the others thought like her. Wanted out of this life before it was too late. That had resonated deep inside her when her cousin Amelia had been mugged by a member of the North End Gang.

More than mugged.

Mother stopped to visit, talking about the new dress she was wearing, and Helen, espying her cousin Karen, kept walking toward the hallway.

"Isn't this exciting?" Karen asked, clapping her hands with glee. "Your first grown-up party?"

Helen nodded, but kept her honest opinion about that to herself. "I got a job," she whispered instead.

Karen frowned. "Why?"

Helen open her mouth to reply, but chaos struck just then. It was a moment before she realized what was happening. That the earsplitting *rat-a-tat* sound was gunfire. Tommy guns. Bullets were flying, glass shattering and people screaming, running, falling.

"Run!"

Someone grabbed her arm, she tried to shake it off, searching for her family, but there were too many people. Too many bullets.

Chapter One

California, 1927

Helen tucked her chin into her neck in order to see over the top of her glasses and get a clear look at the building out of the car window. It wasn't tall like the hundreds, maybe thousands they'd driven past, nor was it made of bricks or stone like so many of the ones that had taken up miles upon miles of the streets of Los Angeles. The city was larger than she'd imagined. That unsettled her and she hugged the baby sleeping in her arms a bit tighter while attempting to swallow the lump in her throat.

Made of wood, the building sprawled out along the street rather than upward like those downtown, and there were few windows, almost as if they didn't want people looking inside. Several tall palm trees grew next to the building, and she had to wonder how trees could grow amongst so much concrete and traffic.

"This is the address, ma'am," the driver repeated.

The streetcars didn't come this far out, which is why she'd had to hire a taxi, yet there was plenty of traffic

traveling up the road toward a gigantic white sign up
on the hill. HOLLYWOODLAND.

Drawing in a deep breath, Helen held it until her
lungs burned. She checked the knot of the scarf tied
beneath her chin, making sure it was tight, then picked
up her purse and twisted to step out of the car without juggling Grace too much. Once on the curb, she
shifted the baby farther into the crook of her arm in
order to slip her purse onto her wrist under the baby
so she could take the small suitcase the driver was
fetching out of the black-and-green-checkered cab.
That suitcase held all of her earthly possessions as
well as Grace's. A shiver rippled her insides, once
again making her wonder if she could do this; yet she
knew she had to.

"Would you like me to carry this inside for you,
ma'am?"

Every nerve in her body was trembling. "No. No.
Thank you." Helen reached out, took the hard-sided
case. "Thank you again for the ride."

"You're welcome, ma'am, and good luck to you."
He climbed back in the taxicab and pulled away from
the curb.

A horn honked as the taxi cut into the traffic and
Helen's stomach sank. Not in criticism of his skills,
but at the departure itself. She was here. In California. Taking the last steps of the journey she and Grace
had traveled. Once again, as she had a million times
already, she wished there was another choice.

There wasn't.

Her throat swelled up. Grace was such a good baby.
Had barely fussed the entire train ride. Only whim-
pered a bit when she'd been hungry or needed a dia-

per change. She was adorable too, with her soft fuzzy blond hair and big dark eyes. The wave of sadness that engulfed Helen made her eyes sting.

She approached the building with caution at first but, remembering that Grace would soon need to be fed, her footsteps grew more purposeful.

It seemed odd that the address was for this—a building rather than a residence, a house or an apartment. But this is where Vera had mailed the letters to, so this is where they'd traveled to. She and Grace. All the way from Chicago.

At the door, Helen paused. *Star's Studio* was painted on the glass in sparkling gold paint. She had no idea what that would mean for Grace, and had to hope it would be good.

She took another deep breath and grasped the handle.

The door wouldn't budge.

She tried again. Jiggled the door.

It was locked. Locked. In the middle of the day.

She peered through the window, but it was too dark inside to see anything.

Flustered she stepped back and glanced down at Grace. The baby was still sleeping, yet Helen whispered, "Don't worry, I won't just leave you on the doorstep."

She wouldn't, but she had prepared herself for this moment—the time where she would turn Grace over and walk away. It was going to break her heart, but the alternative was worse.

The pain of losing her entire family in the raid by the North End Gang on the restaurant two years ago still lived inside her, as did watching Vera die only a few months ago. Pain like that was crippling, but she'd lived through it, and would this, too. Grace's safety was far more important than anything else.

"If I could keep you, I would," she whispered to Grace. "But I can't. You'll never be safe with me. Never."

"Mr. McCarney isn't booking any auditions right now."

Helen spun around and had to squint through the glasses she'd taken to wearing two years ago. They were part of her disguise, as was the dull baggy dress. Through the blur of the magnified glasses she didn't need, she made out a woman walking toward her. She was dressed in a sleek, hip-hugging black-and-white-striped dress, complete with matching head scarf tied on the side, and shoes that clicked against the concrete sidewalk.

Another immense wave of everything from heartbreak to fear washed over Helen. "Mr. McCarney is here?" She glanced at the door. "Inside the building?"

The woman stopped next to the door and frowned as her overly long and hard appraisal went from Helen's toes to the top of her head before it settled on Grace. "Yes, he's here, but he's not taking auditions." The woman inserted a key in the door.

It took Helen a moment to find her voice. "I'm not here for an audition. I just—"

"Whatever you are here for, Mr. McCarney cannot be disturbed." The woman pulled the door open. "By anyone."

Despite the way her heart was breaking and her eyes burning, Helen knew she had to act now, or never might.

"Here," she said, handing Grace to the woman.

Startled, the woman jostled slightly, but took Grace. Hurrying before she changed her mind, Helen set the suitcase on the ground and snapped it open. She pulled out the flour sack she'd filled with all of Grace's things as the train had pulled into Los Angeles this morning. Then she reached in her purse and pulled out the bottle full of milk.

Since the woman's hands were full, Helen set the bag inside the door. Her throat was on fire and she had to fight hard to keep herself from crying. "Her clothes and diapers are in here, and another bottle and cans of milk."

"What? What are you doing?"

Helen could no longer hold back the tears. They burned her cheeks as she set the bottle full of milk on Grace's stomach and kissed her soft head one last time. "Her name is Grace and she's a good baby." Sobs were stealing her breath away. "A—a very good baby."

"What? No. Take her back!"

The woman held Grace out, but Helen backed away. The pain inside her was so strong. Her heart was truly breaking in two. She shook her head. "She needs her father."

"I'm not her father!" the woman said.

Helen grabbed the suitcase off the ground. "Mr. McCarney is." She couldn't see through the blur of tears, but she had to get away, so she ran. Ran. Like she had that night back in Chicago, when tommy guns had been spitting out bullets all around her.

It wasn't just accomplishment or relief, it was knowing this was some of his best work that had Jack

McCarney finally returning to his office from the production lot, throwing down the stack of paper in his arms onto the desk and stretching his hands over his head and popping his knuckles. The last three days had been a hellish race against the clock. Locked in a tiny room at the back of the lot, with his director for almost every single minute of them, they'd finally hashed out the script changes needed to make this film the best it could be.

He loathed script changes as much as he loathed actor changes. But he'd be the first to admit, it would have been impossible to film the script the way it had been originally written. This new version, the reason he'd barely left the studio for over fifty hours, would take Hollywood by a storm.

It was good. Damn good. He'd worked with Malcolm Boyd before, and though the actor wasn't as well-known as who he'd originally cast to play the role of Walter Reeves, Boyd was now a good fit for Reeves and would play the role to a T with Wes Jenkins as the perfect supporting actor.

Full of exhilaration Jack leaned forward and slapped his desk. This was it. His big chance. He couldn't wait to start filming.

He couldn't wait to eat something, either. His ribs were damn near poking out of his shirt.

Jack glanced at his watch, checking to make sure Julia's diner was still open. She hated Hollywood and everything about it, mainly because of the way Bart Broadbent had swindled her family out of several hundred acres of land. Julia had tried, but couldn't get the land back. Bart had already sold it to the folks building Hollywoodland. Fancy houses that only the rich and famous could afford. Julia held on to the last few acres of her land with an iron fist, and was making a nice bundle of cash for herself in the process. Her diner had the best food in the neighborhood. Perhaps the city.

He felt bad that Julia's family had gotten sucked in, but Bart had been known as a dew dropper. The whole lot of Broadbents had been four-flushers, mooching off everyone and anyone.

Recognizing that long ago, Jack had steered clear of Bart and the rest of the Broadbents. He'd warned his brother to steer clear of them too, but like most every other time he'd warned him of something, Joe hadn't listened. Right before leaving, he'd borrowed money from the Broadbents against his shares in the studio.

Frustration washed over Jack as he pushed away from his desk. The Broadbents had been hounding him, wanting to increase their dividends, ever since Joe left.

He refused, but did send them monthly payments, cleaning up yet another mess that Joe had left behind, because that's what he'd always done. Cleaned up after Joe.

If his brother hadn't been such a windsucker, things would be different right now. But that wouldn't have been Joe. He'd thought he was too big to go down. Too high above the rest. Joe had always thought like that, despite the fact that that had never been the case. No matter how famous one gets, there's always someone more famous. Richer. With better contacts and contracts.

That was Hollywood, and why you had to be tough to play here.

Joe had been tough, but he'd also been foolish.

Too foolish. That's what had gotten him blacklisted. Banned from ever acting in Hollywood again for immoral conduct.

Jack almost laughed, except it wasn't funny.

Others were just as immoral, but they didn't flaunt it. That's what had brought Joe down, and the reason he'd left. Why he'd been gone for over two years and most likely would never be back.

It hadn't completely stopped Joe. He was still out there, somewhere, flaunting his Hollywood connections and making promises that would never be fulfilled. The steady flow of women contacting the studio was proof of that. Each one claimed Joe had sent them, promising stardom. Riches. Fame.

There was also a bag full of unopened letters from others who hadn't been able to muster up the money to actually make it to Hollywood, but wanted the same promises fulfilled.

After opening the first few letters, Jack had simply given instructions to put any other mail that arrived for Joe in the bag. Shattering the dreams of the ones who walked through the studio door was more than enough to deal with.

With frustration rising, Jack stood up. Scooping up the stack of papers that were full of script changes, Jack carried them out of his office and down the long corridor to the front lobby. Beverly Hobbs had done a fine job of following his orders about not being disturbed the past couple of days, and he hoped she was as good of a typist as she was a gatekeeper.

He pushed open the door to the lobby, but froze in his tracks. Front office girls came and went as fast as actors, and right now, even though she'd been working here for only a week, he needed this one. Therefore, he cautiously asked, "You have a baby?"

"No." She set the bottle on her desk and lifted the infant to her shoulder. "You do."

Shocked, it was a moment before Jack shook his head. "No, I don't."

She stood. "That's not what the woman who dropped this one off said."

Jack backed up, half-afraid she was going to hand him the infant. "What woman?"

"The one who was at the door when I came back from lunch." She pointed to a sack on the desk. "She gave me that bag of diapers and milk and said the baby's name is Grace and that she needs her father. Mr. McCarney."

His blood turned to ice. He'd thought he'd seen it all. Women had tried all sorts of things to catch his attention, to make them stars, but claiming he'd fathered their baby. That was a first. "Where is she now? The woman?"

"Can't say for sure. She took off running like a swarm of bees were chasing her. Last I saw, Julia from across the street ran out to keep her from getting hit." Miss Hobbs shook her head. "Cars were coming from both directions. It was as if she hadn't even seen them."

He should be concerned, ask if the woman had gotten hit, but he wasn't in the mood to be charitable. "Did she go into Julia's diner?"

"I don't know. The phone was ringing. I had a baby in my hands."

She looked thoroughly flustered. He couldn't blame her.

He spun around and headed for the door. "I'll be

right back." Whoever that baby belonged to needed to come and get her. Right now.

"I leave in half an hour."

"I'll be right back," he repeated, almost to the door.

"I have a date!"

"I'll pay you extra," he said, marching out the door. He didn't have time for this kind of baloney. He'd just been given his shot to move Star's Studio up the ladder and wasn't about to let anything get in his way. Nothing at all. No one at all.

There was a break in traffic, so he shot across the street.

Grant Collins and Max Houlihan walked out of the diner just as Jack stepped up on the curb. He'd worked with both of them in the past and would again if the time came around that he needed to fill the roles of unsophisticated rubes. They were slapstick funny when they wanted to be. But right now he didn't have time to listen to them spill.

"Ham's as good as ever," Grant said, gesturing a thumb over his shoulder. "But you best get in there if you want any. Terry Jones is bellied up to the counter."

Terry Jones outweighed all three of them put together and ate as if he was purely dedicated to adding notches to his belt buckle. He was a heavyweight. Had been a boxer at one time, and was now the best set builder in all of Tinseltown.

Jack was no longer hungry, but even in more of a hurry to get inside. "Good to know," he said, stepping around them to enter the diner.

The tables were all full, so were most of the stools that lined the counter. He had no idea what the woman he was looking for might look like, but recognized enough about the people filling the diner to believe none of them were her. He headed toward the counter and the door behind it that led to the kitchen.

"Hey, McCarney," Terry Jones greeted from where he sat on the first stool. Jones popped an entire bun in his mouth. Whole. And swallowed it like a Labrador, one gulp, no chewing.

Jack didn't know if he should nod, or shake his head. Instead of doing either, he grabbed ahold of Rosie's arm, one of the girls who waited tables, as she walked past. "Where's Julia?"

"Where do you think she is?" Rosie nodded her head toward the kitchen door.

He'd never been in the kitchen before. Had never had a reason to go back there, before today.

Greta, the other waitress, walked out the door, and he had to step aside so she had enough room for the laden tray she was carrying. Both she and Rosie had come to him begging for an audition at one time. Joe hadn't sent them. Nor had he sent hundreds of other women. They'd come on their own. The population of LA grew by the thousands every year. People from all walks of life, from all corners of the world, arrived daily, dazzled by the idea of stardom, thinking all they had to do was arrive in Hollywood and all their dreams would come true.

They had reason to believe that might happen. Movie theaters were springing up across the nation, demanding new picture shows daily. Over eight hundred films had been produced last year alone, and more would be this year, giving the public what they were clamoring for. However, it was the magazines and newspapers that suckered people in. They wrote stories of filmmakers on the lookout for talent. Encouraged people to come to LA. Trouble was, those stories were more fictional than the movies being filmed.

He'd long ago grown tired of being the one to shatter the dreams of so many. The truth hurt, and the truth was, moviemaking was a cutthroat industry. Those who were in, were in, those who weren't, weren't, and most likely never would be. A very small percentage of the people who'd come to him truly had the talent they'd need to make it in the film industry. Fewer had the resolve. It wasn't an easy profession, or as glamorous as people thought.

Rosie and Greta had both been upset with him at first, but had gotten over it.

As soon as Greta was out of the way, he pushed open the swinging door of the kitchen.

Julia was at the stove, but it was the woman washing dishes that caught his eye. He didn't recognize her, and would have if he'd ever seen her before. Although partially hidden behind a pair of glasses, she had an extremely unique set of pale blue eyes. So unique they made him wish the ability to film in color had already been perfected. It would be, some day. And eyes like that would stand out on the big screen. Without the glasses, of course.

"Jack, what are you doing back here?"

He pulled his gaze from the woman and turned to where Julia stood near the stove. Dressed as usual in pink from head to toe, except for the black net that held her dark hair back, she frowned at him.

"There was a woman earlier, running across the street," he said. "Do you know where she went?"

Julia's frown increased as she looked at him, then at the woman washing dishes.

A shiver rippled down his spine as he turned in the direction of the sink again. This time he gave her a long appraisal. From the toes of her scuffed brown shoes to the top of her head, where a mass of glistening brown hair was pinned in a soft roll around the base of her head. Except for several corkscrew bangs that hung down and caught on her long eyelashes as she blinked behind those wire-rimmed glasses and settled that unique light blue gaze on him.

Her eyes weren't the only unique, striking thing about her. The shape of her face was perfect, elegant, her poise graceful, and her skin was flawless. Unblemished and not covered with cosmetics. It was creamy and tinged pink naturally in all the right places. Even her lips had a natural shine about them and were perfectly bowed in the center.

Maybe he should audition her. Even with black-and-white filming, those eyes would stand out. All of her would.

He had to shake his head to get his thinking straight. "You? You're the woman who dropped a baby off at my studio?"

Shock covered her face as her mouth dropped open. "A baby?"

"Yes," Jack said in response to Julia's question without taking his eyes off the other woman. "A baby."

"I thought she was just one more wannabe actress, crying her eyes out over not getting an audition," Julia said.

Anger flared inside him as the woman just stood there, looking at him like he was the oddest thing she'd ever seen. Ignoring Julia's explanation, he said to the woman, "I have no idea who are you, but you must really think I'm a sap. Let me tell you, I'm not." He took a step closer and continued in a low, raspy whisper, "I've met a lot of two-bit dames looking to make a name for themselves, but never have I had one sink so low as to accuse me of being a father in order to further their own ambitions." He pointed a finger at the door. "That's not my child. I know that and you know that, so hightail yourself across the street and collect your baby."

She blinked several times. Then, shaking her head, whispered, "You aren't Joe McCarney?"

"No, I'm not, I'm—" Realization hit like a bolt of lightning.

Damn it, Joe! Jack wanted to shout that, several times over. *You've gone too far this time!*

Chapter Two

Helen's heart was so far into her throat, it was strangling her. Fighting through the pressure, she asked, "Who are you? Where's Grace? Is she all right?"

"I'm Jack McCarney. And your baby, *Grace*, is across the street. At the studio."

"You left her alone?" Helen untied the apron and pulled it off.

"She's not alone. She's with my secretary. The same one you left her with hours ago."

Helen was fighting hard not to run across the street to get back to Grace. She'd fought it all afternoon. A part of her had kept telling herself to get as far away as possible, but the other part of her had refused, saying she had to stay long enough to make sure Grace was fine. From a distance.

At some point, while she'd been crying her eyes out, Julia had offered her a job of washing dishes to pay for room and board for a few days.

Julia assured that was common practice for her. That she often allowed girls needing a place to stay to reside with her in the small house behind the diner until they were able to acquire lodging elsewhere. Julia also hadn't pried. She'd never once asked why she was here, crying her eyes out. And Helen had been too weak to say no, to refuse the offer of a job and accommodation, because it would mean that she'd be able to make sure that Grace would be okay. Would be cared for. Loved.

A shiver rippled Helen's spine as the man before her ran a hand through his hair.

His blond hair.

"What did you say your name is?" she asked. He certainly wasn't the man in the picture with Vera. That man, Joe McCarney, had black hair.

"Jack McCarney," he answered.

A leering glare from his brown eyes settled on her so fully, so completely, her entire body quivered.

Oh, dear Lord, what had she done?

She was almost afraid to ask, but had to. "Are you related to Joe McCarney?"

"I'm his brother."

"Joe McCarney is Grace's father." Hoping to justify what she'd done, she added, "All I had was the address across the street."

"Jack—" Julia started.

"Joe isn't any more that baby's father than I am," he barked.

The disapproval in Julia's face sent another shiver racing over Helen. "Yes, he is," she said. "I have proof."

He scowled. "Proof? What sort of proof."

"A—a marriage license and a wedding picture," she answered. "They are in my purse. I should have left them with Grace, but forgot about them."

"Forgot? How could you forget about your marriage license? Your wedding picture?"

Shaking all the way to her core, Helen didn't have

the wherewithal to point out his mistake. "Is Joe across the street?"

"No, Joe isn't across the street." He grabbed her arm. "But that's where you're going. To collect your baby."

She considered refusing, but if Joe wasn't there, she couldn't leave Grace with this beast of a man.

"You'll be without a dishwasher for a while, Julia," he said while marching toward the door.

"Stop," Helen said, digging her heels into the black-and-white-tiled floor. "I need to get my purse."

"No, you don't."

She refused to move, even though he pulled on her arm. "Yes, I do."

He let her go. "Fine. Get your purse."

She hurried across the room, into the little backroom where she'd cried her eyes out most of the afternoon.

Julia was on her heels. "What were you thinking? Dropping a baby off at Jack's door?"

"I thought it was Joe's door. He's Grace's father. I promised her mother, Vera, on her deathbed that I would bring Grace to him."

"So the baby isn't yours?"

"No, she's not mine. I wouldn't drop my baby off with some stranger." Guilt struck her hard and fast. She shouldn't have dropped Grace off, either. Disgraced by her own actions, she dropped her head. "I didn't have a choice."

"It'll be all right," Julia said, rubbing her arm. "You can come back here. Our deal still stands, a job for room and board, for both you and the baby."

Helen didn't know what to say, other than, "Thank you."

"Jack is Joe's brother. The good son. He's just upset

right now. Joe was blackballed from Hollywood over two years ago, and Jack is still cleaning up the messes his brother left behind when he hightailed it out of the state." Julia shook her head again. "Looks like Joe left him with another one."

Helen's heart dropped. "Joe isn't even in California?"

"No, he left two years ago, and hasn't been back."

"Oh, dear." Helen took off her glasses and wiped at her stinging eyes. Vera had never mentioned that Joe had a brother. She only ever talked about Joe, and how he was coming back. Coming back for her and the baby. Someday.

Perhaps she should have listened to Mr. Amery when he said going to California was a bad idea. That there was no telling what could happen to her and Grace, on the way or once they got here. He'd been kind to Helen after the deaths of her family, giving her a job at his grocery and renting out the apartment above the store to her, and though he'd been a bit begrudging at first, he had let Vera move in as well. Despite all, he'd been very good to both Vera and Grace upon the birth of the baby.

What would happen now? If Joe wasn't in California, what would she do with Grace?

She had to go get her, that was a given.

"I'll be back," she told Julia while picking up her purse. "Thank you, again."

Jack was still in the kitchen, pacing near the door. He stopped and stared at her as she left the back room.

"Are you ready now?"

"Yes." In the three months since Grace had been born, they'd never been apart, and excitement at seeing the baby, holding her, increased the speed of Helen's footsteps. "I'm ready."

"Let's go." Jack pulled open the kitchen door and held it as she crossed over the threshold.

All eyes seemed to land on them, and followed her and Jack as he grasped her elbow and led her through the restaurant toward the door. It was more than uncomfortable, it was unnerving, and, as if she needed an extra reminder, it reinforced exactly why she'd brought Grace to California. She couldn't be seen. She couldn't be dragged back to the life she'd been running from ever since that awful night. Her parents and brother had died in the raid at the restaurant, but she hadn't. She and Karen had run down the hallway, along with a crowd of others, and down to the basement where they raced through a maze of tunnels that had brought them outside in an alley, blocks away from the restaurant.

Her uncle hadn't died either, and upon discovering that she was staying with Karen, had sent men to collect her. Despite Karen's warnings that there was no escaping the family, Helen had run again. She hadn't wanted that life before the raid, and certainly didn't afterward. The violence had only grown after the raid that night. There were shoot-outs in all sections of the city, at all times of the day and night. So many that the newspapers, which she read every night after stocking shelves and scrubbing the floors at the grocery store, couldn't keep up.

Thankfully, her uncle hadn't found her, but it was only a matter of time. She knew that deep inside and *that* was the reason she'd brought Grace to California. She'd been saving every penny to eventually get away from Chicago, but Grace was the catalyst that made it even more necessary. She'd had to get the baby away from the dangers of being anywhere near her.

Her heart sank. She still had to do that.

She had no reason to believe that someone hadn't recognized her or seen her as she'd left Chicago. The possibility of that was real. She'd learned a lot during the past two years and knew the Outfit had eyes and ears everywhere. They'd bought off most every police precinct in Chicago, and she knew it was pure luck that she hadn't already been found and taken back to her uncle.

Karen had said there was only one way to get out of their family and that it included a grave.

The walk across that dining room, with all eyes on her, seemed like the longest one of her life. She had to let out a sigh once it ended, but stepping into the open air wasn't any better. She'd felt safe enough on the train, had sat way in the back and kept her head down; but here, she was in the open. The wide open.

The traffic was minimal and it was hard for her not to run across the street.

When they arrived at the other side, the woman she'd handed Grace to earlier opened the door.

"The baby's is sleeping," she said. "I put her on the couch in your office."

Helen's heart skipped a beat. Grace hadn't rolled over yet, but could at any time, and fall off the sofa.

"Thank you, Miss Hobbs." Jack held the door for her to walk out. "Good night."

"Good night," the woman said, shooting out the door.

"Where is your office?" Helen asked. "I need to check on Grace."

He pointed at a door across the room. Helen hurried in that direction and then down a long hallway to an open door on the left.

Relief filled her as she entered the room and saw Grace sleeping on the sofa. There was a blanket rolled up beside her, so if she had rolled over, she wouldn't have fallen off. Helen walked closer and laid a hand on the baby. It felt so good to touch her again. To see her. Being parted from her had been horrific—more than she could have ever expected.

Jack was in the doorway, staring at her. Helen's throat thickened. No matter how much she'd missed Grace today, how much she loved her, she still had to do the right thing. Find Joe McCarney.

"She's sleeping." Helen had no idea why she said that aloud.

"I see that," he said.

She nodded and then closed her eyes, willing for whatever strength there was inside her to reveal itself.

Jack experienced a bout of anger like never before. Not at her. At Joe. If this was Joe's baby... What? What could he do about it? He didn't have a clue as to where his brother might be.

He didn't even know this woman's name. Wasn't sure he wanted to know. But, beneath her drab clothing, he saw how pretty she was, and that beauty would have attracted Joe's attention.

His full attention.

"I—I know now that Gracie isn't your child," she said quietly. "And I apologize for just leaving her here, but she is your brother's child. Joe's. And this is the address that I had for him."

There was no reason for his stomach to drop to his feet. That statement shouldn't have surprised him. Joe had been giving this address out to women since he'd left. The bag of mail in the closet proved that.

"When did he give you this address?" Jack asked.

"He didn't. If you have another address for him, I'd appreciate if you'd give it to me. I really need to find him. As soon as possible."

The desperation in her voice was almost convincing. Of all the women who'd come begging for an audition, she might be the one who did have what it took to be an actress. Just his luck. "Then how did you get this address?" Another thought struck him. "Why didn't he give it to you? If Joe really is the father to your baby?"

Her gaze fell to the floor. "Grace isn't my baby." She bit her lip and lifted those beautiful eyes back up to him. "Her mother was my friend, Vera. She passed away a few weeks ago. In Chicago."

The pleading in those eyes unsettled him.

"Please, Mr. McCarney, if I can't find Joe, Grace will be an orphan."

The flop of his stomach was merited this time. Chicago. Last he heard, Joe was down in Florida, Miami, but he had been in Chicago a year ago. Working for the circus. *Damn it, Joe!*

Jack took a deep breath, and told himself that he still didn't have enough information to believe this woman.

"Please, Mr. McCarney. All I'm asking is for you to tell me where I can find Joe. Grace needs her father. Her family. She has no one else."

No matter how sincere this woman sounded, he had to be cautious. Joe could be anywhere and if he committed to the idea that Joe was the baby's father, that would make him the baby's uncle—a responsibility he didn't need right now.

He pushed the heavy air out of his lungs. "Why should I believe anything you have to say?"

Something flashed in those unique blue eyes. He wasn't exactly sure what, but suddenly felt a heavy burden stir deep within his chest. A familiar burden that felt too close to the sense of responsibility he'd felt almost his entire life.

"Because I'm telling the truth," she said quietly. "I don't want anything else from you. Just Joe's whereabouts."

Anger and frustration raced through him. He'd spent the last two years cleaning up messes his brother had left behind—wasn't even half done—but wasn't about to get pulled into another one of Joe's problems. Not if he could help it. "I'd need proof."

She tilted her head downward and looked over the rim of her glasses as she dug in her purse. "I have Vera and Joe's wedding picture and marriage license, and I was there when Grace was born."

He bit back a curse and told himself not to jump to conclusions. A wedding picture and marriage license. That would be proof all right. Or damaging evidence, depending on which way he wanted to look at this. Deep down, he knew she could be telling the truth. Women were drawn to Joe, and he to them. He'd almost married one or two in the past. Actually, three or four, until they'd figured out Joe wasn't being faithful. That's what had gotten him blackballed. Infidelity. That time it had been on the woman's part, and her husband, another actor, hadn't liked it in the least. Nor had the people they worked for.

"Would you like to see them?" she asked.

Frustration ate at his insides. He couldn't have another scandal right now. This film meant too much. He'd worked so hard to get back to this point. The cusp of success. Self-made success.

He straightened his spine and rolled his shoulders back, telling himself not to get too caught up in this until he knew the truth. The entire truth. He had a film to make. One that would put Star's Studio at the top of the charts. In theaters across the nation. He was so close, and had worked too hard keeping his reputation clean despite his brother's shenanigans.

She was still standing near the sofa, with an envelope in her hand. He walked in that direction, but only as far as his desk, hating the fact that he was putting off the moment when she might just offer the proof of what she was saying. "What's your name?"

There was a moment of hesitation in her eyes, on her face, but then with a soft sigh, she said, "Helen. Helen Hathaway."

He leaned against his desk. "Well, Miss Hathaway…" He paused as another thought struck. "It is *Miss*, isn't it? Or are you married?" He knew of more than one woman who'd left a husband behind to come to Hollywood. One had told him she'd left five children behind and needed an acting job in order to send money back home in order to feed them. The sad thing was, he'd known she'd been telling the truth.

"No. I mean yes. It's Miss, I'm not married."

Her stammering displayed her nervousness, so did her stance. It looked as if she was about to jump out of her shoes, or run for the door.

He nodded and then finished what he'd been about

to say earlier. "The last I heard about Joe is that he's in Florida."

"Florida?" She turned and stared at the couch, at the baby sleeping there.

"Yes, Florida."

"Oh, dear."

He shot across the room as all color left her face. Not sure what to do, because she hadn't fainted, but was swaying slightly, he asked, "Do you need to sit down?"

She nodded.

He took her arm, guided her a couple of steps backward and onto the opposite end of the couch from where the baby was sleeping.

Despair filled her eyes as she said, "Florida is so far away."

It was, but he wasn't concerned about that. "Do you need a drink of water?"

She shook her head. "No, thank you, I'm fine."

She didn't look fine to him. Not so much as a hint of color had returned to her cheeks. Something inside him, an instinct of sorts, said it wasn't Florida that had sapped the life out of her.

"I'm going to get you that glass of water," he said. "I'll be right back."

Chapter Three

Jack kept one eye on her until he was at the doorway, then he hurried down the hallway to get a glass of water.

Secrecy was just one of the games played in Hollywood. It was played by almost everyone, and was also the one that no one wanted to get caught playing. For the most part, he'd never played that game himself. Hadn't needed to.

He did recognize it though, and there was more to Helen Hathaway than she was letting on.

He could make some phone calls, see if he could locate Joe and question him about the woman's accusations. But that was unnecessary. Would be futile, too. If Joe had married someone, and cared about her, or the baby, he wouldn't need to be searched out.

On the other hand, if it wasn't true, if this Helen Hathaway was looking for something else, Joe might know what that might be.

Jack clamped his back teeth together. He'd put nearly everything he had into this movie. Others had put up a good amount of money, too—not the Broadbents, real investors, and he was determined that not a hint of Joe's name would be tied to this movie. Los Angeles was a big town and the movie industry was growing daily. In many ways. Good and bad. Corruption had already burrowed its way deep inside and studios were walking a fine line.

The powers that be who'd put themselves in charge of the industry wanted all of America to believe Hollywood was the pinnacle of this nation. Where dreams came true, streets were lined with gold, and beds made of rose petals.

It was all baloney. The billboards who put themselves in charge had more skeletons in their closets than those they were blackballing—like his brother. But that was the way it was, and would remain, until a few legitimate studios rose high enough to knock the big five off their pedestals.

And it would happen. Others were getting wise to the way the big companies had taken over theaters. Buying them up across the nation and monopolizing the movies that could be shown in "their" theaters. *Only* their movies. For every big hit, they forced the theaters to show dozens of their low-budget movies, controlling the payouts other films could make.

That was all about to turn around. Which is precisely what he was counting on happening. His new film could be the one that really changed things. It was a good script. With solid actors and a story line that would drive people into the theaters by the droves— theaters that would have the right to show whatever movies they chose. It was all lined up. If he made it with this film, finally he'd have secured his place in the movie industry. Finally he'd have the security he'd wanted for more years than he could count. And he'd have done it *his* way.

If nothing went astray.

An abandoned baby could cause that to happen. Cause trouble he couldn't afford.

He got the water and headed back to his office.

She was still sitting on the couch, but now had one hand on the baby.

There was something about her that struck him deep inside. Had since he'd seen her unique blue eyes, and her nervousness made him curious to know exactly what she wanted, what she was hiding.

She glanced up and, as he'd seen her do several times, tilted her chin downward to look over the top of the glasses. Why would a woman wear a pair of glasses that she couldn't see through? The glasses didn't take away from her beauty, but they did disguise it slightly. So did her clothes. They were loose fitting and drab. Almost as if she didn't want to stand out in any way. Here, in Hollywood, her getup did the exact opposite— they made her stand out like a sore thumb.

He carried the water across the room. "Feel better?"

"Yes, thank you." The smile she offered was forced and she barely took a drink of the water before handing him back the glass.

He set the glass on a nearby table.

"Here." She held up the envelope.

Jack took it, folded back the flap and pulled out a picture. It certainly was Joe smiling back at the camera. The woman beside him was surprising. There was nothing vibrant about her. She was cute, but, well, average. A dime a dozen. Certainly not the type that Joe had been drawn to his entire life.

And certainly not the woman sitting on the couch, either.

Jack tucked the picture back in the envelope and pulled out a folded piece of paper. It was a marriage license. The signature at the bottom was one he knew. Joe had spent hours practicing flamboyant ways to sign his name and had perfected one that he'd used for the last ten-plus years. Ever since both of them had played roles in the traveling shows their parents had forced them to perform in across the nation. Joe had loved it. He hadn't.

Jack put the paper back in the envelope with the picture. "What proof do you have that the baby is this woman's?"

Her glasses had slid down her nose, allowing her to gaze over the top of the rims without dipping her chin. "I was there when Grace was born."

"So, you are friends with her?"

"I was. As I said, Vera died three weeks ago." She glanced at the baby for a second, then back at him with a tenderness in her eyes. "That was her name Vera. Vera McCarney."

He gave a slight nod of respect. It wasn't his job to judge this woman, or the woman Joe had obviously married, but in the end, he was the jury, the only member, who would have to decide what to do about the situation at hand. In order to do that, he needed all the information he could get. "Had the two of you been longtime friends?"

Once again, she glanced at the baby before answering. "No. I met her a short time before Gracie was born."

There was tenderness in her eyes and sadness. Refusing to let what he saw affect him, he walked over to his desk and set the envelope down. "Where?"

"In Chicago."

"But you never met Joe?"

She shook her head.

He pointed to the envelope on his desk. "This may say that my brother married a woman named Vera Baker last year in Chicago, but it in no way provides any proof that that baby is either Vera's or Joe's."

"I was there when she was born."

"You've said that, but I still have doubts that she is my niece. The burden has been put upon you to provide me with the information that might lessen that doubt. Do you have any other information that can do that?"

Her shoulders rolled back as the deep breath she took filled her lungs. She held the air in. He waited, half expecting her to pop like the rubber balloons they used for props.

She didn't pop. As the air slowly seeped out of her, her shoulders dropped. "Vera wrote to Joe, and this is where she sent the letters."

That, he could prove wrong. He crossed the room, to the closet where he kept the gunnysack. Upon opening the door, he picked up the sack and then carried it to the couch. "This bag," he said while setting it on the floor by her feet, "is full of letters to Joe at this address."

Her eyes grew as wide as her glasses. "Oh, my."

She could be shocked by the mail, or by the fact he too had proof. Proof she was lying. He opened the sack and pulled out a handful of letters. "You're welcome to sift through them, find one from Vera." He dropped the envelopes back in the bag. "If you truly believe there is one in here."

"I do," she said firmly. "I know there is more than one. I mailed several for Vera."

A shiver tickled his spine at the possibility that she was telling the truth. The entire truth. Then what was she hiding? It had to do with Chicago. A veil had clouded her eyes, and she'd grown stoic both times she mentioned the town's name. He contemplated that for a moment before asking. "Why didn't Vera mail them herself?"

"She was too weak. Carrying Grace and then giving birth wore her down to skin and bones. She never recovered." She was digging in the bag, pulling letter after letter out, and setting them aside after a quick glance. "She just kept getting weaker and weaker."

He didn't know this woman. For all he knew, she could have kidnapped that baby from someone. His stomach clenched, letting him know that no part of him believed that she was a kidnapper. Not even in the hidden corners of his subconscious. She was hiding something though. Those glasses were proof of that. They were a disguise, he just didn't know for what. Flustered, he grabbed a handful of envelopes and sifted through them, looking at the return addresses. "Vera, you say?"

She nodded. "Vera McCarney."

Before long, they were both sitting on the floor, with the bag between them, sifting through the stack of mail.

"Found another one," she said, tossing an envelope toward at least a dozen other letters with the return address hosting Vera's name.

His skepticism had disappeared after the first letter. Now he had more questions. What was he going to do about it? If he could locate Joe—and that was a big if—he knew his brother. Responsibility was foreign to Joe. Stardom could be to blame, or maybe life in general, the way they'd been raised, traveling from town to town.

Jack withheld the heavy sigh building inside him. He'd like to think differently, but highly doubted even a baby would make Joe change his ways. A child would never fit in Joe's lifestyle.

A hard knot formed in Jack's stomach. A baby wouldn't fit in his life, either. Not even a niece. Not right now. He'd invested every spare cent in this movie. It had potential. *The* potential to put Star's Studio in the running to be one of the top players. Doing so would take all of his efforts. All of his time.

He looked at the envelope in his hand for some time before setting it aside. It had been the last one. The bag was empty, and two piles sat before them, a large one, and a smaller one. Letters from Vera.

Helen sifted through those and picked one up. "I wrote this one," she said. "Vera was too weak. It was the day before she died. I wrote exactly what she wanted me to. That I would bring Grace here, to this address. To Joe."

He took the envelope but didn't open it. Couldn't. It wasn't addressed to him. So that's how it would remain. Unopened. The less he knew, the better off he was. Even in this situation.

As far as the mail went.

"How did you meet Vera?" He set the letter aside. "I'm assuming it was after she married Joe?"

"Yes." Her gaze went to the baby.

"Where did you meet her?"

"In the alley behind the grocery store where I worked."

At some point, she'd removed her glasses and he clearly saw the tears welling in her eyes. She blinked and twisted to discreetly wipe at them with one finger.

A part of him didn't want to know. Didn't want to think his brother would have left a woman destitute, but it certainly appeared that way. "What was she doing in the alley?"

"Looking for food." She looked him straight in the eye, was utterly serious. "She was penniless. Had been kicked out of the place she'd been staying. She was so ill. Coughing." She shook her head but didn't attempt to hide the tears forming again. "I took her to my apartment. She was so weak she could barely walk up the steps. She got better. A little, in the weeks that followed, but then…"

Compassion filled him and he reached over, took ahold of her hand and squeezed it gently. "You did what you could." He looked at the baby. Grace. His niece. "Most likely saved Grace's life."

She nodded and then removed her hand from beneath his and started filling the bag with the letters not from Vera. "Grace is a good baby. Has been from the moment she was born."

Heaviness filled his lungs, his heart, at the idea of a woman searching for food.

If anyone knew what it was like to do that, search for food, to be hungry, it was them. Him and Joe. Nothing during the past ten years had chased away the feelings he'd known as a child. Of being hungry. So hungry the pain had been strong enough to make him cry. As he got older, those same pains made him angry. So angry he swore he'd never become an actor. Never traverse the countryside in a dilapidated wagon singing and doing comedy acts for pennies that never totaled enough to feed them for more than a week at best.

Yet, here he was. In the same business he'd always been in. Times had changed though. And he wasn't acting. Never would act again. Joe had been the actor and had loved it. He'd found work as soon as they'd arrived in Los Angeles.

"Can you contact your brother. Tell him Grace is here?"

Jack didn't look her way. Couldn't right now. She wouldn't like his answer. He didn't like it, either.

He let out the air that had grown stagnant inside his lungs. "You've taken care of Grace since she was born?" He already knew the answer, but was trying to figure out his next steps. Steps that were completely foreign to him.

"Yes."

"And paid to bring her here?"

"Yes."

"What did your family think of that?" Another thought formed. "Or Vera's family?"

There was that flash in her eyes again. A mixture of sadness and fear. "Neither of us have any family. Vera had worked for the circus. That's how she got to Chicago. And she didn't have any family to return to."

Jack wanted to know about her. Helen. But a gut sense said she wouldn't answer any questions about herself. He stood up and picked up the bag once again full of mail. "Is the circus how she met Joe?"

"Yes. He was a magician."

Jack had already known that as well. Joe had perfected several magic tricks over the years, and had
used them to land more than one job. After opening
the closet, he set the bag inside. "Had he continued on
with the circus? Left when it moved on?"

"No. Vera said they both stayed in Chicago. That
Jack had gotten a job at one of the playhouses for a
short time, but then had to return here and said he
would send for her. That's when he gave her this address and said she was to contact him here if she
needed anything."

Of course Joe did. That's what he'd always done.
Passed the buck.

Jack closed the door and stood there for a moment.
The baby had started to fuss and Helen was scooping
her off the couch. That baby was his niece. Joe's baby,
and as inadvertent as that may be, Grace was now his
responsibility.

The mess with the Broadbents was nothing compared to this. What the hell was he going to do?

"I'll pay you," he said as the thought formed.

"Excuse me?"

It might not be the ultimate answer, but it would
do for now. "I'll pay you to continue to take care of
Grace."

She glanced at the baby, and then up at him. Sorrow filled her eyes as she sadly shook her head. "I
can't."

"Why? You have been since she was born."

"Because I promised Vera I'd bring her here. And
I have."

She had all right, and that could open a can of

worms that could take him down. It would be all the Wagner brothers needed to convince the owners of the new theater to break his contract and go with them.

Right now, it was just the two of them, Julia and Miss Hobbs who knew about Grace. He had to keep it that way.

"Just until I find Joe." Then he could send them to Florida, or to wherever Joe was. Let his brother take responsibility for his own actions this time.

She glanced down and the smile she provided the baby might very well be the most precious and beautiful smile he'd seen to date. But then, she closed her eyes and bit her lips together. When she lifted her lids, looked at him, tears had welled in her eyes again. "I wish I could, but I can't."

Money. It had to be the money. Traveling here had probably taken all she'd had. He didn't have much to spare himself, but he did have a bank account that he'd been depositing any royalties owed to Joe from past projects, knowing Joe would return some day and want it. Expect it.

He hadn't used that money to pay the Broadbents because Joe had sold them shares in future projects, not past, but he would use Joe's money for this, his daughter. And not feel guilty about it.

He had no idea what it cost to take care of a baby, so merely said, "Whatever it costs, I'll pay you."

She kissed the baby on the head. He let out a sigh of relief and pulled his billfold out of his pocket. To his shame, he had only a few dollars on him. Pulling them out, he said, "I'll go to the bank and get more tomorrow."

She laid the baby back down on the couch and

picked up her purse. "I'm sorry, but I can't. For Grace's sake, I can't." Turning about, she started for the door.

"Wait! You can't leave!" He started after her, but a crunch beneath his foot made him pause. Her glasses. He'd broken them. She was already out the door. "Wait!"

Tears once again blurred Helen's vision. This time it wasn't just heartache, there was anger inside her, too. Anger that her life would never be her own. No matter where she went. She couldn't continue to put Grace in danger. That's all there was to it.

A baby's cry—Grace's—made her feet stumble, but she forced herself to keep moving forward. Down the hall. In Chicago, after leaving her cousin's house, she'd gone to the edge of the city, where she thought the lack of large businesses would make the mob not as prevalent. That hadn't been true. The neighbor of Amery's grocery store hadn't been run by the Outfit. It had been a smaller mob, one that oversaw little more than the bootlegging of whiskey to the area speakeasies. But nonetheless, they'd been there. Mobsters in big fancy cars, their mugs on street corners.

It was there, late at night, looking out the windows of the grocery store that she'd concluded that there was no getting out. Not for her. Any one of those thugs could have been a stool pigeon for her uncle.

Grace was still crying, and Helen balled her hands into fists as she neared the door of the studio.

She'd created many disguises for herself over the past two years, everything from a young boy to an old woman, but hadn't been able to carry much besides Grace all the way to the railroad station. Therefore, she'd left most everything behind. Other than the drab dresses, head scarves and her glasses.

Her glasses. She'd taken them off because it had been too hard to see the writing on the envelopes. Spinning about, she hurried back toward the hallway.

She told herself it was to get the glasses, that she had to have them, but the moment she stepped into the office door, she knew the real reason. Grace was still crying and Jack stood next to the couch. The bottle in one hand, a can of milk in the other.

"I don't even know where to start," he said, looking at her hopelessly.

Helen hurried forward. "You start by picking her up." She did just that, and snuggled Grace close to comfort her. "Once she's calmed down, you can see to what she needs, whether it's a diaper change or a bottle."

"How do you know the difference?" he asked.

She shrugged. "If her diaper is dry, you fix a bottle. If it's wet, you change her."

He shook his head. "I can't do this. I can't." Holding up the can of milk, he added, "I don't even have a can opener."

"There is one in the bag," Helen said, carefully laying Grace down on the couch. The baby was no longer crying but a diaper change was definitely in order. The bag and most of its former contents were spread out on the floor near her feet. After picking up a clean diaper, Helen asked, "Where is the powder room?"

"Next door down the hall, on the right." He met her gaze. "Thank you for coming back. Thank you very much."

Earlier, while sitting on the floor next to him, she'd

caught herself staring at him. More than once. Couldn't seem to help it. He was extremely handsome, with his blond hair that flopped over his forehead and his dark eyes.

He had the kind of handsomeness that made people stop in their tracks and take a second look. She'd heard about that more than seen it. In fact, she may never have seen it, and truly only heard about it from Vera. That's how she'd described Joe McCarney. Stop-in-your-tracks handsome.

She shook her head, trying to clear her thoughts, and bent down to pick up Grace. "We'll be right back."

"I'll be here."

She found the powder room and as she saw to changing Grace, she couldn't help but wonder who would see that the diaper was properly washed, or that the bottles and nipples were cleaned after each use, or all of the other things that needed to be done to see to the care of a baby. She hadn't known any of those things in the beginning, but did now, and had cherished doing all of them.

It had been a long time since she'd had someone to love. Grace had filled that hole since the moment she'd been born. She'd told herself from the beginning that Grace wasn't hers to love, that her only duty to the baby was to find her father.

She hadn't done that.

She hadn't fulfilled her promise to Vera. The promises she'd made to Grace.

Despite her fears, she couldn't leave. She'd tried twice, and couldn't do it. Giving Grace a hug, she whispered, "Don't worry, sweetheart, no matter what, I won't let anyone hurt you. I promise."

She left the powder room with more resolve than she'd had in a long time. Jack was still in the office, had returned all of Grace's items to the bag and had it sitting on his desk.

"Thank you," he said again as soon as she entered.

The relief on his face was so evident she had to bite her lips to keep from smiling. There was no denying that the idea of staying with Grace a bit longer filled her with joy.

"I had no idea what to do," he said. "She started crying as soon as you stepped out the door."

"I heard. Your shouting probably scared her."

He shrugged and shook his head. "I don't know what to say. I've never been around a baby before."

"I hadn't, either," she admitted. That had been frightening at first, but had quickly turned into joy. More joy than she'd known in a very long time.

"I'll pay whatever you want, for you to take care of her until I can find Joe."

Helen held her breath for a moment. Could she do it? Stay with Grace? "I came back for my glasses," she said, needing a bit more time. She was nearly out of money, so wouldn't get far, if she did leave.

"About those." He glanced down at his desk. "I stepped on them by accident."

She looked down, saw the crushed frames and broken glass.

"Why do you wear them? You don't need them."

"Yes, I do." Not to see with, but to hide behind.

"I'll buy you a new pair."

It was almost as if the smashed glasses were a symbol, one that told her she couldn't hide for the rest of her life. She already knew that, just hadn't known how to get out. How to get far enough away that she wouldn't have to hide. That had been her goal, why she'd saved every penny she could. Yet, until Grace, she hadn't had the courage to leave.

That's why she'd stayed put, in the little apartment above the grocery store, stocking shelves, scrubbing floors, reading newspapers every night, and wishing she could go outside, enjoy the sunshine, the rain, even the snow and wind, every day.

"Tomorrow. I'll buy you a new pair, tomorrow."

Helen pulled her eyes off the glasses. A new pair wouldn't make a difference. Tomorrow would be no different from today. She took a moment to think back over the past few days. Traveling on the train she'd experienced a small amount of the freedom she'd sought the past two years. Before then in another sense. Guilt arose when she thought about that. How she'd wanted out when she should have been thankful her family had been alive and well.

She hadn't been thankful about that, not enough, and today, she'd been so worried about herself, about getting away again, that she'd left Grace with someone who didn't have the ability to care for her. Jack could learn. She had, but that wasn't the issue. The true issue was whether she was really willing to let her past, her fears, have so much control over her that she was willing to let Grace suffer while Jack learned to take care of her. Is that who she was? Who she'd become?

If so, why hadn't she left as soon as she'd handed Grace over? Ran back to the train station and used the last of her funds to buy a ticket that would have taken her as far away as possible?

"Do you need to return to Chicago immediately?"

"No." Helen closed her eyes at how quickly she responded. Heaviness filled her as she opened her eyes and looked at Jack. She had no idea what to say, what to do. It was as if she was caught in a trap even stronger than the one she'd lived in the past few years.

Chapter Four

If Jack had been alone, he might have spewed an entire sentence of curse words, but he wasn't alone. The woman standing before him was hiding something, and she was holding his niece. His niece. And he didn't have a clue as to what to do about that. About either of them. He'd never been so out of his element as when Grace had started to cry. Nor had he ever been so relieved as when Helen had shown back up in the doorway.

He'd also never seen fear in someone's eyes like what had appeared in hers when he'd asked if she had to return to Chicago.

Damn it to hell, this shouldn't even be his problem. It should be Joe's.

Which is precisely what made it his. And why it fit so well. Every time he was almost there, almost to the point where everything was good and right, Joe stepped in. It had been that way his entire life. So why should it change now?

Angry like he hadn't been in some time, he spun around. Ran a hand through his hair, and tried to think. Nothing came to him, much like a few minutes ago, when Grace had been crying.

He huffed a breath of scalding air, full of anger toward Joe for once again leaving him with a mess to clean up, and then drew in another breath. His hands were tied, like they had been so many times before.

Unlike his brother, he'd always accepted that honesty was the best policy, so he turned around. "I have to be up front with you. I don't have a clue how to take care of a baby, nor do I have a clue where Joe is. Last I heard it was Florida, and I will call some connections I have there, see if they've heard from him, know where he is, but it could be days, weeks, before I learn about his whereabouts."

She didn't make a move, or say a word, other than to glance down at the baby in her arms.

Frustration had his nerve endings tingling. "And there's more. I have a movie to make. The actors have been hired, the sets have been built, the script's written. We start filming in the morning. I have two months, eight weeks from start to finish, to get it filmed, edited and ready to show. If that doesn't happen, I'll have to lock the doors of the studio permanently." He'd never admitted that realization, not even to himself, but it was the truth. The movies he'd made the last couple of years had been small-budget productions, and the minimum runs they'd been given in theaters had barely been enough to pay the salaries of his crew and the actors, especially once the Broadbents had been given payments toward Joe's debt.

Her gaze was on him, and remained there as she nodded.

At a loss, he let out a sigh. "I know that's not your problem. That none of this is your problem." He wished it wasn't his problem, either, but it was. That little girl in her arms was his niece and like it or not, he couldn't turn his back on her. "But I don't know what to do, other than to ask you what it will take for you to agree to continue to care for Grace for the next eight weeks?"

"Eight weeks?"

The fear in her eyes returned full force. He didn't want yet another issue, but couldn't deny that it was his only option to deal with it. Whatever it was. "You have to level with me, doll. Tell me what's really going on. Why you're acting like some moll on the lam."

Her head snapped back as if she'd been struck a blow on the chin. "I'm not a moll, and I'm not your doll, either."

There was fire in her eyes, which was surprising considering how meek she'd been a moment ago. He hadn't meant she was a gangster's gal, or his doll, but that really had struck a nerve with her. Which he was going to take advantage of now that he had her full attention. "Then what are you?"

A frown filled her face, but not her eyes, they were still snapping.

"Why are you hiding and what are you running from?" he added.

She stood stock-still for so long he wondered if she was going to answer. When she did finally move, it was to lift the baby in her arms up against one shoulder and pat Grace's small back. He held his silence. Watching her movements. Once again, the idea of filming her entered his mind. He had to push it away, which wasn't easy. Her movements were elegant, smooth. Graceful. It was her thoughtfulness, that really held his attention. How she was contemplating her next move. The audience would see that too, and wonder, just as he was, what she was about to say.

"I came here fully expecting to give Grace to her father, that he'd know how to take care of her."

"And then?" he asked.

She shook her head.

He could tell she was being honest, and honesty brought honesty. "I haven't talked to my brother in over two years, but would doubt he'd know any more about taking care of a baby than I do."

"Why haven't you talked to him in two years?"

He was tired of standing, and figured she was too, so waved at the sofa, silently inviting her to sit down.

She watched him cautiously as she crossed the room and then perched herself on the edge of the cushion, almost as if prepared to jump up and run for the door all over again.

He sat in the chair next to the sofa, but it wasn't standing that he was tired of, it was this—another obstacle. "I haven't talked to Joe in two years because he was blackballed from acting in Hollywood and left the state. I tried to smooth things over, but…" He shook his head. There hadn't been anything he could do. No one had wanted to hear him defend his brother. He'd told Joe that, and that he wasn't going to lose his standings for Joe's mistakes. Not again. That's when Joe had sold out to the Broadbents and left town.

"What had he done to become blackballed?"

"Misconduct." He shrugged. In truth, Joe's actions had been no different than half the men in Hollywood, more maybe, he was just the one unlucky enough to get tangled up with the wrong doll. The movie industry wanted the world to believe they had standards and every once in a while, they pulled out a stool pigeon to prove a point. That had been Joe. Jack understood all this, but that didn't mean he condoned Joe's actions. Fooling around with a married woman was wrong and one married to a topliner was downright reckless. He shook his head. "Joe had been a good actor, had become popular, and he'd let that popularity go to his head."

She frowned. "Will he be back? To Hollywood?"

"I honestly don't know, but I doubt it."

Letting out a heavy sigh, she glanced down at Grace. "Not even for his daughter?"

Jack didn't know. Long ago he'd stopped trying to figure out his brother. There were times Joe had been there when he'd needed him. When they'd been in their teens and their parents had died. Joe had gotten them to California and then taken on any and all menial jobs he could get, while insisting Jack go to school. Filmmaking was new and raw then, and Joe hung in there when others hadn't and finally worked his way into acting. The money he'd made then had not only kept them both in food and clothes, it had funded the start of Star's Studio.

Although he hadn't wanted that in the beginning—he'd wanted to try something completely different from what he'd always known—he'd stuck with it because Joe had wanted it.

They'd made money, more than they would have elsewhere, and he owed his brother for that. For all he had, and always would. He'd never forgotten that, either. Nor would.

"I won't know that until I talk to him." He'd make some calls in the morning, to a couple of the film com-

panies that were popping up down in Florida. He'd
heard through the grapevine that Joe had been down
there, looking for work a few months ago. Trouble was,
Joe might not call him back. They'd been at cross-
roads when Joe had left, and nothing had happened
to resolve that.

"I have no idea when that might be," he admitted.
"But, I can promise, that if you give me eight weeks,
enough time to get this movie made and into theaters,
I'll then take over full responsibility for Grace. I'll pay
for all of her needs starting right now. I just need you
to take care of her."

"Eight weeks…"

The tremors in her voice shifted his train of thought.
He knew actors. There were people who could instantly
step into a role, become a character completely, then
there were others, that no matter how hard they tried,
they couldn't act. Couldn't pretend to be anyone other
than themselves.

He'd put her in that second category. She also
couldn't hide something else. She was scared. Beyond
scared. Her hands were trembling and she kept glancing at Grace, almost as if the baby might pop up and
fly away like some little bird.

"What aren't you telling me?" he asked.

She looked away while gnawing on her bottom lip.
Even her arms were trembling. So was her chin.

"What's preventing you from accepting my offer?"
he asked.

"Nothing."

His hope rose. "Nothing?"

She shook her head. "Everything."

Huffing out a breath, he asked, "Which is it? Nothing or everything?" Maybe all of his imagining her on the big screen was because she *could* act. Or lie. Had been lying all along. "Is Grace not who you say she is? Is she your baby and you made all this up about Vera and Joe?"

"No." Her shoulders squared as she leveled a glare on him. "Everything I have told you about Grace and Vera is true. The letters say as much."

He didn't need to read the letters. He knew she wasn't lying. He was just stuck between a rock and a hard spot. "I'm sorry. I do believe you." Standing, he rubbed at the tension in the back of his neck. "There is one other thing that I haven't mentioned yet. Another reason I need you to care for Grace."

"What is it?"

"Right now, while I'm making this movie and getting it out to the public, I can't have word spread that I've taken in Joe's abandoned baby. This is Hollywood. The rules change daily. That could be enough to have me blackballed for still associating with my brother." His own words sickened him. "I know that sounds selfish, but it's the truth. I can't argue for it or against it, it's just what it is right now."

"So you want me to pretend like Grace is my baby?"

He didn't want to face her, but did. "I want you to go on taking care of her, not saying anything, one way or the other." He wasn't proud of this, but he had to think of his future, of what this movie meant, perhaps even more now than ever. He had Grace to think about. Her future.

Chapter Five

Helen couldn't move, not even breathe. Her entire life had been full of not saying a word one way or the other. And she'd been pretending Grace was her baby. Right down to her heart. Right from the beginning.

Then her heart began to pound, her mind spun, but it wasn't all because of her, or Grace. It was because of him. She could relate to his predicament. She didn't know anything about making a movie, had only seen a couple in her entire life, but she could relate to being put in a situation without any control or any way out. He wasn't seeking a way out, just some time to get things in order, so he could take care of Grace.

"You and Grace can stay at my apartment," he said. "I'll pay for everything. Milk, food, clothes."

Could she do it? Take care of Grace for another eight weeks? That part would be easy. No different from what she had already been doing. Others had helped her during her desperation, despite the dangers that may have put them in. Especially Mr. and Mrs. Amery. They'd let her live above their grocery store, brought in a doctor for Vera.

Maybe this was her chance. A chance to see if she

had gotten far enough away. The thrill that stirred in her stomach surprised her, as did how fast she made up her mind. "That won't be necessary. Julia said Grace and I could stay with her."

The look of surprise on his face made her lips tremble. They wanted to smile. She wanted to smile.

A twinkle sparked in his eyes and a dimple formed in one of his cheeks as a grin formed. "You mean you'll help me?"

"Yes. I'll stay. Take care of Grace for eight weeks."

He grimaced slightly. "Maybe nine? Depending on how filming goes?"

Her smile broke free, but she was able to contain the rest of the emotions fluttering in her stomach. "We'll see. I can't promise how long Julia will need a dishwasher."

He frowned. "A dishwasher?"

"Yes, she offered room and board in exchange for washing dishes." Julia had said the deal still stood, and Helen sincerely hoped it would last for at least eight weeks.

"How will you be able to take care of Grace while washing dishes?"

"I'll manage just fine." Now that her mind was made up, she was anxious to get settled. An excited anxious, which hadn't happened in some time. Securing her hold on Grace, Helen stood. "This little girl will need to eat soon."

"I found the can opener," he said while walking toward his desk. "But wasn't sure if I should open the milk or not."

"I'll feed her at Julia's and get her settled in for the night."

He glanced at his watch. "The diner is already closed for the night. I'll walk you over to the house." He picked up the bag and nodded toward the door.

The diner was only across the street, yet she didn't protest his offer.

He shut off the office light and walked beside her down the long hallway. "We start filming first thing in the morning, but I'll make time to get to the bank."

Money was a necessity, she'd understood that for years. It was that it was earned fairly that she was concerned about. "I won't accept money from you for taking care of Grace, but I will accept a case of canned milk for her, and more when that's gone. That's all we'll need."

He looked at her quizzically, but didn't respond as they crossed the front room of the studio. At the door, he opened it, waited for her to step outside and then shut off the light. He also locked the door after closing it.

She didn't know what time it was, but darkness had settled, the street quiet. So quiet it echoed in her ears.

A moment later, her steps faltered as a shiver rippled her spine. "What was that?" she asked, referring to a strange sound. Like a yip and then faint howl from a dog.

"Haven't you ever heard a coyote before?"

She tightened her hold on Grace. "No. Never." The sound came again, and it was unnerving.

"Don't they have coyotes in Illinois?"

"Possibly, but not in Chicago."

"You lived there your entire life?"

"Yes."

"And never left the city?"

"No."

He took her elbow and stepped into the street. "Well, Los Angeles isn't as big as Chicago, yet. It's growing though, every day more land surrounding the city is bought up and developed. That growth is invading on the coyotes' and other critters' native hunting grounds."

Another shiver rippled through her. "Native hunting grounds?"

"Yes."

That sounded so primitive, and made her wary. "You're just saying that to scare me."

He frowned. "Why would I do that? I have no reason to try and scare you. This area has always had coyotes. It was cropland and orchards at one time. Julia still has a large plot of land behind her place that grows produce. The crops bring in the rabbits and the rabbits bring in the coyotes."

That made sense, but didn't make her feel any more comfortable. Neither did the darkness. She'd never been overly brave when it came to that. Junior had always called her a scaredy-cat because she'd refused to go anywhere in the dark alone. She'd overcome some of that, but those yipping sounds were enough to make a grown man quiver.

Not Jack though. He didn't appear nervous at all.

He was tall, much taller than her, and broader. His white shirt showed the thickness of his arm muscles, and that did provide her a small sense of comfort. "Do they attack people?"

"Coyotes?"

"Yes."

"No, they are more afraid of you than you are of them."

She doubted a coyote, or any other animal could ever feel the same amount of fear toward her as she did toward them. "You don't know that."

"Yes, I do."

They stepped up on the curb in front of the diner and then walked along the front of the building. There were no streetlights here, no light except for the moon, which wasn't nearly as bright as she wished it could be. "How? How do you know that?"

"Because unlike humans, animals are smart. They won't attack anything bigger than themselves."

"Unless cornered," she said, recalling she'd been told that at some time. "What if we corner one?"

"We won't corner one. Coyotes are smarter than that."

That didn't satisfy her. "How do you know that?"

"Because I've seen plenty. They sneak into the back filming lot all the time, but as soon as they see a person, they run." He led her around the corner of the diner building.

It was even darker back here, and she shivered again, held Grace tighter. There was a cluster of trees between them and Julia's house, she could make that much out, and she wasn't looking forward to walking on the little pathway that led through the trees.

The trail narrowed and she had to either step behind or in front of him.

He paused.

She nearly stumbled.

"There's nothing to be afraid of."

She denied the truth. "I'm not scared, I just like being prepared." That said, she came up with a plan. "We'll need to run if we see a coyote and I'm not sure of the way."

He chuckled. "Do you have any idea how fast a coyote can run?"

"No. Do you?"

"Yes. Faster than both of us put together." He tugged on her arm and started walking again. "You really are a city girl."

She hung close to his side, and chose not to reply. She might be a city girl, but also had good reason to be afraid of the dark. Chicago might not have had coyotes, but it had all sorts of things that could attack you late at night.

In the dark.

Like this.

"Don't fret, we're almost there."

She forced her feet to keep moving as they grew closer and closer to the cluster of trees.

Jack bit the inside of his cheek to keep from laughing. He might never have seen someone as scared as she was right now. Someone who'd never heard the sound before could be scared by a coyote's howl. There was an eeriness to it like no other. But it was also easy to get used to. He remembered falling to sleep to the sound. It had been a long way between towns while his parents had been acting in playhouses across the center of the nation. During good years, they'd traveled by trains. Not so good years, it had been a wagon and horse. Once it had been a mule, one that had been too stubborn to move most of the time.

He and Joe had spent hours pulling that stupid critter forward, and had slept a lot of nights beneath that wagon. Remembering listening to coyotes was a good memory. That meant it hadn't been raining or snow-ing. There had been nights he'd probably have frozen to death if Joe hadn't snuggled up against him. Kept him warm.

A walk down memory lane wasn't what he needed right now.

"So," he started, looking for something else to focus on. "You lived in Chicago your entire life, but don't have any family there?"

"No. None."

He nodded, but didn't say anything because concern tickled his spine. He should be able to see lights on at Julia's house. It was just on the other side of the grove of trees.

Side by side, they stepped through the trees, and he surveyed the house. The dark house. "Julia must have already gone to bed."

"Is it that late?" Her voice quivered slightly.

"No, actually, her car is gone," he answered, nodding toward where it was usually parked. "She must have had somewhere to go tonight."

"Maybe someone borrowed her car," she said hopefully.

"Let's go see," he said, stepping forward.

A few minutes later, Jack wasn't sure if he was happy or not. No one answered the door and the place was locked tight. He couldn't leave them here, not without Julia home, and Grace was getting fussy. Hungry. Wet. Both maybe. He didn't know.

He had offered to take them to his apartment, and would, if necessary, but he wasn't so sure that was a good idea.

Grace let out a solid wail.

Helen talked softly to the baby, but her fussiness

continued. Not an all-out cry like before, but it sounded like that's what she was working up to.

Good idea or not, he didn't have a choice. "Let's go."

"Go where?"

"To my apartment."

"But—"

"Julia's not home, and Grace is hungry, or wet or something." He took hold of Helen's elbow again and turned her back toward the trail that led through the grove of trees. "I'll give you a ride back here in the morning."

This time she was too busy dealing with Grace to worry about coyotes. He led her all the way to his car in the studio's parking lot, and held the door open while she climbed in, trying her best to hush the fussy baby.

"It's not far," he said, dropping the bag in the backseat before closing the door and walking around to the driver's side.

The three miles to the apartment went quickly, in some ways. To Grace, it appeared, it was way too long. She was crying in earnest by the time he parked the car.

"She'll quiet down as soon as she's fed," Helen said, as if apologizing.

Like before, the sound of Gracie's sobs did something to his heart. Though his niece would never remember this night, she was far too young, he could remember being hungry. It was a miserable feeling.

"This way," he said, grabbing the bag out of the backseat as soon as Helen had climbed out. "Through that door and up the stairs."

There was a total of sixteen apartments in the building. His was on the second of four floors. Solidly built of bricks, the walls were thick so he wasn't overly concerned that Grace's crying would disturb anyone. If it did, too bad.

Helen talked quietly to the baby, telling her everything would be all right very soon, as they hurried to the building and up the stairs. He unlocked the door and let them in, then hit the light switch, kicked the door shut and set the bag on the table near the door so he could open it all at the same time.

He found the bottle, milk and can opener. Unsure what to do, he set them on the little table. "Here, I'll take her. The kitchen is straight ahead. You get the bottle ready."

"Thank you," Helen said. "I'll hurry. I've rarely heard her cry like this."

The moment he took Grace and placed her up against his chest, she stopped crying. Her little body shook slightly from the remnants of her sobs, but as her eyes met his, her little petal-shaped lips formed a smile.

A warmth like he'd never known filled his chest. It was as if his heart opened up. He hadn't felt anything like that in a long time. It was like an explosion of emotions he'd forgotten lived inside him.

"You must have a way with her," Helen said, picking up the can of milk and the bottle.

"No," he answered honestly, "I think she has a way with me."

She frowned slightly, but then smiled. "She's very easy to love. I'll be right back."

He slid Grace higher onto his shoulder, so her little face was in the crook of his neck. Easy to love. He could believe that. Patting Grace's back gently, he crossed the room to the window that was opened a few inches. A sense of protectiveness filled him as he stood there, holding his niece.

His niece.

Joe's daughter.

"I'm here, Gracie-girl," he whispered softly. "Don't fret. No matter what happens, your uncle Jack will always be here for you. I swear you'll never go hungry. Never be cold." He dipped his head and kissed the top of the soft curly blond hair covering head. "Never be alone. Not as long as I'm alive. I swear."

She nuzzled the side of his neck and then lifted her little head, looked up at him with a pair of big brown eyes. A couple of teardrops still sat on her cheeks, yet she grinned. An adorable, toothless grin that would have stolen his heart if she already hadn't accomplished that.

He stood there, holding her, thinking, until Helen reappeared, with a bottle in hand.

She used the tip of one finger to wipe away the last teardrop from Grace's face. "She's going to fall asleep while drinking this bottle. Do you mind holding her a moment longer? I'll get a diaper and change her now that she's calmed down. Then she'll be ready to sleep for several hours."

"I don't mind. Get whatever you need." He nodded toward a door on his left. "The bathroom is right there. The other door is the bedroom."

Helen glanced toward the doors and then back at him. An odd quiver tickled Jack's spine as their gazes locked. His attention had been focused on Grace, but suddenly the full magnitude of the situation came to light. Of the two of them living here. With him.

There would be consequences to that.

It's only for one night, he told himself. *One night.*

Chapter Six

Helen's mouth was dry. Completely dry. Like towels left on the clothesline with no wind to soften them. Her heart was thudding, hard and fast. The sight of Jack standing there, holding Grace, shouldn't affect her this way. He was just a man holding a baby. But he was doing so with such care and attention.

Grace made a cooing sound. It was soft, but enough to kick Helen's senses into gear enough that she pulled her eyes away.

She then spun around, and though her legs trembled, she walked over to the bag on the table near the door and collected a diaper. Purposefully not making eye contact with Jack, she walked back across the room and told herself not to notice how carefully he handed Grace to her.

Once in the bathroom, she took a moment to collect herself, and then quickly changed Grace and returned to the front room.

It was empty.

The bedroom door was open. She peeked into the room. He wasn't in there.

Quietly, she crossed the room and looked into the kitchen.

He wasn't there, either.

Her sigh of relief didn't last long. Uncertainty took its place. Where could he have gone? As much as she didn't want to admit it, his presence had become reassuring.

That was now gone.

As gone as he seemed to be.

Grace must have noticed as well, because she started fussing again.

"It's all right, sweetie," Helen whispered. "Let's get you fed."

Picking the bottle off the short table in front of the sofa, she sat down. The softness of the furniture practically surrounded her. It had been a long time since she sat on something so comfortable. The upholstery was a soft velvet and dark green. There were two chairs of the same material, with high backs and wooden arms and cushions as thick as those she sat upon. Leaning back, she held the bottle up to Grace's lips.

Grace latched on to the nipple like she hadn't eaten in years rather than hours. Helen had to smile, and nestled down into the softness, enjoying the sweetness of the moment. That's what happened when she sat like this, holding Grace. The baby made it possible for her to block out the rest of the world.

The bottle was almost empty by the time Grace's hunger was satisfied. Her eyes were closed and her lips moved only now and again. Experience had taught Helen not to remove the nipple too soon, so she sat still for a few minutes, or longer, waiting for Grace to fall completely asleep.

Helen leaned her head back as her own eyelids grew very heavy. She was so tired and the sofa was so comfortable. She would just rest her eyes for a few moments. Not fall asleep. That wouldn't happen. She hadn't slept in weeks. Certainly not on the train. Before that, between taking care of Vera and then Grace, and working nights at Amery's store, she'd learned to survive on catnaps.

Even though she wondered where Jack had gone, the apartment, with its thick brick walls, made her feel secure. It was odd to feel that way in the heart of the city, but that's how it had been back in Chicago, too. It was much harder to be found, picked out, in a crowd.

There was a sound. A soft one. She considered ignoring it, but then snapped her head up, realizing she couldn't let her guard down. Not anywhere.

Jack was walking through the door, carrying a box. Helen released the air from her lungs as relief once again washed over her. Heat rushed into her face too, at the way he smiled. She glanced down at Grace.

"Is she asleep?" he asked while quietly closing the door.

"Yes," Helen whispered in return, lowering the empty bottle onto her lap.

"I got her a case of canned milk." He carried the box toward the kitchen.

Surprised, and feeling a sense of guilt, she said, "I didn't mean you had to do that tonight."

"I know, but I also knew Nick would still be at his store."

She watched as he disappeared into the kitchen. "His store is open this late?"

"No, but the speakeasy in the basement is, and he's

usually there until ten." He returned to the living room. "Nick owns the store at the end of the block. If you need anything, just tell him I sent you. He knows I'm good for it."

Although she doubted she'd ever go to the store, she nodded. "That will be enough milk for several days."

He rested his elbows on the top of the tall-backed chair. "Where does she sleep? In bed with you?"

Helen hadn't thought that far ahead. "I held her on the train, before that she slept in a basket."

"A basket? How big of a basket?"

She shrugged. "A regular basket."

"That couldn't have been big enough for her to even roll over."

"She hasn't rolled over yet."

"Because she's never had room."

Helen grinned at his logic. "That may be. The book says it should happen soon. Her rolling over."

"What book?"

"The one I bought about babies."

"Didn't know they existed. Books about babies. It makes sense though. I might have to borrow it."

He was grinning and nodding his head. Once again, Helen had to pull her eyes off him. "The book explains that babies should sleep in something with sides on it, so when they do roll over, they don't fall on the floor. It's in my suitcase." Her suitcase was still at Julia's. That wasn't the end of the world. Other than a few articles of clothes, the book was the only thing in it.

He was now scratching his chin. Then, as if he'd just thought of something, he held up a finger and walked toward the bedroom. "I'll be right back."

The light clicked on, but she couldn't see into the

bedroom. There was noise. It wasn't loud or disturbing, but she was curious as to what he was doing. She set the bottle on the table, careful to not jostle Grace, and leaned over, trying to see into the room, but it was to no avail.

He appeared in the doorway a few minutes later. "Bring her in here." Frowning slightly, he then asked, "Do you need help?"

"No," Helen replied, standing up carefully. "Just don't want to wake her."

He stepped into the room as she walked around one of the tall-backed chairs. Helen was curious, yet moved slowly, cautious as to what he wanted her to see.

She crossed the threshold. The room was rather large. A bed, with decorative metal head and foot rails and neatly made with a rust-colored chenille bedspread, sat in the middle of the room with a window near the head for the breeze to blow on whoever slept there. There was a large tan-colored vanity, complete with padded stool and mirror on one wall, and a matching chest of drawers on the other. That's where he stood.

"Bring her here," he said, grinning so broadly a dimple had formed in one cheek.

Helen looked at him and the dresser again. The bottom drawer had been removed and was sitting on top of the dresser. "Why?" she asked, even while walking across the room. Like in the living room, the floor was mostly covered with a large patterned rug that was so plush it completely muffled her footsteps.

"To see if she fits. I put a folded blanket on the bottom and covered it with a sheet. It's larger than a basket, and has to be more comfortable."

Helen couldn't say exactly what happened inside her, but it felt as if something was melting. Warmth bubbled beneath her breastbone at his thoughtfulness and ingenuity.

"Lay her down. See if she likes it." He grasped the edge of the drawer. "It's solid."

Gently, Helen laid Grace into the drawer. The baby let out a little sigh, and as if knowing she had more room than ever before, she flopped her little arms out at her sides.

"Look at that," he whispered. "I think she likes having more room."

"I think you are right." Helen's eyes smarted at how kind his actions had been. The milk. The drawer. Not wanting him to notice, she glanced around.

"She'll sleep like a baby in that." He chuckled softly at his own pun.

She pinched her lips together, keeping a smile at bay. "You are probably right again, but you won't get any sleep." Helen glanced toward the neatly made bed with matching lamps hosting marbled glass shades sitting on small tables on each side of the bed. "Not with her in here. She wakes up in the middle of the night for a bottle."

"That won't bother me," he said. "And you'll easily hear her from the bed."

Helen's heart rate increased. "I c-can't sleep in your bed," she sputtered, her cheeks on fire.

"Yes, you can, and will," he said. "I'll sleep on the couch."

Helen's cheeks burned hotter at the way he was looking at her, as if she'd just implied they would be sleeping in the same bed. That wasn't what she'd been thinking. It was his apartment. His bed. "I'll sleep on the couch. We can carry the drawer to the other room, put it on the table. It'll be near the kitchen for when she does wake up and I need to fix her bottle."

"The two of you will have more privacy in here," he said, as if he hadn't heard her explanation.

"She usually needs to be changed in the middle of the night, too." Helen followed him out of the room. "You can sleep in the bedroom with the door closed, so none of that will wake you."

"None of that will bother me." He picked up Grace's flour sack of possessions and walked toward the bedroom again.

She turned around and followed. "But it's your bed."

"Exactly. So I get to say who sleeps in it." He set the bag on the bed and grabbed a pillow. "I'm assuming your things must still be at Julia's?"

Taken aback by the change of subject, she merely nodded.

"All right, then, it's late, and we are both tired." He walked to the door. "Let's get some sleep and we'll face tomorrow when it arrives. Good night."

A second later, the door shut. Helen questioned opening it and following him again. But accepting that would be useless, that she wouldn't win this argument no matter how hard she tried, she stood still, looking around the room. Noticing things she hadn't noticed before. The closet door. The sheer curtains on both windows, the pictures on the walls.

She moved closer, examining both men. Jack and Joe. Dressed in suits and standing side by side in front of the studio. Joe had his arm around Jack, and they were both smiling. Looked genuinely happy.

A sense of melancholy washed over her. Her mother had loved taking pictures. She'd taken pictures of everything. Everyone.

It had been over two years since that dreadful day, but there were times when it felt like yesterday. The pain was still there. And the guilt.

Helen turned away from the picture, and wondered, as she had many times before, what had become of those pictures Mother had taken. Of all the possessions her family had owned. She'd never gone back to the house.

Shaking her head, she attempted to dispel other thoughts that wanted to come forward. Things she wanted to forget, as well as some she wanted to remember. Neither would do her any good right now. Nor would they do Grace any good.

She glanced at the bed, and telling herself it was only for one night, she sat down to remove her shoes. Tomorrow Jack would take her and Grace back to Julia's, where they would stay for the next eight weeks, and then…

Well, like Jack had said, she'd face it when it arrived. That was a good philosophy.

Her mind wasn't easily convinced though, even after she shut off the light and lay down on the bed. As usual, when her head hit the pillow, her mind kicked into high gear, coming up with all sorts of things that prevented her from falling asleep. It had been that way for a long time now, but the alternative was worse. The nightmares that plagued her when she did fall asleep. They could be horrific at times. Plenty of times she'd purposefully kept her thoughts running in circles, just so she didn't fall asleep. Didn't dream.

Tonight, her mind was going in circles all on its own, and coming back to one thing. Jack. The way he'd looked while holding Grace. How readily he smiled. How handsome he was. How he was sleeping on the other side of the door.

Helen flipped onto her side, as if that would change the directions of her thoughts.

Jack wasn't entirely sure what woke him, and lay still for a moment, listening through the sounds of the morning traffic filtering in from the window. He couldn't make out any sounds coming from the bedroom, and wondered if Grace had woken up in the middle of the night. He hadn't. Not that he could remember.

He sat up and stretched his arms over his head to get the kinks out of his back. Despite all, he'd slept remarkably well. Even though his mind had had a hard time shutting off last night. Knowing Helen was just on the other side of his bedroom door had given his imagination plenty of ammunition to keep him awake. He'd have to get ahold of Joe as soon as possible. Find a resolution to this situation. Quickly.

Two months from now, he'd have more time to work out a solution. Possibly. If all worked out in his favor, he might be busier then than he was now. That was what he'd hoped for. Still did. This was his chance to succeed, and he wanted that. Wanted to succeed. To know that he'd never be reliant on someone else for money, or food even. Not like when he and Joe had been kids living hand to mouth.

He glanced at the clock on the wall and stood. Filming was scheduled to start in two hours, and he had things to do before then.

He rose and started for the bathroom, but paused as the bedroom door latch clicked. A full-fledged smile formed and he slid up against the wall to watch. The door barely cracked open and little more than a pert nose appeared as Helen peered out of the narrow opening. She looked toward the sofa, and seeing it empty, pulled the door open wider.

Taking advantage of the moment, he stepped away from the wall and darted in front of her. "Boo!"

She jumped backward. "Oh!"

He laughed.

"That was not funny," she said, with one hand pressed to her chest. "Not at all."

"I thought it was." He also thought she was even prettier this morning than last night. Her hair was hanging loose, a tumbling cascade of shimmering brown that fell way past her shoulders. He liked it. Most women wore their hair short.

Twisting, she glanced over her shoulder. "You could have woken Grace."

He looked over her head. The drawer was still on the dresser, and Grace lying in it. Fast asleep. "I didn't hear her wake up in the middle of the night."

"She didn't," Helen whispered. "She hasn't woken since I laid her down."

"She must like her new bed." Even though it was a mere dresser drawer, a sense of pride filled him at the idea of his niece liking the bed he'd given her. His niece. That reality was growing on him. It had been a long time since he had family near.

"Yes, she must, or she was just extremely tired from staying up well past her bedtime."

The smirk on Helen's face was not only cute, it

showed she had a sense of humor. Something he hadn't seen before. He liked that too. "How did you sleep?"

Her cheeks turned bright pink and she quickly looked away.

He noticed something else then. "Did you sleep in your clothes?"

She attempted to smooth out the wrinkles of the material covering her trim waist with both hands. Cheeks turning redder, she huffed out a breath and then pointed at him. "Did you?"

Inclined to tease her, he shrugged. "I didn't want to shock you."

Even her confused frown was adorable.

He winked. "I assumed seeing me sleeping on the couch stark naked would shock you. Maybe not."

"Oh!" She slapped a hand over her mouth.

He laughed and touched the tip of her chin. "So, yes, I slept in my clothes, and now that you're awake, I'm going to get a fresh suit out of the closet and get ready for work."

Careful to not wake the sleeping baby, he collected his items quietly and then went into the bathroom. The image of Helen, with her pale blue eyes, stayed with him the entire time he washed up, shaved and put on clean clothes. So did his smile.

The smell of coffee filled the air when he left the bathroom. Following his nose, he walked to the kitchen. His breath caught in his lungs at the sight he found. Helen was at the table, feeding Grace a bottle. Sun rays shone through the window, landing on them, but it was the serenity on Helen's face as she looked down on Grace that was downright spectacular.

She glanced up. "I made coffee. I hope you don't mind."

He had to clear his throat before his voice would work. "I don't mind."

"I noticed you have a basket of eggs, I can fry them for you once Grace is finished eating."

"How about I fry them while she eats," he offered. "How do you like them?"

"I have no preference," she answered. "But I can do it, she won't be much longer."

He walked toward the refrigerator. "I'm perfectly capable of frying eggs," he said. "I do it all the time." For some odd reason, he wanted to show her just how capable he was, not only at frying eggs. The episode of not knowing what to do for Grace last evening had been embarrassing. He'd never been so out of his element.

"She is almost done," Helen said. "You might get splatters on your suit."

He removed his suit coat and draped it over a chair, then walked to the fridge. "I have others."

"Will you give us a ride to Julia's this morning?"

Disappointment hit so hard he almost dropped an egg. There was no reason for that. It was better for everyone for them to stay with Julia. Especially him. "Yes. As soon as we are done eating."

Besides the eggs, they ate bread and jam. Helen insisted upon cleaning up the kitchen. They left afterward. Their conversation focused on Grace, and what the book she'd purchased said about babies.

As soon as he turned onto the road leading up to the studio, traffic quickly slowed to a crawl, and it wasn't until they were but a block away that he discovered why.

"What's wrong?" Helen asked.

"I'm not sure." Keeping one hand on the wheel, he gestured up the road. "Something must be happening at Julia's."

"Julia's?" She leaned over to see around the vehicle ahead of them. "Oh, my! Those are police cars."

A shiver zipped up Jack's spine at the fear in her voice. He reached over and laid a hand on her arm. It was shivering, and icy cold. "I'm sure everyone is all right," he said, trying to assure her, even while hoping there hadn't been a break in, or something worse.

It didn't seem to help. He felt her body stiffen beneath his hand, and remain that way, as if frozen stiff. Turning before the diner, he pulled into the studio parking lot and parked the car in his usual spot. "You can wait in my office. I'll go across the street and see what's happening."

She didn't argue, and was trembling from head to toe. He climbed out and walked around the car. Opening her door, he took Grace from her. Holding the baby in one arm, he reached in and took Helen's arm. "I'm sure it's nothing."

Her eyes were full of fear as she looked up at him.

"Come," he said softly. "It'll be fine. I promise."

"I…" She shook her head.

"Don't worry." Jack eased her out of the car. "You're safe with me. I promise." He wondered what was happening next door, but was more concerned about her. She was seriously trembling.

He wrapped his free arm around her and led her to the studio. She tucked her head against her chin and nearly dashed for the door. Once inside his office, he helped her sit down on the couch and then laid the blanket on the floor. Grace was cooing and smiling, clearly unaffected. He knelt down and laid the baby on the blanket. "You be a good girl, Gracie. Uncle Jack will be right back."

Still on his knee, he turned to Helen. "I'll go across the street and find out what's happening. No one is here yet, so you won't be disturbed." He wasn't sure why he was inclined to say that, but the way she still had her chin down, and her shoulders tucked in, made him think she didn't want anyone to see her. As if she could hide inside her own skin. "I'll be back in a few minutes."

She covered her mouth with both hands, which were still trembling.

That concerned him even more. "Would you rather I stayed here with you?"

She lowered her hands to her lap. "No, we'll be fine. Please go see what's happening."

He grasped her hands, squeezed them. "All right. I won't be long."

She gave a small nod. "Thank you."

He questioned whether he should leave her, but instinctively knew she wouldn't come out of the stupor of fear until she knew why the police cars were at Julia's. Anxious about leaving her in this condition, he left the room quickly and jogged down the hallway. Once outside, he ran across the street.

A crowd stood outside the door. "What's going on?"

"Seems Julia helped a couple of girls escape during a raid last night. The coppers are here to find them," a man answered.

Jack might know who the guy was, if he cared to

think about it hard enough. Right now, that wasn't important. "Was one of them Rosie?" She wasn't the type to be happy waiting tables and was one Julia would go to rescue.

"Sure is. They're searching the place, looking for her."

"Where was the raid?" he asked. Not that it mattered, he just hoped it was a speakeasy and not an opium joint. Girls that got mixed up in those rarely got away.

"Don't know. Had to be downtown. That's the precinct these bulls are from."

Jack didn't wait long enough to scan the cop cars—he'd heard enough and jogged back to the studio.

Helen wasn't on the couch. She'd moved to the floor, sitting beside Grace, but jumped to her feet as he opened the door.

The fear now burning in her eyes sent him forward. She met him in the middle of the room. Her eyes asking far more than any spoken words could. "Is—?" A sob escaped at the same time tears formed.

Something let loose inside him. "Everyone is fine." He pulled her close, holding her head against his chest. "It was just a raid downtown. Julia helped some girls escape and they are looking for them."

He felt her relief, and held her tighter as she melted against him.

"I told you it was nothing to worry about," he whispered. "Nothing at all. Julia has been known to rescue more than one girl who has found themselves in trouble."

He pinched his lips together as soon as the words were out of his mouth. She was sure to assume he was including her in that explanation. He hadn't been, but now realized that was true. He just didn't know what her trouble was, other than it didn't have to do with Grace. He was sure of that.

Chapter Seven

Helen's heart still raced, but her fear had subsided a small amount. She wasn't sure if that was because of Jack's arms, or the reason he'd claimed the police were at Julia's place. She was extremely thankful that she and Grace hadn't been there. Not last night, and not now. The police might have asked who she was, where she was from.

Even though she didn't want to, she knew she had to, so she eased backward, slipping out of his hold.

Dropping her hands to her sides, she squeezed them into fists against the tremors still quaking inside her. "You're sure Julia's all right?"

"Yes, I'm sure. She can hold her own. Everyone knows that."

She had no reason to believe he was lying. And truly didn't think he was. Yet couldn't dispel the doubt inside her. Not so much doubt as fear. She sucked in a breath. "A raid on what?"

He shrugged. "I don't know for sure. Rosie was involved."

Her heart leaped into her throat all over again. "Rosie?"

"They are looking for her." He reached out and took her hands. "You and Grace shouldn't go over there right now."

The warmth of his hands holding hers kept her heart racing, but it also gave her a grounding, a comfort that she sincerely needed. "No." Swallowing at the lump in her throat, she shook her head. "No, we shouldn't."

"Do you want to go back to the apartment?" He glanced around. "Or you could stay here."

No, she couldn't. Not with the police next door. "Would you mind if we went back to your apartment?" Trying to come up with a reason, she glanced over at Grace. The baby was no problem, so she couldn't use her as an excuse.

"No, I don't mind. I think both of you will be more comfortable there."

He gave her hands a squeeze before releasing them and walking toward Grace. Helen closed her eyes for a moment. Telling herself she shouldn't go back to his apartment, but she couldn't stay here. Not with the police searching the area.

His hand touched her shoulder. "Ready?"

She opened her eyes, took a deep breath and nodded. Would this ever end? Would there ever be a time when a police car didn't scare the dickens out of her? Fearing they were in cahoots with the family and looking for her?

No. There wouldn't be. That was her life.

The ride back to the apartment was uneventful, thank goodness, and the familiarity of the apartment eased her nerves considerably.

"I'll be home sometime after six," Jack said. He'd already carried the case of milk back into the kitchen.

"There's a phone downstairs in the hallway near the mailboxes. I'll write down my office number and leave instructions with Miss Hobbs to come get me if you call for any reason."

"There's no reason to do that," she said. "We'll be fine. No reason to call you."

A frown tugged at his dark brows. "I'll write down the number just in case." He crossed the room and disappeared into the kitchen again.

Just because he wrote it down didn't mean she'd use it. There was no need for her to say that. She wouldn't leave the apartment, never even open the door.

Moving to the kitchen doorway, she watched him write on a piece of paper on the table. Much like the bathroom, the kitchen was very modern. Built-in cupboards took up two walls, painted the same pale yellow as the curtains on the windows. The stove with its side oven, the refrigerator and the sink were white and the floor was covered with white-and-black-checkered linoleum.

"Nick's grocery store is at the end of the block. Out the door and to the left." He pulled out his billfold and set several dollars on top of the paper he'd written on.

"Thank you, but we won't need anything."

He tucked his billfold into his back pocket. "Well, if you think of something that either of you need, go ahead and buy it." He held out his hands, clearly inviting her to hand Grace to him.

She stepped forward and handed him the baby.

He bounced her in the air. "Anything at all that this little girl needs."

Grace giggled. He laughed and kissed her little head before handing her back.

"I'll see you two, tonight."

Helen followed him to the door, trying to think of something to say. As he grasped the doorknob, she settled for "Thank you for letting us stay here today. For bringing us back here, for, well, everything."

His smile produced that dimple in his cheek as he pulled open the door. "You're welcome. Have a good day."

"You, too."

He stepped into the hallway. "There's an extra key to this door hanging on a hook in the kitchen."

"All right." She was thankful to hear that, and would collect it as soon as he left.

He nodded. "Well, then, have a good day."

"You, too," she said once again, anxious to lock her and Grace inside, away from the outside world. Like it or not, that was her life.

He stepped out of the way and closed the door.

Helen hurried into the kitchen and found the key. After returning and locking the door, her entire body seemed to relax. She stood there for a moment, thinking about Jack. He certainly was far more handsome than other men, especially when he smiled. Not only did that dimple form, but his eyes shone. Sparkled. Much like Grace's did.

She glanced down at the baby, who was smiling up at her. "Your uncle Jack is a nice man," Helen whispered. "Don't you think?"

Grace giggled.

The sound filled Helen's chest with glee, smoothing over her earlier fear. She'd started out taking care of Grace out of necessity, but almost immediately, she'd recognized the joy it gave her. She'd promised Vera that she'd love Grace for her, but now, she loved her for herself as well.

"Because you are so easy to love, little lady," she said, pressing her lips to the top of Grace's head. "So very easy to love."

Another sense of relief filled her. If Joe was anything like his brother, Grace would be well taken care of, have a good life.

A few hours later, Helen decided the little apartment was exactly the type she wanted someday. A lovely breeze blew in through the windows, drying the diapers and few other articles of clothing she'd washed and draped over the string she'd tied between two kitchen chairs. She'd also scrubbed the floors and all the kitchen appliances. They hadn't been dirty, she just wanted to do something for Jack for letting them stay there.

That is what drove her to examine the contents of the cupboards, and upon finding a supply of canned foods that would work with the contents of the fridge, she determined what to make for an evening meal.

She seemed to have an endless supply of energy today. It could be because she'd slept remarkably well, despite waking up to check on Grace a couple of times. Or it could be because for the first time in a very long time, she wasn't looking over her shoulder all day. No one knew she was here, in this apartment, except Jack.

Feeling completely safe, and at ease, she'd taken a bath and washed her hair, leaving it hanging loose to dry. Someday, when she had the freedom to, she'd have it cut short, like the women she'd seen on the train.

At six o'clock on the dot, just as he'd said, Jack arrived home. The meal was complete and the table set. An odd, but not uncomfortable, nervousness wrestled inside her as he walked through the door.

"Good evening," he said, removing his suit coat and hanging it on the coat rack that stood beside a small table near the door. "How was your day?"

"G-good. How was yours?"

"Very productive. Got several scenes shot." He pointed toward the bedroom. "Is Grace sleeping?"

"Yes, she ate a short time ago."

He grinned. "I hope she left some for me. It smells delicious."

Her nerves wouldn't settle. She clasped her hands together, hoping that helped. She also hoped he'd like the canned ham she'd baked. She'd stocked them at the grocery store, but had never cooked one, or even tasted one. "Grace doesn't eat table food yet."

He chuckled. "I know, and I haven't even read that book of yours yet."

His teasing made her grin. "Well, I assumed you'd be hungry."

"You assumed correctly. Do I have time to peek in on Grace?"

The fact he already cared so much for Grace warmed her heart. That was exactly what she'd hoped for. Of course, when she'd been hoping that, she'd thought it would be Joe, not Jack, but either way, it made her happy. "Yes."

"Be right back." He winked one eye before walking to the bedroom.

Her heart did a complete somersault. With cheeks burning, she hurried into the kitchen to remove everything from the oven.

"You did go to the grocer."

Helen carried the platter of sliced ham to the table. "No, I didn't."

Jack's brows were furrowed as he stared at the various foods on the table. "Then where did all this come from?"

"Your cupboards and what was left in the fridge."

"Nifty." His tone held disbelief.

Disbelief filled her, too. "Don't you know what's in your cupboards?"

He pulled out a chair and nodded for her to sit in it. She did, but kept her gaze on his face, waiting for his answer. Everyone knew what was in their cupboards. Or what was not in them.

"No," he said, sitting in the chair across from her. "I don't eat here very often. Eggs for breakfast is about it."

"Then where do you eat?"

"Julia's a lot of the time." He shrugged while filling his plate. "Other places when she's not open. This looks fantastic."

Too distracted to say much more than "Thank you," she sat on a chair. Then, curious, she asked, "How did the food get in your cupboards?"

He chuckled. "I go shopping every so often, just in case I'm too busy to go out."

"Too busy doing what?"

He took a bite of ham before answering, "Working on a script."

She bit her lips together, watching his face as he swallowed, hoping the food tasted as good as it smelled. The aromas had been making her stomach growl for the last hour.

"You must have been a cook back in Chicago," he

said, cutting another piece of ham off the slice on his plate. "This is delicious."

Happiness bubbled in her stomach. "No, I stocked shelves in a grocer." She quickly forked food into her mouth, having said more than she should have. More than she'd told anyone, even Julia.

"Your mother must have taught you, then, and she must have been a good cook."

He was smiling, and eating as if he was truly enjoying the food.

"She was a good cook," Helen admitted, refusing to let her mind go any further down a road that wouldn't do her any good.

"Mine wasn't." He forked another slice of ham off the platter in the center of the table. "I think the only times I saw her pick up a frying pan was to chase my father with it when she thought he was paying too much attention to another actress."

Although the image he'd just described was a bit horrific in her mind, he was still smiling, his eyes sparkling. "Your mother was an actress?"

Chewing, he nodded. "We all were," he said after swallowing. "But don't let that fool you, it wasn't nearly as wonderful as people think." He shook his head. "I was so glad when I got old enough that I no longer had to go on stage and could work behind the scenes instead."

"Like you do now?"

"No, I was merely a prop boy then, and it wasn't in a studio." He didn't appear repulsed, but there was a tone of disgust in his voice.

"Where was it?"

"Theaters or playhouses once in a while, but usually

barns, community halls, churches, even open fields. Wherever we could set up a stage and hang a curtain." His plate was empty and he set down his fork. "My parents were vaudeville actors. We traveled the nation, stopping wherever and whenever to put on a performance. If my father thought there were enough people willing to shell out the money for tickets, we stopped. If not, we moved on to the next town. Both Joe and I performed, too. Dancing and singing when we were little. The opening act. I look back now and laugh at how awful we had been. How awful I'd been. Joe would get so mad at me. He loved performing as much as my parents did, especially afterward, when people would crowd around to meet the actors. I hated that and couldn't wait to pack up and leave."

Helen couldn't remember being so interested or fascinated by someone, and wanted to know more. "You don't like crowds?"

"I don't mind crowds, I just don't like being crowded. I didn't like all the attention either." He propped his elbows on the table and clasped his hands together. "It was hard on a kid. Being hugged and kissed by women of all ages and sneered at by other kids. It wasn't so bad when we traveled with larger shows. Then there were enough people that I could slip away, but when it was just the four of us…" He shrugged. "There was no place to hide then."

Her heart went out to him, fully understanding. "Where are your parents now?"

"They died when Joe and I were in our teens. Mother from pneumonia in Idaho and a few months later, father from a couple of roadway robbers in Northern California."

A flash of alarm had her pressing a hand over her heart. "Roadway robbers?"

He nodded. "They followed us after a performance, to steal the money we'd made. They got it, and Dad died two days later from a blow to the head that he'd taken. We'd been on our way here, to Los Angeles, so that's what Joe and I did, came here."

Helen stared at the plate in front of her. She didn't know what to say, how to express the sorrow she felt for him.

"How did your parents die?"

"A fire," she replied out of habit. It was a lie. One she'd created out of necessity. An explanation of how she'd ended up alone on the streets of Chicago. "I wasn't home, but my mother, father and brother had been."

"How old were you?"

"Seventeen."

"How old are you now?"

She let the air out of her lungs. Lying to him was harder than it had been to others. A part of her wanted to tell him the truth. That had never happened before. Not even with Vera. "Nineteen."

"You've had a tough couple of years."

Needing to move the focus off herself, she said, "You did too. More than a couple."

"Everyone does in one way or another, but life goes on."

She couldn't help but stare at him. For all he'd just said, how hard all that had to have been, he sounded so optimistic.

"All we can do is go forward, look toward the future and leave the past behind." He stood up and picked up his plate. "Thank you for all of this. It was delicious."

A bit surprised by his change of subject, she stood. "You're welcome. It's the least I could do for letting us stay here."

"You don't owe me anything, I owe you." He set his plate on the counter and stood there for a minute. "I have to tell you something."

He turned around and the seriousness of his expression sent her heart to her throat. A dozen things flashed through her mind, before one settled on Grace. "Did you find Joe?" She held on tighter to the dishes in her hands, bracing herself for his answer.

"No." He stepped forward and took the plate from her hand. "But I did talk to Julia."

Relief, along with a bout of guilt for having forgotten about the police at the diner this morning, washed over her. "Did they find Rosie?"

He set her plate on the counter by his. "The police, no. Because Julia hid her in a cabin in the woods until things cool off."

"Why? What happened?"

"Rosie got herself mixed in with the wrong crowd. Called Julia from a dope den last night." He shook his head. "That stuff is as deadly as coffin varnish."

She knew how deadly that was. Prohibition laws hadn't stopped people from drinking, it only made it more dangerous. Bootleg liquor was made from anything people could find, and often proved poisonous. Her father had prided himself on knowing the good stuff from the bad. That's what he'd specialized in. Bootlegging for the family. She'd heard about opium dens, too. How people walked in and were carried out, straight to the morgue. If she'd needed proof Los Angeles was as deadly as Chicago, she had it now. Just like liquor, mobs were behind the dens. They had been in Chicago and probably where here, too.

"Julia said she picked up Rosie before the raid happened, along with three other girls, but somewhere along the line, it spread that Rosie had called in the bulls."

"Did she?"

"Julia said Rosie only called her, but it doesn't matter. Rosie needs to lie low for a while because someone did make that call. The owners of those places are in tight with the police, and neither one of them want to get caught with their hands in each other's pockets. If they can make a patsy out of Rosie, they will."

Further proof hadn't been needed, but she got it anyway. No rock unturned. Helen's entire being grew jittery and to combat it, she started clearing the table. "Is Rosie all right?"

"Yes, but she'll be staying in the cabin for the time being. The other girls Julia got out of there are staying with her, too."

Helen carried a stack of dishes to the sink. She didn't know Rosie well, but knew she wouldn't like hiding out. Neither had she, but it had suited her better than it would one as vivacious as Rosie. From her dyed red and permed hair to her bright lipstick and flashy clothes, everything about the waitress had shouted *look at me*, and that's exactly what Rosie had wanted. To stand out. Get noticed. Become famous.

The exact opposite of her.

"You know what that means, don't you?"

Helen didn't move away from the sink, not exactly sure what he was talking about.

"You and Grace will need to stay here."

That hadn't even crossed her mind. It would have eventually. Probably.

"I picked up your suitcase. It's down in my car."

She turned and walked to the table for more dishes. Why didn't that upset her? The idea of staying here? With him? It should.

As if she'd heard her name, a sound came from the bedroom. It wasn't a cry, just more a call out from Gracie saying she was awake and ready to be picked up. Helen set down the dishes she was holding.

"I'll go see to her," Jack said.

Helen merely nodded. Her mind was too cluttered for anything else. She was no longer the naïve girl who had thought that a typing certificate and a job would change her life. That had been nothing more than a silly notion, because at the time she'd still been in the dark about so many things. Mother had run a strict household. It hadn't been until after the raid that Helen had realized how sheltered she'd been. How she'd been molded into a quiet and shy child who didn't ask questions.

Her mother had been diligent about not having her exposed to the world outside of their house. She'd grown up knowing the streets were full of bad people. It hadn't been until she was fourteen and Amelia, who had been older by several years, had been mugged by members of the North End Gang that she'd come to understand her family constituted a large number of those ruling the streets.

The North End Gang had been encroaching on the Outfit's territory, and the mugging of Amelia had been a warning of what was to come. An all-out war between the North End Gang and the Outfit. There had been no one to stop it. The police precincts on the North End belonged to that gang, just as thoroughly as the precincts the Outfit oversaw.

It had been during those months that Helen had decided she wanted out. A naïve thought for sure. Even if the raid hadn't happened, and she'd gone to work typing at the laundry, she'd have still been as embedded as ever because the Outfit owned the laundry, which is why she'd been offered the job in the first place.

Helen huffed out a breath and glanced around. Is that why she didn't mind staying here, at Jack's apartment, because just like back in Chicago, when she'd wanted out, all she'd really done was hide?

She had Grace to worry about now. Did that make staying with Jack more appealing? That the protection he would be providing his niece, also extended to her?

Jack lifted Grace out of the drawer, smiling back at the big grin she displayed. He'd wondered how Helen would take to the news that Julia didn't have room for her and Grace right now. Even if Julia did have room, he'd have had to stop them from going back there. He had enough going on without worrying about who might be looking for Rosie and what they might do to anyone who got in their way.

Dope was a big thing out here right now, growing bigger due to prohibition laws. People would forever search for something to alter how they felt. That's what it came down to. Booze. Dope. People drank it, smoked it, because they wanted to feel different. But Jack had never been tempted to try the stuff himself, instead finding that euphoric feeling others got from booze and dope by focusing on something he could do, something he could achieve. That had become the studio, and he'd dedicated his life to it.

Joe had too. They'd worked hard getting it off the ground, building it up from nothing.

Looking down at Grace, who was still smiling up at him, he had to admit that today had been the first time he'd looked forward to locking the door of the studio at the end of the day. Matter of fact, this morning had been the first time he'd had any sort of pangs about going to work.

The second time he'd left the apartment, when he'd had to leave Helen and Grace here alone. He'd felt torn at the idea of wanting to be in two places at one time.

He pondered that for a second, looking down at the grinning baby in his arms. The future he dreamed about hadn't ever included others. Not even Joe. He'd been the responsible one for so long, the idea of being accountable only for his own actions appealed to him. He couldn't remember a time when he hadn't been the one following others, because he was the one cleaning up what was being left behind. Even the campsites when they'd been traveling as a family, while the others loaded up to move on, he'd been the one making sure the fire was out and snatching up belongings others had forgotten to put away.

As the age-old sense of resentment rose up inside him, he squelched it, telling himself dwelling on the past would get him nowhere. The future, what lay ahead, was where he'd always kept his attention, and would continue to.

"Filming went great today, Gracie," he said, looking down at her.

She grinned. He smiled in return and lifted her high into the air.

"Great I say. This movie is going to change everything. Everything."

She let out a tiny giggle and he laughed aloud at her expression. Her eyes opened wider as he spun about again and her little legs kicked at the gown covering them.

"You like that, don't you?" he asked.

Taking her giggles as an answer, he jiggled her about while walking through the living room and into the kitchen.

"Look who is awake," he said, gently grasping Grace's hand and making it wave at Helen.

"I heard the two of you laughing," Helen said, wiping her hands on a towel as she stepped closer.

Grace was cute when she smiled, with her chubby cheeks and twinkling eyes, but Helen—she was beyond cute. She was beautiful. When she smiled, her face lit up. Those magnificent eyes shone like nothing he'd ever seen. She was like nothing he'd ever seen.

She touched the tip of Grace's nose. "Laughing up a storm, that's what you were doing. Laughing up a storm." Looking at him, she asked, "Do you want me to take her?"

"No." He gestured toward the sink behind her. "I'd rather hold her than do dishes any day. But we'll stay in here and keep you company."

Her cheeks turned pink. "I wasn't expecting you to do the dishes."

He could stand here looking at her all night and never stop enjoying it. That wasn't like him. There had been a woman or two who had turned his head, but never held his attention like she did. "Then tell me, how would you do dishes while taking care of her?"

Her smile was laced with slyness as she turned and walked back to the sink. "I have my ways."

He sat down in a chair and propped Grace on his thigh. "You do, do you?"

She laughed. "Yes, I do."

The sound of her laughter was as entertaining as Grace's. Like music. He huffed out his own laugh as he watched her return to the task. "Doing the dishes was always my job."

"While you were traveling with your family?" She washed at a speed he'd never seen before, placing each item on a towel covering the counter.

"Yes. There were never as many as you have there. We only had the one frying pan and a few plates and bowls."

Using a second towel, she started drying the dishes and putting them in the cupboard, again with speed and preciseness. "If your mother didn't cook, who did?"

"Me." He hadn't thought of the meals they'd eaten along the road in years. Mainly because he hadn't wanted to. The past was in the past. "There wasn't all that much cooking to it. It usually was either eggs or potatoes."

The way she looked at him out of the top of her eyes reminded him of the glasses on his desk. The ones he'd known she hadn't needed even before accidently stepping on them.

"Why potatoes and eggs?" she asked.

"Because they are easy to steal in the middle of the night, and easy to carry while running when someone woke up and took chase." He hadn't thought about that in years. Him and Joe racing out of gardens and chicken coops. He laughed. "Plenty of eggs got broken in those escapes."

She was shaking her head, but smiling.

He shrugged. "It's the truth."

Laughing again, she said, "I don't doubt it is."

He did his best to look shocked. "It's that easy for you to believe I was a thief?"

Her eyes narrowed thoughtfully for a moment before she snapped the towel, folded it neatly and draped it over the edge of the sink. "You really aren't a very good actor, are you?"

Laughing along with her was as natural as walking. In fact, he hadn't felt this relaxed, this normal, for a long time. "No, I'm not."

She held out her arms to Grace who had become strangely fussy and rosy cheeked. "Here, I'll go change her."

Jack handed over Grace. "Another job I'll gladly let you handle."

He stayed in the kitchen while she carried Grace into the other room, glancing around. Everything was put neatly away. Actually, everything was sparkling clean.

She must have been cleaning all day. He'd been thinking about her all day, wondering what she was doing, if she was scared, still worried about the police. She'd been scared this morning. Truly frightened stiff.

"Jack! Jack!"

A shiver rippled his spine at the urgency in her voice.

Chapter Eight

Helen's heart was pounding so hard it hurt to breathe. "Feel her forehead. She's running a temperature."

Jack reached into the drawer and touched Grace's forehead. "She doesn't feel that warm."

"Yes, she does," Helen insisted, fearing the absolute worst. "It's tuberculosis. I know it is." She grabbed Jack's arm. "I know it is. The doctor said it could happen."

"What could happen?"

"Tuberculosis!" Her eyes stung as tears fell and she couldn't catch her breath. This couldn't be happening. She'd been so careful. So cautious. "No. No." Air was catching in her lungs.

"Hey." Jack took ahold of her upper arms. "Breathe," he said close to her face. "Catch your breath."

Helen tried to suck in air and push it out, but it hurt. Everything hurt. "She could die!"

"She's not going to die." His hold on her arms tightened. "She's fine. She's not even crying."

"She's running a temperature!" All the things she'd witnessed with Vera flew through Helen's mind. "She can't go to a sanitarium. Can't."

"She's not going to a sanitarium."

"That's what they wanted to do to Vera. Why she had to stay hidden."

"Vera?" He shot a glance over his shoulder at Grace. "That's what her mother died from? Tuberculosis?"

She saw the concern in Jack's eyes. Everyone knew how widespread tuberculosis had become. It was an epidemic. And awful. The amount of suffering that she'd witnessed Vera enduring flashed in her mind. A baby couldn't survive that. "Yes. They wanted to put her in a sanitarium. She was afraid of what would happen to Grace."

He pulled her forward and his tight hold lessened some of the hysteria that had been consuming her.

Laying her head against his chest, she absorbed some of his strength. His calmness. "She was afraid they wouldn't let Joe take Grace if that happened. That Grace would be confined to one her entire life. It's in her letters to him."

He grasped her shoulders and stepped back enough to look down at her.

There was concern in his face, and understanding. Everyone knew that when a child entered a sanitarium, they rarely left.

"Let's not jump to conclusions," he said. "I know a doctor. I'll go call him. Have him come look at Grace."

The doctor is who wanted to put Vera in the sanitarium. Would have insisted if she'd had the money that required. "But what if—"

Jack shook his head. "We aren't jumping to conclusions. Dr. Baine is an excellent physician. I'll be right back."

It wasn't until she heard the door close that Helen

realized Jack had softly kissed her forehead before he'd let her go and left. She touched the spot then, flustered at focusing on such a small thing, dropped her hand. She couldn't think about things like that, about herself, not with Grace sick.

Lying in the drawer, looking around, Grace certainly didn't appear ill, yet, as Helen laid her hand on the baby's forehead, her suspicions were once again confirmed. Grace was warmer than usual. She hadn't been earlier. Could the signs of TB show up that quickly?

She had read all the pamphlets the doctor in Chicago had given her, but her mind was muddled now. TB had been declared a national epidemic, with sanitariums the only hope for those infected. Vera had read the pamphlets too, and from the moment Grace had been born, she insisted the baby be kept away from her in order for Grace not to contract the disease.

Helen lifted Grace out of the drawer and held her close. Pressing her lips to the baby's forehead, she could feel the heat even more intensely. Her fears reignited and she started walking, pacing the floor and praying.

It felt like hours before Jack returned.

Helen hurried to the bedroom doorway.

"The doctor is on his way. How is she? Getting worse?" he asked.

A sob stuck in her throat as she said, "No worse, but no better. She's still warm."

He put an arm around her and steered her toward the sofa. "Let's go sit down while we wait for him. How long was Vera ill?"

"I don't know. She was very ill when I met her. It

was the end of February and very cold. I thought that was why she was ill at first."

They sat on the couch. He kept his arm around her and felt Grace's forehead with his other hand. "When was Grace born? What date?"

"March eighteenth. She'll be four months on the eighteenth of this month."

"You're sure Vera had tuberculosis?"

"Yes, the doctor who delivered Grace confirmed it. He insisted Vera and Grace go to a sanitarium, until he learned that she didn't have any money." She glanced up at him. "They require enough money for a burial before they'll admit anyone."

He nodded. "I know."

Helen drew in a deep breath. Vera had been adamant about not calling in a doctor because another one had already suggested she go to a sanitarium. But Mrs. Amery had called one in, declaring Vera was too weak to deliver Grace without assistance. "After he'd learned she didn't have any money, he told me to get some bleaching powder to wash the handkerchiefs Vera used for her cough and to not let Grace near her." Helen ran a knuckle under Grace's chin. "I did that. Relentlessly."

"I'm sure you did."

Helen closed her eyes as regret filled her. Why did it appear that everything she did was wrong? Right down to this, taking care of Grace.

By the time the doctor arrived, Helen was not only convinced Grace had tuberculosis, she was convinced the doctor would verify she was the worst person to be in charge of the baby. He'd be right too, in more ways than one.

Fighting back tears, she handed Grace over to the gray-haired man who carried her into the bedroom and closed the door.

"She'll be fine," Jack said, once again laying an arm around her shoulders. "He's good and thorough."

Whatever resolve she might have left dissolved. She would have fallen if Jack hadn't put his other arm around her and held her tight.

"You're worrying too much," he said, resting his chin on the top of her head.

Helen wrapped her arms around his waist and held on to him with all her might. She'd been on her own for so long, and even while knowing her burdens couldn't ever be shared, she was so thankful to not be alone right now.

He was still holding her when the doctor opened the bedroom door.

Her legs grew weaker and her stomach clenched. There were no telltale signs on the doctor's face. He wasn't smiling or frowning, merely standing in the open door, looking at them.

"You two can come in now," he said.

Jack guided her forward into the bedroom. Gracie was on the bed, looking around as if everything in the world was normal and right.

Helen sat on the edge of the bed and pressed a hand to Grace's forehead. It was still warm. She glanced up at Jack, letting him know her findings.

He laid a hand on her shoulder while asking the doctor, "Is it tuberculosis?"

"No." The doctor smiled brightly. "All in all, you have a very healthy little girl. I can tell she's had excellent care."

Helen's relief was tenfold of any she'd ever known. For a moment. Glancing up at Jack first, then the doctor, she asked, "Then why is she running a temperature?"

"I'd estimate she's about four months old, isn't she?" Dr. Baine asked.

"Yes, almost," Helen answered.

"Let me show you." The doctor leaned over and gently pulled Grace's bottom lip down. "See this, how her gum is red and slightly swollen?"

"Yes," Helen replied wondering what could have caused that.

"She's getting her first tooth," Dr. Baine said.

Helen looked closer into Gracie's mouth. "She is?" She'd read about that in the book, but it hadn't said anything about that making Grace ill.

"That will make her run a temperature?" Jack asked.

Helen glanced up at him, wondering if he'd read her mind as she lifted Grace off the bed.

"Yes, a low one. Nothing to be concerned about." The doctor clasped his bag shut. "Some babies run temperatures, some don't. There is no real rhyme or reason to it. She might be fussy for a few days, until the tooth comes through, or you may just suddenly notice it. Same with all her other teeth. Keep a spoon in the refrigerator and let her chew on that. It'll help."

"I will," Helen answered, thankful for the suggestion.

"You're sure about the tuberculosis?" Jack asked.

"As sure as I can be without further tests." Dr. Baine's expression grew serious. "You know for sure she was exposed?"

"Yes," Jack answered. "In Chicago. Her mother died from it shortly after giving birth to her."

A full frown pulled the doctor's brows down as he looked at her. "You aren't her mother?"

A different sort of fear rippled Helen's spine.

"No, she's not," Jack said. "I mentioned on the phone that Grace is Joe's daughter. Helen brought her out here to me after Grace's mother died."

"Where is Joe? I've wondered what happened to him," the doctor asked.

"Florida, I think." Jack laid a hand on Grace's back. "What further tests?"

The doctor's expression said he understood as clearly as Helen did that Jack hadn't called him here to talk about Joe.

"As you know, Jack, Los Angeles has one of the most prestigious sanitariums in the nation. The best treatment people can receive. They've also made progress in the diagnosis of TB, as well as prevention. There's a test I could give Grace. It's noninvasive, little more than a skin prick, and will let us know if she has contracted the disease for sure."

"Then give it to her," Jack said.

"I can't here," Dr. Baine said. "You'll have to bring her to the hospital and then back again two days later so we can read the results. It's fairly new, but the results have been excellent. Very accurate. It's also on the expensive side."

Helen bit her lip, but Jack didn't blink an eye.

"When should we bring her in?" he asked.

"Tomorrow morning, say nine o'clock?"

"We'll be there." Jack held out his hand. "Thanks for coming over so quickly."

Dr. Baine shook Jack's hand. "My pleasure." He nodded toward her. "Nice meeting you, miss, and Grace."

Helen had no idea how to express her sincere gratitude. "Thank you." She snuggled Gracie closer to her chest. "Thank you so very much."

The doctor patted Gracie's back. "You're very welcome. I'll see you in the morning."

Helen nodded. She'd go anywhere, do anything for Grace.

"I'll walk you out," Jack said.

The doctor picked up his bag. "Good, you can tell me about your next picture show. I've heard rumors it's going to be shown in that new theater being built downtown and I'm already looking forward to seeing it."

"It's not a rumor." Jack slapped the doctor on the shoulder. "You'll be invited to the premiere."

As the men left the bedroom, Helen pressed her lips to the top of Grace's head and let the relief completely wash over her. She'd been frightened before, scared, but never like this.

The full implications of all that had happened slowly seeped in. By the time Jack appeared in the doorway, her nerves were back to jittering beneath her skin.

Jack stopped in the doorway to the bedroom, simply looking at Helen and Grace. Concern for others came naturally to him, but it had been ages since he'd been this alarmed. He'd been as worried about Helen as he'd been about Gracie. Cared as much about her as he did his niece. How that had happened in such a short period of time was unimaginable. He could understand it with Gracie, she was Joe's daughter. Family. Of course he'd care about her, and tuberculosis was no baloney. It had killed more people than World War I. And still was.

"I'm so sorry," Helen said.

He leaned a hand against the doorframe. Right now, it would be safer for him to keep his distance. Those eyes of hers did things to him. He could read them like a script, and feel her emotions deep inside. Not reacting was impossible. Which is what he'd done earlier. Hugged her. Held her. He couldn't do that again. There was too much at stake. Not just to his reputation, which is what he'd explained to the doctor while asking him to keep Grace's identity under wraps. But to him. He wasn't just responsible for Joe's messes now. He was responsible for them. To them, Grace and Helen.

"So sorry."

"For what?" he asked, pressing his hand harder against the doorframe.

"Everything." She looked down at Grace. "Overreacting. I didn't know teething—"

"I didn't, either, but now we do." She looked so sad. So forlorn. Not hugging her, not trying to offer something to make her feel better would soon be impossible. "And after the tests, we'll know even more. I'll go put a spoon in the refrigerator like Dr. Baine said."

He drew a couple stabilizing breaths on his way to the kitchen, but if they helped, the relief had disappeared when he shut the refrigerator door. Helen was standing there. Holding Grace and looking like she needed more than a hug.

"I have money," she said. "Not a lot, but it should be enough to pay for the tests and Dr. Baine's visit this evening."

He wasn't disgusted, but was bothered, hurt, that she thought he wasn't willing, or able, to pay for Grace's needs. He wasn't completely destitute. "I've already paid for tonight's visit and will pay for the tests. Why wouldn't I? She's my niece."

"Yes, she is your niece, but she's not your responsibility."

"Yes, she is," he insisted. "She became my responsibility the moment you introduced me to her. Before then actually, I just didn't know about her."

Sorrow filled her eyes. "I'm not trying to upset you."

Guilt stabbed him like a prop knife. He hadn't meant to sound angry. He wasn't angry, just frustrated. "You aren't upsetting me. I just don't want you worrying about it. The money. I have more than enough to provide for her."

"Until you find your brother."

He bit his tongue. There was no telling what Joe would do about the situation. He might come to California, or he might want to have Grace delivered to him—wherever that might be. That stuck Jack dead center. Joe couldn't know any more about taking care of babies than he did, and like him, would most likely want to hire Helen. Joe would take advantage of that. In more ways than one. "It's been a long evening. We should get this one into bed." He held out his arms. "I'll hold her while you fix her bottle."

Helen was hesitant, but then handed him Grace.

He carried her into the living room. Turning either of them over to Joe would never be to his liking, but he didn't have any control over that. Holding Grace a bit tighter, he sat down on the sofa.

Grace cooed.

The sound warmed his entire chest cavity, and damn if that didn't make his eyes burn. He held her up, in front of his face. She gave him one of her toothless grins. Until that moment, he hadn't realized the immensity of the barriers he'd put up around himself, the ones that were breaking loose, threatening to tumble all the way down. A tiny shiver tickled his spine. Had he focused so hard on work for so many years because he'd been afraid of this? Of loving someone. Because when you loved someone, your life wasn't your own. You owed that person your everything…your responsibility. He knew that firsthand, and had been trying to escape it for years.

He was still contemplating that when Helen arrived, bottle in hand. Passing Grace to her, he stood. "I'll be back."

Helen frowned, but didn't ask where he was going, even though her eyes demonstrated she wanted to. He didn't offer an explanation. Didn't have one. He wasn't sure where he was going, just knew he had to get away for a while. Clear his mind.

Once in his car, a six-cylinder Chrysler that he'd bought brand-new three years ago, he closed the door but didn't start the engine. He'd paid cash up front for the car, believing everything had been on the right track. The studio had released four movies that year, starring Joe. Money had started to roll in. Real money, and the future had looked bright and clear. Then the debacle with Joe had struck.

Jack started the car and shifted into First. Exiting the parking lot, habit had him turning left. Joe had been the reason those four movies had done so well, he'd been the star fans had flocked to the movie theaters to see. Other studios knew that, and Joe should have known that meant he had to keep his nose clean.

Joe *had* known, just hadn't worried about it. He'd never worried about consequences.

Jack shifted gears again, heading toward the studio. That had been his destination. He rarely went anywhere else. Didn't have the time to. It had taken all he had to keep the studio from going down with Joe.

As they had years ago, a plethora of emotions rolled through him. Anger. Frustration. Blame. He'd thought he'd come to grips with all that. Evidently, he'd just buried it. Or maybe those emotions were part of the reason he'd pushed forward harder than ever. To prove that he wasn't his brother. Something he'd been doing his entire life.

For as long as he could remember, he'd been compared to Joe. Told to be more like him. Joe had lit up while on stage, and their parents had wanted him to do the same. Claimed they'd make more money if he could make the audience respond the way Joe did.

He'd tried, for their sakes, but it had been impossible. Acting just wasn't in him. That's what made it easy for him to spot it in others. It took more than just wanting to be an actor, it took an ability that was as natural as walking. Because even that, how they moved, had to fit the character they needed to portray.

His chest was heavy when he pulled into the studio lot. His mind had shifted, too. Was on Helen now. There was nothing false about her. She couldn't hide her true self. Nor could she hide how much she loved Grace. She had been truly petrified at the idea of the baby being ill.

He'd never met someone like her. Probably because

she was as far away from the world he'd lived in his entire life as a person could get. The acting world was full of players, and Helen wasn't a player.

He climbed out of the car and entered the studio, going straight to his office. At his desk, he opened the script lying there, tried to focus on the section they would film tomorrow. This film was different than all the others he'd created. It was a drama. The story of two men returning from the war. There was a touch of comedy, here and there, and a small amount of romance. Melodramas weren't new, but this one was different. The plot focused on the challenges the two men faced attempting to make it home against everything the world threw at them, including a blinding and deadly snowstorm, which was going to be an extra challenge to film in sunny California. That's also what made it different. People who hadn't experienced a snowstorm would be drawn in wondering how the men would survive, and those who had would be able to relate and empathize with the men's life-threatening obstacles.

His mind went back to Helen and the obstacles she'd faced. He couldn't say that he knew another woman who would do what Helen was doing. Give up her own life for the infant of someone she'd barely known.

He had to wonder if he should release her from their agreement, before she was exposed to the reality of Hollywood. The reality that was kept hidden.

The ringing of the phone surprised him. It was late. Almost ten. Long ago, he'd refrained from answering the phone. That's why he had a secretary. To field all those calls of people wanting an audition.

His heart froze for a split second and then he

grabbed the receiver. "Hello," he said, half expecting Helen on the other end.

"Jack?"

It wasn't Helen, but a voice he knew. "Joe."

"How are you?" Joe asked, before saying, "It's good to hear your voice."

"Yours too," Jack answered with a sense of dread pressing down on him. "You must have got the message I left for you this morning."

"I did. And am so glad you called. I've missed you, Jack. Missed you."

Chapter Nine

Helen thought she'd lived through the longest nights in her life. Those where she'd been too full of worry and fear to sleep to even close her eyes. She'd been wrong. The night that had just passed went beyond all those of the past. Jack had never returned to the apartment. As if she realized that too, Grace hadn't slept, either. She'd fussed and cried, harder than ever. No matter what Helen had tried. Diaper changes, bottles, even the spoons Jack had put in the refrigerator, nothing soothed her.

She had walked the floor all night, holding Grace, and every moment that hadn't been focused on comforting the baby had been fixated on Jack. She imagined the absolute worst. Everything from a car accident to a run-in with the mob or police. She also fretted over whether he'd regretted bringing her and Grace here. To his apartment.

She hated this feeling of helplessness more than ever. Which had to stop. She'd survived the last two years on her own, and would again. Fact was, she wasn't on her own. She had Grace, and right now getting her to the hospital for the tests was the most important thing.

Most likely exhausted from her rough night, Grace had eventually fallen asleep. Helen laid her in the drawer and carried their suitcase into the bathroom. After changing her clothes, she put up her hair and then stood in front of the mirror to tie the scarf snugly beneath her chin.

The image reflected in the glass showed the bags under her eyes, but her glasses would...

She no longer had her glasses. They had been her disguise for over two years. She never went anywhere without them.

Huffing out a breath, she closed the suitcase. This wasn't Chicago. Nor was this about her. She had to put her fears of being recognized by a member of the Outfit behind her—for Grace's sake—this morning.

It was far more important that she find a taxi driver who knew where the hospital was that Dr. Baine worked at, and would take them there.

Suitcase in hand, she opened the bathroom door. The case almost slipped out of her fingers at the sight of Jack standing near the apartment door.

"Good morning."

He was smiling and acting as if, well, as if he'd been there all night. A bolt of anger struck inside her like lightning.

"I spent the night at the studio." He hung his suit coat on the coatrack. "Had to make sure everything was ready for filming since we don't know how long Grace's tests will take." He turned and walked toward the kitchen. "I'll fry us some eggs. We'll have to leave in an hour, the hospital isn't far, but there is plenty of traffic this time of the morning."

Helen was floored, but the anger was still there, and she wasn't sure what to do with it. Especially as her heart thudded against her rib cage.

"How did Grace sleep?"

He'd disappeared into the kitchen. "She didn't."

He poked his head out the doorway. "She didn't?"

"No. The teething kept her awake all night."

"And therefore you, too."

She had to look away. He appeared too concerned, not only for Grace, but for her.

"Why don't you lie down then, just for a little bit? She's sleeping now, I checked on her."

Why hadn't she heard the door? Heard him? Maybe he'd arrived while the water had been running, which meant he'd been there awhile. Tossing those thoughts aside, she shook her head. "There isn't time."

"I could call Dr. Baine. Ask if we can come in later."

"No. I'm not tired or hungry." Frustrated, she added, "Grace needs those tests this morning."

His eyes narrowed slightly, as if he was questioning her reaction. She didn't care. Anger still simmered inside her.

"All right, then. What can I do to help get Grace ready?"

She walked to the bedroom. "Nothing. I changed her right before she fell asleep and have a bottle ready."

He followed her into the bedroom. "Then we might as well leave."

She stepped in front of him and lifted Grace out of the drawer.

He attempted to make small talk, asking questions

about Grace, if she'd found the spoons he'd put in the refrigerator and if they'd helped, but must have tired of her one-word answers because they drove to the hospital in silence.

Helen knew she had no real cause to be angry with him. It was out of the goodness of his heart that she and Grace were at his apartment. Yet, she was angry. In a way she hadn't been ever before. It made little sense, especially when she should be focused on Grace.

Upon entering the hospital, they were escorted down a long corridor. Everything was stark white and the smell reminded her of the bleaching powder she'd used to wash Vera's bedding and handkerchiefs.

"Good morning," Dr. Baine greeted them, stepping out of a room to meet them in the hallway. "I figured you two, or three, I should say, would be early. We're ready for Grace." He gestured toward a short bench. "You two can wait here. It won't take long."

A nurse, a dark-haired woman dressed in white, had stepped out of the room behind him. As she stepped closer, Helen tightened her hold on Grace.

"Don't worry," the nurse said, reaching for Grace. "She'll be fine."

"She didn't sleep well last night," Helen said, attempting to justify not handing over the sleeping baby.

"Teething can do that," Dr. Baine said.

"Give her to the nurse," Jack whispered in her ear. He'd also put his arm around her shoulders. Helen wished he wouldn't do that. For as much comfort as it provided, it also caused chaos. Inside her. Had last night and did again this morning.

"She'll be fine," he added.

She released her hold on Grace and the nurse lifted

the baby out of her arms. As the nurse started to walk away, Helen's heart jolted. "Wait."

The nurse and the doctor looked at her.

"I have a bottle in my purse. She might need it."

"You can give it to her afterward," Dr. Baine said. "This won't take that long." A moment later, they disappeared behind a door.

"Have a seat," Jack said. "You must be exhausted."

"No," Helen answered, although she lowered herself onto the bench. Her stomach was gurgling and her hands trembling. "We should have asked them what they are going to do to her."

Jack sat beside her and stretched an arm out along the back of the bench. "Dr. Baine said last night that it was little more than a pinprick."

"Yes, but how much more?"

Jack grinned patted her shoulder. "Sometimes not knowing is better. Besides, they'll tell us all we need to know afterward."

That was true, but it didn't settle her nerves.

He tugged her closer to him, and against her better judgment, she didn't resist. Even when her cheek rested against the side of his shoulder.

"It's tough, isn't it?"

She nodded.

"We are doing all we can." He sighed heavily. "All we can."

A niggling sense said he was referring to something more than the tests. The heaviness that came then nearly crushed her insides. He was a busy man and suddenly learning he had a niece, and having to provide for her, had not been something he'd expected.

"I don't like hospitals."

His change of subject was so unexpected, she sat up and looked his way.

He shrugged. "Don't know how people can work in them. They give me the heebie-jeebies."

"Why?"

"No reason, except for the look of them, the smell of them and the fact they are full of sick people."

She had to grin at his expression and statement, and then nodded. "I've never been in one before."

"Never?"

"No. Never."

"I haven't too often. Never been in one for myself, but have visited them to see people. A friend of mine was in a car accident last year. I went to see him before he passed away."

"A good friend?"

"Yes. He helped me write the script I'm filming right now. The plot was his idea."

Interested because it gave her something else to think about, she asked, "What is the plot? And the name, what's the name of the film? If it has one already."

His face lit up. "It does. It's called *Home Bound*, right now, but I've been known to change the name after seeing the final product."

"Why?"

"Because sometimes, after seeing it all together..." He shrugged. "It feels different than the script did, and a new name fits it better."

She found that interesting, even though a bit hard to understand. "So what is *Home Bound* about?"

"The journey of two men coming home after the war." Thoughtfulness filled his face.

"Do they make it home?" she asked.

"I don't know yet, haven't shot that scene."

His grin said he was teasing. She'd been to the theater only twice, and both films had been funny. Full of overexaggerated car chases and bumbling police officers. "Is it funny?"

"There are some funny parts."

"Like what?"

He frowned. "You really want to know?"

"Yes."

"Well, in the beginning, when they get off the ship that had brought them back to America, they get their luggage mixed up. The two men are different sizes, so the clothes in their bags don't fit either one of them. Then they meet up again on the train taking them to their hometowns while wearing the wrong-sized clothes and realize the mix up."

Images of what he described played out in her head. "I bet that is funny."

"That's also when they realize that they know each other. That they live in neighboring towns. And they decide to travel home together. We just started filming yesterday, but it's already turning out better than I'd expected even. The two actors are great together. They had the entire crew laughing. We were still laughing hours later."

There was pride in his voice and on his face, as well as delight. He obviously really enjoyed making films. "I'm sure the audience will be laughing, too."

"That's our hope. Getting reaction from the audience within the first couple of scenes is imperative. It makes them engage, want more, to the point they become engrossed, wondering what will happen next."

"What does happen next?"

"I can't tell you."

"Why not?"

He grinned and nodded toward the end of the hallway. She quickly turned, and jumped to her feet as Dr. Baine carried Grace through the door. Jack stood too, and as soon as Grace saw him, she smiled and started cooing.

"She did excellent," Dr. Baine said. "Not so much as a peep."

"She is a good little girl," Jack said, tickling her beneath her chin.

Helen took Grace and kissed her forehead.

"What did the test consist of?" Jack asked.

"It's called the Pirquet test." Dr. Baine pulled Grace's left sleeve up, uncovering a tiny bandage. "It's being used worldwide to indicate the presence of tuberculosis."

"And if she has it?" Jack asked.

Dr. Baine shook his head. "We'll discuss that at the time. I don't know what the living conditions were like before Grace came to live at your apartment, but the environment she's in right now is exactly as it should be. Clean. Plenty of light and fresh air, and no spittoons. It was believed that saliva is what transmitted the disease, but studies are showing otherwise. That a person actually has to breathe them in. That's why fresh air is so important. Make sure she gets as much as possible."

The doctor was looking at her and Helen nodded. "I will."

"You can remove the covering later on today, and keep an eye on the area. If you notice it's red or swollen, I need to see her immediately, otherwise, you'll need to bring her back the day after tomorrow."

"That's it?" Jack asked.

"Yes."

It wasn't over, Helen knew that, but still her heart felt lighter than it had in some time. "Thank you."

"You're welcome," Dr. Baine said.

Jack had pulled out his wallet. "How much do I owe you?"

"You can pay for it after we know the results," Dr. Baine said. "The front desk will have a bill made out for you then."

"All right." Jack shook the doctor's hand. "Thanks again." Looking at her, he said, "Let's go home."

More than ready to leave the hospital, Helen nodded.

"Not so quick," the doctor said.

Helen's heart skipped a beat as she and Jack looked at each other and then the doctor.

He pointed at her. "Were you around her mother?"

"Yes. She lived with me."

He nodded. "I think we should give you the test, too."

The cost was the first thing Helen thought of.

"You're right," Jack said. "Can you do it now?"

"Yes."

"Then do it," Jack said, reaching to take Grace.

"I—"

Jack shook his head. "No arguments. Grace and I will be right here."

"It's as much for Grace as it is you," the doctor said. "In fact, it's more likely that you could have been infected than Grace."

Helen understood that and the importance of not infecting anyone else. She handed Grace to Jack and followed the doctor through the doorway. She'd always been very careful around Vera, giving as much of herself as possible, while ensuring that she wouldn't catch the disease, ensuring that it was at least one way she wouldn't put Grace at risk.

Just as he'd promised, the test didn't take long and was little more than a pinprick in her forearm. It was barely a matter of minutes before she and Jack left the hospital.

"Are you hungry?" he asked once they were all in the car. "We could stop at a diner for some breakfast?"

"No, I'm fine," Helen said, using her scarf ties to tickle Grace's nose. "I can make you some eggs at the apartment."

"You won't mind?"

"Of course I won't mind." Helen glanced out the window, at the people strolling into the hospital, and then down at her brown dress. This certainly wasn't Chicago. Her drab attire here made her stand out rather than hide in a crowd.

"Then let's do that," Jack said. "Get both you and Gracie back home. Does your arm hurt?"

"No. It was just a little prick with a needle," Helen answered, her mind more focused on her attire.

"Look, that's what we need."

Helen glanced up. They'd stopped, waiting for cars to go by so he could turn. She glanced around. At buildings, cars, fashionably dressed people. "What?"

"That woman. The buggy she's pushing. There's a park not far from the apartment, Grace could get all the fresh air she needs."

Helen saw the woman and the buggy. It was white, made of wicker, and had a bonnet over the top to shield the sun. The woman pushing it was wearing a bright yellow dress, with matching scarf and purse.

"Wonder where you'd buy one of those," he said.

"A store I suppose. I'm sure they are expensive." A buggy like that would be costly, so would the woman's clothes.

Traffic cleared and he took the corner. Once they were rolling along again, he gestured toward Grace. "Looks like she needs a toy or something too, the way she's playing with your scarf."

"She's never done this before," Helen said. Grace was engrossed with the ties of her scarf. "I'll tie one of the spoons to it when we get home, maybe she'll chew on it then. She didn't want anything to do with one last night."

"She seems happy now."

Grace did, making Helen wonder if all of the fussing last night was because he'd been gone. That was silly. Grace was too small to realize who and who wasn't nearby. She, on the other hand, wasn't, and had been beside herself. It seemed like that's all she'd thought about. Him. It was as if her mind wasn't her own. Even now, he had to have been embarrassed, taking her to the hospital in her frumpy clothes.

"What's wrong?" Jack asked as he pulled up next to the apartment building.

"Nothing," Helen answered quickly. She opened the car door to step out, juggling Grace and her purse.

Jack hurried around the car and grabbed the door, holding it out of the way as Helen climbed out. After shutting the door, he held out his arms. "I'll carry Grace."

"I can."

"I know you can, but I want to." He did want to, and waited until Helen handed her over.

As soon as he had opened his eyes this morning, realizing he'd fallen asleep at his desk, he'd shot to his feet and raced home. He hadn't meant to leave them alone. Not all night, and having done so had filled him with regrets that had grown upon learning that both Helen and Grace hadn't slept well. If at all.

He was surprised he'd slept. He'd sat at his desk for hours after Joe had hung up, waiting for his brother to call back. Joe hadn't said he would—Jack was just hoping. As soon as Joe had heard about Vera's death, he'd hung up. Before Jack had a chance to mention Grace or Helen, or find out where Joe was.

He'd called the operator, asked her to ring back the number that had just called him. She hadn't been able to because it had been long distance, out of her exchange.

Joe had been stunned by the news of Vera. So shaken, Jack wished he'd broken the news more gently. He hadn't though. Rather than asking where Joe was, how he was doing, he'd blurted out that he'd received news that Vera had died in Chicago. Joe had asked how, when. Jack had said TB, last month.

The line had gone so quiet the static had echoed in his ears. He'd finally asked if Joe was still there. Joe had said he was, but that he had to go. That's when the line went completely dead. No static. Nothing until the operator had come on and told him to hang up because the call had been disconnected.

Helen was in front of him, walking up the steps, and he wondered if he should tell her about talking to Joe. Why? He didn't know anything more than before talking to his brother. She'd probably question him, point out things he already knew. That he shouldn't have been so callous.

Joe hadn't been. Not at first. He'd sounded happy, ready to talk.

"I'll start frying your eggs right away," Helen said, stepping aside for him to insert the key in the door.

"That's all right," he said, opening the door. "I better get to the studio." He kissed the top of Grace's head, handed her over and left. Traipsed down the steps he'd just walked up, with a whole other set of regrets pressing down on him.

He'd been furious at his brother when the scandal hit. Joe had insisted it wasn't anything to worry about, that he'd take care of it. Joe had, in his own way, taken care of it, by selling off shares and skipping town.

Joe had called a couple of times those first few weeks, but Jack had been up to his eyeballs in the aftermath of it all. Getting rid of Joe hadn't been enough. They'd wanted the studio shut down. *They* being the studio owners of The Big Five. The owners had gotten together and laid down rules they expected everyone else to follow only because it benefited them and their studios, not the smaller ones like his.

Though he hated to admit it, the Broadbents had played a part in that not happening. They bought and sold any and everything, and had their hands in more pockets than anyone knew. In the end, the big players backed off, knowing there was more than one way to shut down a studio.

Jack climbed in the car. That's what he'd been fighting. The collapse of the studio. It had been a tough game. Still was. The other studios had refused to show his movies in their theaters, had offered his actors extravagant salaries to break the contracts they'd signed with him, and, on more than one occasion, paid to have others smear his films and to insult those who dared to claim they'd enjoyed one of his films.

What had kept him going was the results his films received outside of Hollywood. The privately owned theaters who could show whatever movies they wanted and requested more from him. They had become his bread and butter because he wasn't solely trying to make stars out of anyone. His actors were good, but so were his story lines and his final products were what people wanted. Enjoyment. They didn't want to just see a well-known name on screen, they wanted a story they could relate to.

He started the car and pulled onto the road. The Big Five were after one thing—to monopolize the entire industry. They were tying up actors, writers, producers and directors with contracts so tight there was little creativity left. Production chiefs and publicity managers ruled entire studios. Vertical integration, that's what they were doing. Tying up every aspect of the filming industries under one roof.

What they were overlooking was that when there was that much money involved, others wanted in. Those others weren't always the most scrupulous people. Gangsters from New Orleans, New York, Chicago, Detroit, had all hit town. Top eggs back home, they were hot on the trot to get in on the action. Especially one known as the Outfit in Chicago. They'd sent more than one egg. Word was, they sent an entire unit of sab cats to sabotage others getting too close to deals they wanted sole access to.

They were also building theaters, ones where every studio could show their films. One was right here in Los Angeles. A big extravagant building downtown. It was scheduled to be completed in two months. So was his movie. If all continued to go right, his movie would be the first one shown in that theater.

He'd been surprised when they first came to him, offering the deal, and he'd asked if Joe was behind it. Somehow connected. They said no, that they'd seen his movies, and that the only thing behind it was the money that could be made, by all of them.

The money he could make off that one showing would be enough to pay off the Broadbents completely, and leave him plenty to invest in his several movies yet to come.

The parking lot of the studio was full, and he had no doubt filming had already started. He had a good crew, people he trusted, and would make sure they got their just rewards when this film hit it big.

He might be the studio owner, but it wasn't all about him.

"Any calls?" he asked walking through the front door.

"No, sir," Miss Hobbs replied. "Other than those wanting auditions."

Heading toward the hallway, he started to tell her to come get him if Helen or Joe called, but stopped. Helen might not provide her name, Joe might not, either. "Come get me if anyone calls."

"Anyone?"

He understood the implications of that. "No, not

those you know for sure are only requesting auditions, but anyone else."

She nodded and went back to typing while he opened the hallway door. He didn't go straight to the film set. There was someone else he had to see first.

Chapter Ten

Helen opened her eyes and licked away the dryness from her lips and the roof of her mouth. The fog from being deep asleep was heavy and she blinked, trying to dispel it enough to see what had woken her. Grace was asleep beside her on the bed. She didn't even remember falling asleep. After Jack had left, and she'd fed Grace, she'd lain down beside her, thinking she'd rest for only a few minutes.

A sound penetrated her thinking, a knock.

Surely it wasn't on the apartment door.

It came again. Louder. Confirming it was on the apartment door.

Recalling how she hadn't heard Jack walk in this morning, she jumped off the bed. After double-checking that Grace was still sleeping, she hurried out of the bedroom.

At the door, she grasped the knob. "Who is it?"

"I have a delivery for Helen Hathaway."

She froze. Her mind was blank, but she searched it anyway. Wondering if someone had seen her this morning. Knew she was here.

"Ma'am?"

Shaking her head, having no idea how long she'd stood there, stock-still, she swallowed, but her throat was so dry there was nothing to swallow. "From who?" she managed to croak.

"Jack McCarney. It's getting heavy, ma'am, can you let us in?"

What could Jack be sending her? Why didn't he just bring it home later?

A thud sounded, along with a somewhat strangled, "Ma'am?"

"Just a second." She released the knob and grabbed the spare key from the side table. After unlocking the door, she opened it only a crack.

There were two men standing there, holding a crib, legs up and almost over their heads.

"We don't want to set it down because it's only going to go through the door sideways," one said.

He was tall and gangly, the other was shorter, and red faced.

The red-faced man said, "We had to carry it up the stairs this way."

"Oh." She stepped aside, pulling the door open as wide as it would go.

"Where do you want it?" the first one asked as they maneuvered the crib in sideways through the door, legs first.

She didn't have a clue. "Right there will be fine."

"In the middle of the living room?" the second one asked.

"It has wheels," the first one said, sounding flustered. "Set it down. Slowly."

The crib did indeed have wheels. Little black ones. Made of metal, and sparkling white, the crib was stunning. Metal pipes made up the two sides, while the two ends were solid metal with curved tops. She pressed a hand to her lips at the sight of the little lambs painted on both ends. Inside and out.

"We'll be right back," the tall man said.

Pulling her gaze off the crib, which was difficult, she asked, "Why?"

"The mattress," he said.

"Among other things," the other said, following the first one out the door.

A short time later, Helen confirmed Jack was certainly more amazing than she'd even imagined. The delivery men made a total of four trips up and down the stairs. Hauling in the crib mattress; a buggy, wicker, identical to the one they'd seen that morning; a high chair, wooden, with a little bear eating a pot of honey painted on the back of the seat; a rocking chair and a variety of packages wrapped in paper and tied with string.

Helen stood there, amongst the array of items, for some time after the men had left. It was as if Jack had been inside her mind. Knew all the items she'd dreamed Grace would someday have. These items had to have cost a fortune.

Remorse rose up as she took another long look at the items. She was the one who had promised Vera that she'd take Grace to Joe. Joe. Not Jack. He was doing all this out of the goodness of his heart. She'd not only thrust Grace on him, but herself too. Yes, he'd asked her to watch Grace while he made his movie…

His movie. She was even impeding on his ability to do that and it was up to her to do something about that. About all of this. Exactly what, she wasn't sure, but she didn't want to be a burden to him.

The crib was in the bedroom, as were the new baby clothes and diapers; the high chair in the kitchen; and the buggy, the only place it would fit was along the wall near the bathroom, so that's where it was stationed when Jack walked through the door.

"Oh, good, it arrived," Jack said before she had a chance to speak.

"Yes, it arrived. All of *it*." Shaking her head, she asked, "Why would you do all of this?"

His grin was a bit sheepish. "I didn't. Not really. Carter, my prop man, said he knew exactly what we'd need, and said he'd have it delivered."

Confused, she said, "No one is supposed to know about Grace, not until your movie is completed."

He held up a finger. "No one needs to know she is Joe's daughter. Except for Dr. Baine, that was out of necessity, but he won't share that with anyone. I trust him. And Carter. I trust him too." He touched the buggy. "Where's Grace? Has she tried any of it out?"

"She's in the crib, asleep."

He took a step toward the bedroom, and though it took courage, Helen swiftly blocked his path.

"Where she is going to stay."

He frowned. "What's wrong?"

"This!" She gestured toward the buggy and then the rest of the room. "All of this."

He huffed out a breath as if her question was ridiculous. "Grace isn't going to fit in that dresser drawer for long, and how is she going to learn to eat food if she doesn't have a high chair? You need the rocking chair so you don't have to carry her around when she's fussy.

You can rock her back to sleep instead." He pointed at the buggy. "And Dr. Baine said she needs fresh air."

"All that may be true." Helen couldn't deny babies needed things, nor could she blame the indignation that flashed in his eyes. "But you aren't the one responsible for supplying her them. That is your brother. Joe. She's his child."

He threw his arms out at his sides. "I don't know where Joe is."

She took a deep breath in preparation for the speech she'd practiced all afternoon. "I realize that, and I realize all of this is my fault. The fact that Grace and I are here. There is nothing I can do about that, but there is something I can do about—"

"Stop right there." He took ahold of her arm. "What happened? Why would you be this upset over me buying Grace a bed to sleep in, or a chair to sit in?"

"I'm not upset about them, I'm upset about how we've disrupted your life. You have a movie to make, you told me that it's imperative you get it completed in eight weeks."

"And I will. We shot several more scenes today."

It was only an assumption, but it was something she thought about all afternoon. "But you ended early, so you could be home in time for supper."

The look on his face confirmed she was right.

"You were late this morning, too, because of taking us to the hospital."

He let go of her arm. "I have good people working for me, they can take care of things while I'm gone."

"But it's your movie, Jack."

"I'm fully aware of that."

She considered a lot of things this afternoon, and

had come to the conclusion that Jack had spent his entire life taking care of others, and was doing so again, because of her. She couldn't live with that. Well, she could, but didn't want to. She was already living with too many things she couldn't control. "I'm fully aware of that too, and I want to make sure you get your movie done."

He frowned. "I don't understand. You already agreed to take care of Grace."

"And I will continue to, but I need to do more." She did need that. Needed to be in control of something. She had fought so hard in the last two years to be independent. To not depend on anyone, desperate to not give over the reins of her life to anyone ever again. But she was beginning to do that with Jack, to rely on him too much, to long for the way he made her feel. And she couldn't let herself. The thought had risen so quickly inside her this afternoon, and remained so strong that she had to do something about it. "I want you to tell me what I can do, besides taking care of Grace, that will help you get your movie done."

He shook his head. "Nothing."

It was as if all the air had left her body. "Nothing? There has to be something."

He shrugged. "There's not. Other than taking care of Grace."

She wasn't exactly sure what she had wanted him to say, but that definitely wasn't it.

"And the apartment, the cleaning and the meals you've made, that's a lot of help."

He was trying to placate her. She held in the sigh that wanted to be expelled, and grew even more determined to find a way to help. Really help.

* * *

Two days later, Dr. Baine told her exactly what she'd wanted to hear. Both her and Grace's tuberculosis tests were negative. That was such good news, and such a relief, but she still felt like a burden to Jack. Actually, it was more than a burden. She felt useless and didn't like it. He was up early every morning and gone all day. She fixed him breakfast and always had supper waiting, but it wasn't enough.

She enjoyed hearing him talk about the movie he was making, all the different aspects, and couldn't help but imagine that there was something she could do to help him. Each day she racked her brain to come up with a viable idea, but she didn't know anything about making a movie.

Several days later, she was on her hands and knees in the kitchen, scrubbing the floor, when she heard the apartment open and close. It was only midafternoon, but as it had started doing each time he arrived home, her heart thudded against her rib cage, and sent a warmth throughout her entire body.

"Hello!"

He was in the doorway before she had a chance to rise to her feet.

"Hello," she replied, swiping a clump of stray hair away from her face as she sat back on her knees. It was the oddest thing, but at times, when she looked at him, her mouth went completely dry and she embarrassed herself with silly thoughts about how it would feel to kiss him.

He grinned, and stepped forward, holding out a hand.

Her heart beat harder as she placed her hand in his

and rose to her feet. His eyes were locked on hers, and for the life of her, she couldn't look away. That also happened at times, and never failed to leave her breathless.

After a moment of concentrating on breathing, she asked, "What are you doing home this time of the day?"

"I'm here to get you and Grace."

"Why?"

"Because Julia said she needs to see for herself that you and Grace are doing fine."

His thumb was rubbing the inside of her wrist, making it hard to focus on anything else. Concentrating, she finally was able to say, "The diner is closed now."

He nodded. "Exactly. That's why she wants you to come now, so she'll have time to visit."

She hadn't seen Julia for over two weeks, but Jack had given her regular updates on how things were going, particularly about Rosie and how everything had blown over, that she was once again working at the diner.

Helen bit her bottom lip. Julia might have an idea of what she could do.

Jack's grin grew, and then winking one eye at her, which made her cheeks warm, he twisted about.

"I'll get Grace," he said. "You get whatever she needs to spend the afternoon visiting."

Helen quickly dumped out the bucket of water, rinsed out the rag she'd used to scrub the floor and grabbed two prefilled bottles of milk out of the refrigerator. In the bedroom, she collected several diapers, and stuffed them and the bottles in her purse before grabbing her scarf.

"It looks like you need a bigger purse," Jack said. "We could stop and buy you one."

She finished tying her scarf beneath her chin and picked up the purse that was stuffed so full she could barely hold the handles together in one hand. "There's no need for that."

Jack couldn't pull his eyes off her, much like when he'd arrived and saw her sitting on the kitchen floor. A prettier woman simply didn't exist, and when those blue eyes shone like they were right now, she was beyond beautiful.

"Oh," she said, putting the overstuffed purse back on the bed. "Let me get the bonnet that matches her dress. She looks so adorable in it."

He glanced at the baby in his arms, who was adorable with or without a bonnet. Along with all the furniture, he'd ordered several frilly dresses for Grace. He should have ordered some for Helen, too. She wore the same two dresses over and over. Although they were always wrinkle-free and clean, he was going to have to do something about that, and the purse.

While he held Grace, Helen put a bonnet on her and tied it beneath her chin.

"Ready," she said.

The excitement in her voice thrilled him. He felt bad about having to leave her home alone, all day, every day. "I take it you're excited to see Julia."

"Oh, yes."

"You should have said something, I would have taken you there before now." A tinge of guilt struck him. "Or I should have thought of it."

"Applesauce," she said, stepping out of the apartment door.

It wasn't nonsense to him. He locked the door behind them. "You must get lonely and bored being here all day, every day."

She glanced up at him as they walked down the steps. "No. Grace and I are not lonely or bored, and you are much too busy to think about such things."

He had been busy, and would continue to be. All was going well, though, including the splicing together of the scenes they'd already shot. He really couldn't be more pleased, but that shouldn't mean he was too busy to not think of her. In fact, it didn't. Busy or not, she was on his mind all the time. He couldn't wait to leave the studio and return home to spend some time with her. She always had some news of what Grace had done during the day. He liked hearing about them, but the enjoyment truly came from watching Helen tell him. She was so animated, so excited over each small accomplishment.

A smile was always on her face, much like the one there now, as she climbed in the car. It was bright enough to light up the world.

He'd changed his mind about seeing her on the big screen. Mainly because he didn't want to share her with anyone. However, he had all sorts of other thoughts when it came to her, and trying to dispel them was growing harder and harder. He tried to keep things relaxed, tried to act indifferent to her living at the apartment, but in truth, it was damn near killing him. There were times when her shallow breathing and the intensity of those pale blue eyes made his pants too tight. He'd escape into the bathroom until he had enough control over his body to face her again.

Jack shifted in the seat of the car as his thoughts evoked a reaction inside him. Her loose-fitting dresses were another thing that sent his mind reeling. He could imagine that her body was free of any restricting undergarments beneath the brown drab material. That struck him hard at night, while lying on the sofa, knowing she was just on the other side of his bedroom door.

He parked the car next to Julia's diner and walked Helen inside, then drove the car across the street to the studio lot.

Beverly Hobbs greeted him as he entered the building, and for the first time, he took in the outfit she was wearing. A red-and-white polka dot dress, with matching scarf tied sideways around her head and red shoes. He couldn't help but think how nice Helen would look in a dress like that.

He paused next to her desk. "Miss Hobbs, I need to send you on an errand."

"All right." She picked up a pencil, held it over a pad of paper. "What is it you need?"

He hadn't told anyone, other than Carter, his prop man, about Grace and Helen staying with him. He didn't want others to know Grace was Joe's daughter, abandoned daughter, but that didn't mean he was keeping them hidden. "I need some women's clothes, outfits similar to the one you're wearing. Four or five of them. And a purse. A big one. Big enough to hold baby bottles and diapers."

She still held the pencil, but hadn't written anything down, and he knew a knowing nod when he saw one.

"Miss Hobbs?"

Smiling, she looked at him and shrugged. "How do you think your niece ended up with gowns and matching bonnets, and shoes? Carter asked me to type up a list for him to send over to Hudson's. He'd forgotten clothes, so I added them."

"My niece?"

She shrugged again. "I put two and two together."
Tapping the pencil to her chin, she said, "I'm assuming these clothes are for the baby's mother. I can guess
her size, that shouldn't be an issue."

"Helen's not Grace's mother. She died shortly after
Grace was born. Helen was a friend of hers and has
been caring for Grace since she was born." He wasn't
sure why it was important that others understood that,
but it was.

Miss Hobbs pressed a hand to her chest. "Bless her
heart. I know exactly where to go to buy her a few outfits. How long do I have? Shopping takes time."

He shrugged. "I'd like them by this evening, before
I go home."

"Oh, ducky! That I can do." She grabbed her purse
from beneath the desk. "She can wear them to the party
tomorrow night. The invitation is still on your desk. I
RSVP'd for you." Holding up a hand, she said, "The
phone will go unanswered while I'm gone."

"That will be fine." Not worried about a few missed
phone calls, he pulled out his billfold and handed her
all the bills he had. He'd forgotten the party tomorrow,
but there was a party, for some reason, almost every
night, and he had far more important things to fill his
time. "Will this be enough?"

She shuffled through the bills. "I can make this
work." After putting the money in her purse, she asked,
"Do you know her favorite color?"

"No." Even after living in the same apartment for
weeks, he knew very little about Helen. "I don't. But
her eyes are blue."

"Perfect!"

Chapter Eleven

Jack was anxious about the scenes they were about to shoot. Carter had insisted feathers were what they needed. That they would look more like snow on film than anything else. Better than the real thing. So, feathers were what they were using. White feathers. Millions of tiny, white feathers.

So far, Carter had been right. The sand painted white had worked well, and now they'd find out if the feathers would work for the blizzard scenes. Jack hoped like hell that they would. That many feathers had cost more than a pretty penny.

"Places! Places!" Newton Hindman shouted. "Pll-laaaaceeees!"

Groups of crew members and actors broke apart, and following the director's orders, moved to their prospective spots.

As he walked to his spot, scanning to make sure all was set to start filming, Jack caught sight of Helen opening the door to the back lot. He changed directions and walked to the door.

"Done visiting already?" he asked, touching the tip of Grace's little nose, making her smile grow.

Helen's smile increased, too. "Julia had work to do, and I didn't want you waiting on us."

He nodded toward the set behind him. "We are just getting ready to shoot another scene. Do you want to watch?"

Her entire face shone. "Could I? I'll stay out of the way and won't say a word."

He sucked in a quick breath at the way her excitement made his chest swell. "Sure. I'll get you a chair, you can sit by me."

A crew member quickly found another tall chair and positioned it next to his, right behind Newton's chair. Jack introduced her to Newton, and then held Grace while Helen set her purse on the floor and climbed up onto the chair.

"It's like an adult high chair," he said.

"It is," she whispered. "Minus the tray."

He chuckled, handed her Grace and climbed up on his chair. They were tall so he could see over Newton's head and watch the scene play out, directly behind the center camera.

"We are about to film the blizzard scene," he told her.

She gestured toward the set, the painted background of trees and snow, and the platform covered with sand. "I like the white sand, it looks like snow."

He tipped his head toward her. "Glad to hear you say that, you've probably seen more snow than any of us here."

She nodded. "It does snow more in Illinois than California."

"Ready!" Newton raised a hand, and waited until silence echoed in the air, then dropping his hand, he shouted, "Action!"

The first few minutes in this final act were meant to be slapstick funny, and considering Helen's reactions as the two actors pretended to slip and fall on the snow, they were. Eyes sparkling, she covered her mouth with one hand to smother her giggles as Malcolm Boyd made an exaggerated show of falling onto the ground. He was the taller of the two main actors, and his long legs flayed in the air as he landed on his back.

Wes Jenkins, much shorter and stockier, hurried over to help, but again, with the perfect amount of exaggeration, he slipped and landed atop Boyd.

Helen's shoulders shook as she laughed harder. On her lap, Grace seemed almost as enamored by the actions as she did.

The actors did a great job of attempting to help each other up, and then, eventually, of showing their exhaustion and staying put.

"Cut!" Newton shouted. "That was perfect! Copacetic! Take five while we get the snow in place!"

Helen leaned toward him. "The feathers?"

"Yes." He'd told her about them, and about hoping they would work.

"Thank you for letting me watch this. It's so exciting!"

"I'm glad you arrived in time," he said, although his attention had shifted to Malcolm Boyd, who was walking their way. Tall, dark and handsome, that's what Malcolm's résumé said, and it was accurate.

"Where have you been hiding this doll, Jack?" Malcolm asked, winking at Helen.

Helen's arms fully engulfed Grace as she cast an unsure look his way.

Jack stretched his arm along the back of her chair.

"This is Miss Hathaway, and Grace." Nodding at Helen, he said, "This is Malcolm Boyd."

"Miss Hathaway," Boyd said, making a show of bowing.

Jack's insides clenched. He didn't want a scandal concerning Joe to interfere with this movie, but he also didn't want Helen to acquire a bad reputation on account of Joe. On account of him hiding exactly who Grace was. If he'd had more time to consider the options he might have chosen his next words more carefully, but if his secretary had figured out who Grace was, others might too, and it would be better to have the truth come from him. Especially when it came to Helen not being Grace's mother. "Grace is my niece."

Boyd frowned. "Your niece? Joe has a daughter? Last I heard, he was down in Florida. Is he still there?"

"Yes," Jack answered, even though he didn't know if that was where Joe was or not. "Grace is staying with me for the time being." He had left several other messages for Joe, but had yet to hear from Joe again.

"That whole debacle was a raw deal," Boyd said. "Joe was a patsy. The brothers didn't like how he was outshining their main star."

There were plenty of people who felt that way. He and Joe hadn't been the only set of brothers to start a studio. At one time, the Wagner brothers were their idols. Already well established, the Wagners hadn't paid them much attention until Joe's popularity had soared after a couple well-received movies. The affair that Joe had been blackballed over had been with the Wagner brothers' main actor's wife. She was their top actress, and the blame was all put on Jack. Rumors started that he was attempting to break up their marriage. No one seemed to notice that Rita Wells had other affairs, before Joe, and hadn't stopped seeking out men other than her husband afterward, either. Joe, however, had been the only one blackballed.

"Two minutes!" Newton shouted.

"Hope you enjoy the filming," Boyd said to Helen, and gave her another wink before walking away.

Jack liked Malcolm, but that second wink was one too many. Actually, the first one had been one too many.

"What did he mean about Joe being a patsy?" Helen asked.

He still hadn't told her about Joe's one and only phone call. "I'll tell you later." He nodded toward the top of the backdrop, where two stage hands sat atop ladders, holding bags of white feathers.

Her eyes grew wide, and her smile returned. "I can't wait to see this."

"Places! Places everyone!" Newton shouted.

Always serious, with a permanent frown that kept the tips of his bushy dark brows angled together, Newton ran a tight ship. He didn't mince words or waste a minute. All of which Jack appreciated. He also appreciated how Newton had hung with him through thick and thin. The director had been given other offers, good offers that Jack couldn't have blamed him for taking, but Newton claimed he liked it here. That The Big Five studios would never give their directors enough freedom to make a decent movie. All they wanted were scenes of half-dressed women and shirtless men.

Jack agreed for the most part, and did his best to give Newton full control of directing every scene.

"This scene starts the final stretch of their way home," he said to Helen.

She nodded, but never took her eyes off the set.

"Ready!" Newton shouted, holding up a hand. Dropping it a second later, he added, "Action!"

In the same positions as when they'd stopped shooting, Boyd and Jenkins were serious as they helped each other up. Then they slowly started moving, as if trudging through the snow. They stopped near a sign that listed how far it was to each of their hometowns.

"Cue snow!" Newton shouted.

Shivering, both Boyd and Jenkins rubbed their arms and stomped their feet as feathers slowly started falling on them.

"Amazing," Helen whispered. "It looks like snow. It really does!"

The actors started walking again and pulled the collars of their coats up over their ears.

"More snow!" Newton shouted.

Feathers fell faster. At first it looked good, especially how a few feathers stuck to their coats and hair, but then too many started sticking to them, more and more. Soon they began to look like...chickens. Big. White. Chickens.

Jack held his desire to curse up a storm, knowing Newton would see exactly what he was seeing.

"Cut! Cut!" Newton shouted, jumping off his chair. "They look like chickens! Skinny chickens!"

Boyd and Malcom were both flaying their hands, attempting to get rid of the feathers sticking to them from head to toe. What the hell was he going to do?

A muffled giggle had him glancing toward Helen. She had a hand over her mouth, but couldn't hide the mirth in her eyes. He glanced back at the actors, who still looked like chickens, but at that moment, he saw them through her eyes.

Although still frustrated he couldn't help but laugh.

The room went silent for a moment, all eyes on him. There wasn't much he could do at this moment, so he let out another laugh. Others then followed suit, including Helen.

To his surprise, even Newton let out a belly roll. Shaking his head, he said, "Don't know about this one, Jack. It looks like a pillow exploded on them."

"It was good, but..." He huffed out a breath. He couldn't have his actors looking like chickens on screen. The scene was supposed to be dramatic. Show the extremity of their journey during a blizzard. His budget was minimal for this film, mainly because that's all he had, but he still had standards to meet, and actors who looked tarred and feathered were not up to those standards.

Helen bit her bottom lip, not sure if she should speak or not. She didn't know anything about filming a movie, but did know a little bit about feathers. Jack and the director both looked frustrated.

Reaching out, she laid a hand on his arm. "Jack?"

He turned, and though there was annoyance on his face, he offered her a smile. "Yes?"

Half afraid he'd think it silly or no help, she bit her lip before saying, "There was a laundry near where I lived in Chicago, and one time a feather pillow accidently split open. They used a fan to blow the feathers off the rest of the clothing. The owner had told me about it." That had been the very day she'd applied for the typist job at the laundry.

"A fan?"

Her stomach jittered with nerves, as she nodded. She hadn't seen it happen, but Mr. Stamper had told her all about it.

Jack turned to the director. They shared a thoughtful gaze and then both looked at her.

She nodded again.

"I like that," the director said. "Not only would it blow the feathers off them, it would look more like a blizzard." He spun around and shouted, "Get me a fan. More than one!"

Jack patted her shoulder. "Thanks."

"I don't know if it will work for sure," she warned.

"But it's a good idea and worth a try."

A sense of accomplishment, or pride, or something akin to that filled her. She held her breath as two fans were set up and turned on. The director, Newton Hindman, had the actors walk before the fan several times, watching as the feathers caught air and gently blew away.

Just when she thought her lungs might bust from the air that needed to be let out, he clapped his hands.

"This will work!" Newton shouted. "Two minutes!"

"I've never seen Newton smile like that," Jack said. "Thanks."

"I'm glad I could help." Helen couldn't hold back her smile. Helping him, even in this small way felt better than anything. It was such a little thing compared to all he'd done for her and Grace, but it felt so good.

When filming started again, her heart quickly jumped into her throat. With the fans blowing the feathers about, it looked as if the men were seriously trudging through a blizzard. When one fell, it wasn't funny, but serious, especially when blood appeared on his temple. He kept stumbling, past another sign measuring the miles to his destination. It was the tall one who was injured. Malcolm Boyd.

The way he'd approached her and winked earlier had unnerved her, but now she felt sorry for him. The way he stumbled and crawled back to his feet. It truly felt as if he was fighting with all he had to get home.

The other actor kept helping him up, helping him move forward through the blizzard.

Even though she'd seen someone put the sign up, she still held her breath when the two stumbled up to it. It showed both of the names of their hometowns—one was straight ahead, the other to the left.

Boyd gestured for the other actor to leave, go toward his hometown. The other man refused and looped his arm around Boyd to help him onward, toward his home instead.

"Cut!"

Helen didn't realize she'd grabbed ahold of Jack's arm until he patted her hand.

"It's just a movie," he said.

"I know, but they are so close to being home and have traveled so far." She knew that from all that he'd told her about the movie, how the two men had been friends from neighboring towns before going to war, and how they'd missed their bus after a long and enduring train ride. Wanting to be home in time for Christmas, they'd decided to walk. She felt as if she knew the characters, and wanted them both to make it home safe and sound.

"I hope every person who sees this film feels the same way," he said.

She tightened her hold on his arm. "They will. I know they will."

He was looking at her, and try as she might, she couldn't look away. Even when her heart started pounding fast.

The director barked out an order, and Jack pulled his eyes off her. A wave of disappointment washed over her.

She had to take in a deep breath and tell herself that he hadn't been thinking about kissing her. That she was being silly. Foolish actually. She hadn't been hoping he'd kiss her, either, because that would have been just as foolish.

Trying not to think about that, she watched as the crew members rolled away the background of trees and snow, and pulled out one that had a house painted on it, far in the distance.

As much as he'd told her about the movie, Jack had refused to give away the ending, always saying she'd have to see it. "They are going to make it home in time for Christmas, aren't they?" she asked.

He lifted a brow and shrugged.

"Do you want me to take Grace?" he asked a moment later.

Helen hadn't even realized Grace had dozed off. The chair had arms, so Grace's weight wasn't an issue. "No, she's fine."

Her attention went back to the set, but her thoughts stayed with him. Her hand stayed on his arm too, and when the filming started again, she held on tighter. The tall man was bleeding harder and the shorter one had to work to keep them both moving, nearly dragging the other one toward the house. He shouted toward the house, but with the wind blowing and the snow falling, no one could hear him.

When the taller one collapsed, she gasped.

The other man tried to get him up, but couldn't. He kept trying and trying, yelling for help and begging his friend to get up as the snow piled up on top of them.

Unnerved for the men, she leaned closer to Jack. "They have to make it. The house is right there. They can't die. Not that close to home."

He wrapped his arm around her. She leaned against him, needing the comfort, the assurance.

The actors finally got up, but a few feet later, the tall one went down, limply. The other one fell to his knees.

"Cut!"

"No!" Helen slapped a hand over her mouth. Face on fire, she said, "Sorry."

Jack laughed. "Think we got a winner with this film, people!"

There was a round of laugher and clapping. Helen hid her face against his shoulder for a moment, feeling eyes on her.

When Newton started barking orders, she looked up at Jack. "They are going to film more, right?"

"Yes."

"Good." Rabid dogs couldn't have dragged her off her chair. Whether it was just a movie or not, she had to know that these two men made it home.

The background the crew rolled out this time was of a house, closer, and on the far side of the set. When Newton shouted action again, a woman was on stage in front of the house, with a hand shading her eyes as she looked about. She squinted as if seeing something, but then shrugged and turned around.

Helen wanted to shout, tell her not to go back inside.

The two male actors were on the other end of the stage, with a snow-filled backdrop and piles of feathers. The shorter one managed to get the taller one on his back, and holding the other man's arms over his shoulders, he slugged forward, dragging the other man. Then, just when it appeared they might make it, the shorter one went down, face first.

Helen's heart rejoiced as the woman appeared again and rushed forward. Others followed her. They gathered around the two men in the center of the stage, and with urgency, the new actors helped the other two up and toward the house.

A satisfied sigh left her chest at the same time Newton shouted "Cut!" again.

"That's a wrap!" he added. "Great work everyone!" Newton then stood and turned around. "Great work to you, too. Fans were exactly what we needed."

Helen nodded, still glad she'd been able to help, but the other thing that he'd said had her mind whirling. *That's a wrap.*

Turning, she asked Jack, "Is that how it ends?"

His expression was unreadable. "Why?"

"I'm happy for the one, but what about the other one? Does he make it home to his family before Christmas?"

"There's one more scene in the script."

Satisfied, partially, she asked, "Will you film it now?"

He climbed off his chair. "No, we've already filmed it. There are still more scenes from earlier in the film to shoot over the next few weeks."

Confusion followed her disappointment. "Why would you do that?"

He lifted Grace out of her arms. "Because that's how it's done. Scenes are never filmed in the order they are shown."

She climbed off the chair and picked up her overflowing purse. "Why?"

"For many reasons."

"Such as?"

"Schedules, weather, set changes. To name a few." He put a hand on her back and guided her toward the door. "Thanks for being here today. Those fans were a very good idea."

"I'm glad it worked so well."

"It certainly did." He opened the door leading back inside.

She stepped into the hallway. "It didn't even seem like we were outside."

"Well, there were walls around us, just not a roof," he said. "Beyond the closed lot, we have an open one. We film scenes out there, too. Several for this movie. And we have an indoor set that we use just as often."

"It's so much more complicated than I realized."

"But you enjoyed it?" he asked, gesturing toward his office door.

"Immensely." She had, and was impressed by how talented he was. The movie was sure to be a hit. A big one.

"Jack? Got a minute?" Newton asked from the doorway.

Jack patted her back. "I'll just be a minute. I'll meet you in my office."

She nodded and continued down the hallway, but upon opening his office door, Helen froze. His secretary was there, Miss Hobbs, standing near the sofa.

"Hello," the woman said brightly.

Slightly taken aback, considering their past encounter, when she'd practically thrown Grace in the woman's hands and run away, Helen barely managed to respond. "Hello."

"I owe you an apology," Miss Hobbs said. "I do hope you'll forgive me, but when given orders, I follow them, and I'd been ordered that Jack wasn't to be disturbed that day."

Helen had to appreciate that. Had to appreciate anyone helping Jack. Even a beautiful woman with very fashionable clothes.

"I do hope you'll like what I picked out," Miss Hobbs continued, waving toward the sofa. "I believe they'll fit."

Helen glanced at the sofa, her brow puckered in confusion as she looked at the numerous packages sitting there.

"Jack didn't tell you, did he?"

Goose bumps sprang up on Helen's arms. "Tell me what?"

"That he asked me to go shopping for you."

Helen's stomach sank as she glanced down at her brown dress.

"Did he tell you about the party?"

Helen shook her head. "What party?"

"The one Jack has to go to. The Wagner brothers are hosting it at a private club downtown tomorrow night. They own one of the biggest studios, and are trying to cozy up with the folks who are building the new studio. My friend works at another studio and she told me that word is the brothers are trying to convince them to give them the opening night instead of Jack."

A shiver raced over Helen. She tightened her hold on Grace still sleeping in her arms. "But they can't. He signed a contract with them."

"This is Hollywood. Deals are broken every day."

Alarm filled Helen. "Does Jack know?"

Chapter Twelve

The knot in Jack's stomach had grown tighter, harder, all day long. The Wagner brothers were at it again. He should have expected it. This was the part of the business he hated. The game playing. It was also the part Joe had thrived on. He'd not only shone on stage, he'd always been the life of the party. Jack had never minded staying behind, letting Joe shine.

Except, this time, he didn't have that choice, and without a massive opening night, his movie wouldn't stand a chance.

The very movie he'd spent another day working on. He'd known this movie would stretch him to the limit. Being so financially strapped, he was doing far more than producing this one. From writing all the script changes to building sets. He didn't mind the work, it just didn't leave time for anything else.

He rubbed at the tension in the back of his neck. There was another reason he didn't want to attend the party tonight. Helen. She'd insisted he needed to go and had agreed to go with him. He appreciated her support, but taking her tonight would be like leading her directly into a wolf's den. One look at her, and every producer at the party would be all over her.

A heavy sigh left his lungs. He could understand why she wanted to go, though. She'd been cooped up in his apartment for weeks.

A knock on the door had him spinning about. "Come in."

Miss Hobbs pushed the door open. "Is there anything you need before I leave?"

"No, thank you."

She nodded. "I'll be at your apartment in an hour and half, then, to watch Grace."

"Thank you." He probably should say more. She was going above and beyond her duties in offering to care for Grace while Helen attended the party with him. So was Helen.

She'd been so happy watching the filming yesterday, so enamored and so endearing when she'd given them the fan idea.

He closed his eyes, not wanting to remember the fear on her face when he'd entered this office later. He'd tried hard to convince her that the owners of the new theater wouldn't break their contract with him, even while knowing that was a very real possibility. Especially after he'd made a few phone calls and learned what Beverly had said was very true. That was indeed the word on the street. The Wagner brothers were trying to nudge him out.

He wouldn't let that happen, and he wouldn't let anyone get to Helen, either. She was too innocent for this business. For this town.

Grabbing his suit coat off the back of his chair, he started for the door just as the phone rang. He considered ignoring it, but then reach across his desk and lifted the receiver.

"Jack? Jack, is that you?"

Anger lit up inside him and he tossed his jacket on the desk. "Joe! Where the hell are you?"

"I'm sorry, Jack, I've been busy. You know how it is. Always have a show to put on."

He leaned a hip against his desk. "Where are you? Florida?"

"No, I'm in South Carolina."

"South Carolina? There aren't any studios there. Or are you still with the circus?"

"No, I haven't been with the circus since Chicago. That's why I'm calling, Jack. Do you know where Vera is buried?"

He frowned, not at the question, but at the desperation in Joe's voice. "No, well, Chicago I'm assuming."

"Can you find out?"

"Yes." Helen would know. "I can find out."

"I need you to find out, Jack, and buy a headstone. A big one. Nice one." There was a long pause. "She was a good woman, Jack. A real good woman. Sweet and kind, but I had to leave. Had to."

He shook his head, but refrained from commenting. There was no reason to leave a wife and baby. "I'll find out where she's buried, but there is something else you need to know, Joe."

"Thanks, I appreciate it." Another silence happened before Joe asked, "What else would I need to know?"

The desperation was gone—now he just sounded uninterested. Jack squelched the ire building again. "You have a child, Joe. Vera had a baby before she died."

Whatever he said was muffled, then there was a long silence, before Joe said, "A child? A boy or girl?"

"Girl." Jack's heart softened. "Her name is Grace."

"Where is she? How old is she? Is she...healthy?"

"She's three months old and as healthy as a horse." There was no need to mention the tuberculosis scare. The negative test results had removed the fear of that from his mind. "She just got her first tooth recently."

"You've seen her?"

"Yes. She's here. In California." Saving himself from a dozen questions, he continued, "A friend of Vera's brought her out here, looking for you. Her name is Helen. Helen Hathaway. Do you know her?"

"No, I didn't know any friends of Vera's, but the baby, Grace you say, she's there, with you?"

"Yes. At my apartment."

"And she's healthy?"

"Yes. She's been well taken care of. *Is* being well taken care of." *And loved*, he said, only to himself. Helen loved Gracie like her own child.

"I—I gotta see what I can make happen here, Jack." Now there was an urgency in Joe's voice. "Get things together so I can come home. Back to California." Another silence. "This Helen, you say she's taking good care of my baby?"

Something inside Jack tightened. "Yes, Helen is taking the best care of her. Hasn't let her out of her sight since Grace was born. The two are inseparable." He wasn't sure why he said that, except for the fact it was true. It was also what had been plaguing him all day. He'd convinced her to stay, to help him, and was now pulling her down deeper into his bucket of trouble.

"And you, you're helping her?"

"Yes," Jack answered, holding back a sigh. "I'm helping her."

"Thank you, Jack. Thank you. You're the best brother a man could ask for. Have always been." After another pause, he said, "I'll let you know my plans. I'll call and let you know my plans." He sounded odd again, and his last statement was barely a whisper, "I love you, Jack."

The line went dead. Not just silent this time. Dead, with static, and then a buzz.

Jack hung up before the operator came on and instructed him to, and ran his hands through his hair. Nothing had changed. Never would. It was like a curse of the younger brother. The one not as good-looking, not as good of an actor, not as willing to hurt others.

He pushed away from his desk, hating the way he was thinking. Joe was his brother and had done a lot for him. He loved him. Always would.

He also wished like hell that Joe was the one going to this party tonight.

Helen sat on a bar stool, wearing one of the dresses that Beverly had purchased. The purple beads of the hem bounced against her shins as she shifted, crossing her legs at the ankles to keep them from shaking. She'd told herself all day that she could do this. Attend a party. It was for Jack, and something she could do to repay him for his kindness.

A part of her still couldn't believe she'd done it. Put on the shimmering purple dress and was now here, at a private club downtown, but she had. And was.

From the moment Beverly had told her about the party, that someone was attempting to undermine Jack and all his hard work, she'd known she had to go. Knew if she didn't, Jack wouldn't.

He'd tried to say it wasn't that important for them to go, but she saw through that. It was very important.

She kept telling herself everything was going to be fine, that this party was nothing like the only one she'd ever gone to, back in Chicago. The one that had been raided. Even though this party was very different—the people, the gaiety, the sheer glamour of it all—deep inside her, anxiety swarmed.

Jack stood behind her, talking with men he'd introduced her to. She couldn't remember their names. He'd introduced her to a number of people since they'd arrived a short time ago, and she was very thankful for his continued nearness.

Jack laid a hand on her shoulder. "Do you need another drink?"

She shook her head. The glass of iced tea she'd ordered still sat on the bar in front of her. That was what her mother had told her to order two years ago. Iced tea.

"How about something to eat?" Jack asked.

Swiveling the stool in order to look up at him, she shook her head. "No, thank you, I'm fine." She glanced around the room, at the people dressed in clothes so fine they looked like movie stars. Because they probably were. She'd never seen anything like the room, either. How everything sparkled. There was even an ice sculpture near the food. A huge swan made of crystal-clear ice was surrounded by platters and platters of food the likes of which she'd never seen.

He sat down on the stool beside her and twisted it so he faced her. "Thank you for coming with me. I wish I could say we won't be here long, but I don't know how things are going to play out." He nodded toward a large crowd near the tables laden with food. "Those are the Wagner brothers over there, along with their producers, directors, actors."

She laid a hand on his knee as he huffed out a long breath. "Are the owners of the theater here?"

He shook his head. "Not unless they are hiding in the bathrooms."

She tried to offer him a smile, but knew it fell short.

"I'm sure Grace is fine."

"So am I," she answered. Leaving Grace with Beverly had been the easiest part of the night. Beverly was more than capable, and Grace was a good baby.

A tall blonde woman—wearing a very fashionable, and short, black dress—was walking toward them with a sly grin curling up her red lips as she ignored others along the way. The diamonds glittering around her neck could have more than paid for a train ticket anywhere Helen could have wished to go.

The smell of her perfume arrived before the woman did, and Helen leaned back. Jack's fingers wrapped around her hand, holding it against his knee as the woman stopped in front of him.

"Jack, darling," she said, kissing the air near Jack's cheek.

"Rita," he said rather coldly.

"I haven't seen you for ages," she cooed.

"It hasn't been that long. This is Helen. Helen, this is Rita Wells."

The woman didn't even look her way, which saved Helen from having to respond, but also filled her with disdain.

"Come dance with me, Jack, darling. So we can catch up."

"Sorry, Rita, that's where Helen and I were just headed." He stood and tugged on her hand.

Helen rose beside him. The smile on his face was strained, and that's what seemed to ignite some determination inside her. Jack clearly didn't like this woman, therefore, she didn't either. "Excuse us," she said to the woman.

Jack led her toward the other side of the large room where a band was playing and people were dancing beneath huge glass chandeliers. "We don't have to dance if you don't want to," he said.

"Yes, we do," Helen answered. "She's watching."

The grin that appeared on his face was more natural, and that eased some of the tension inside Helen. "She's an actress, isn't she?"

"Some say she's the best actress in Hollywood right now."

Helen shot a glance over her shoulder. "She is very pretty."

"On the outside." He stepped on the dance floor and pulled her up next to him. "Not everyone is like you. Beautiful on the inside and out."

Her cheeks grew warm, and then warmer when he hooked her waist with one hand and planted his cheek next to hers.

"Ready?"

She laid her free hand on his shoulder as he lifted their clasped hands into the air. This she could do. Dance. It was one of the things she'd missed upon graduating school. The dances. "Ready."

It didn't take but two steps for her to catch his rhythm

and him hers. Cheek to cheek, they glided across the floor, spun around, and glided back across the floor.

"You've been keeping secrets from me," he said, releasing her waist so she could twirl about beneath their arched arms. "You're a very skilled dancer."

At the end of her twirl, she glided up against his chest. "So are you."

The smile on his face was the most enchanting thing she'd ever seen. As was the glint in his eyes. Something broke free inside her, true enjoyment, and she embraced it. With their footsteps matching the beat of the music, they danced face-to-face, and kicked up their heels as they tore up the dance floor, laughing aloud.

She'd never been so happy, so carefree. Her spirits became as high as those of the others in the room, where the merriment truly echoed off the walls.

After several songs they were both winded, and Jack led her off the floor. He was jubilant, laughing and joking with others as they headed toward the bar.

"Where have you been keeping this doll, Jack?" someone asked.

"Away from you," he answered with a laugh as he pulled her through the crowd.

Caught up in the fun, Helen laughed too, and this time, when she was handed a glass of iced tea, she drank the entire thing.

People gathered around them, asking Jack about his latest movie, and when they would question him about her, his answer became, "She's my assistant. The best one I've ever had."

Pride nearly bubbled out of her. She knew he said that only because he couldn't explain who she really was, but that didn't matter. She liked the idea of being able to assist him—like she had with the feathers—and wished she could do more. Be more involved in his life. In this life of fun and merriment.

They danced several more times and ate plates full of food that looked too fancy to eat, but tasted too good not to, and laughed. Jack made it impossible for her not to laugh, especially when telling about the feather incident to a small group of people who had gathered around a table with them. He also told them about her fan idea, and how it had worked perfectly.

When he said it was time to leave, she was almost sad. It had been a very long time since she'd enjoyed herself so much. It wasn't until they were in the car, driving home, that she remembered the purpose of the party. "Were the owners of the new theater there?"

He shrugged. "I've never met the actual owners, but the people running the theater for them sat at the table with us."

Surprised, she asked, "The ones you told about the feathers?"

"Yes." He glanced at her and winked. "It doesn't hurt for them to know that filming a movie isn't all the cat's meow."

The lightheartedness of the evening still lived inside her. "I suspect you're right."

He reached over and squeezed her hand. "Thanks again for coming. It helped a lot."

"It was fun."

"You mean it?"

"Yes." Sensing there was more, she asked, "Why?"

"Because we have another one to go to night after tomorrow."

"We do?"

"This is all part of movie making."

She let the idea settle for a moment. Which was un-necessary because she already knew that she'd go with him. It hadn't been nearly as unnerving as she'd first allowed it to be while sitting next to the bar like a flat tire. She did have one worry. "Do you think Beverly will be able to watch Grace again?"

"I'll ask her. She's turned out to be an excellent sec-retary. One of the best I've had."

"Julia might be willing to watch Grace, if Beverly is unavailable."

"Good thinking." He parked the car and turned off the engine. "I know it's asking a lot of you. More than what you bargained for."

She shook her head. "If you recall, I said I wanted to do more. To help more. I still do."

He took ahold of her hand, held it while looking at her. "You've been doing more since the very begin-ning."

Her mouth had gone dry and her heart was thud-ding in her ears.

He leaned toward her. Her heart flew into her throat at the same time a rush of excitement filled her. He was going to kiss her. Kiss her. What should she do? Kiss him back? She didn't know how. Had never kissed a man before.

He lifted her hand and kissed the back of it. "I can never thank you enough for all you've already done."

The disappointment that filled her was like noth-ing she'd ever known. That had not been the sort of kiss she'd been thinking about. Which had been a very foolish thought.

* * *

Jack drew in a deep breath and held it as he opened his car door. He let it out slowly before he said, "I'm sure Beverly is ready to call it a night."

The night air was hot, the exact opposite of what he needed right now. He'd almost kissed Helen. Seriously kissed her. It had taken all his will not to, because he wasn't like his brother. Never had been. There was too much at stake for him to kiss her, to cross that line and put them in a greater mess than they already had. Once again he had to be the responsible one. Even as the desires ate away at him, he would now lead her up to his apartment and sleep on the lumpy couch, all the while knowing she was only a few feet away, in his bed.

Damn it, Joe.

He shook his head while walking around the car. This wasn't Joe's fault. He could blame a lot of things on his brother, rightfully so, but not this. Not Helen. Joe had nothing to do with her. No, this was all on him.

Jack drew in another deep breath before opening her car door and taking her hand. She stepped out. He told himself to let go of her hand, but he didn't, despite the tumult inside him. She was temptation in the finest sense. Tempted him in ways he'd never been tempted. Dancing with her couldn't be to blame, either. She'd grown on him long before tonight. He couldn't remember being this sweet on a woman, not that there was anything sweet about the way he was feeling right now.

They walked to the building and up the stairs in silence. Once inside the apartment, he excused himself, went into the bathroom and splashed water on his face while Helen and Beverly discussed Grace's evening. He needed to keep things on the level.

She'd caught eyes tonight, just as he'd known she would, and he made sure every set looking her way got a return stare from him. One that let them know she was hands-off. That caused a few lifted brows, but no one challenged him on it. Unlike his brother, he'd never been known as a drugstore cowboy, and never would be. There was nothing false about him, particularly his silent warnings to the other men tonight to keep their distances from Helen.

Upon exiting the bathroom, he offered to walk Beverly down to her car, not so much out of politeness as need. The desire to kiss Helen was still living inside him and he needed a bit more time to get himself under control. A bit more time before he returned to the apartment, before he was alone, with her.

But the few minutes it took to walk Beverly to her car and wait until she drove out of the parking lot was not nearly enough time. He was still wound tighter than a live wire.

Playing by the rules had always been his strong suit. Nothing ever pushed him so far that he got reckless, and it shouldn't now.

Especially now. He needed all his faculties intact. If this movie didn't get done, and done right, and premiered, he'd be belly up. And then he'd be absolutely no use to Grace or Helen, let alone Joe. He couldn't, wouldn't ever, inflict the kind of childhood he'd had on his niece.

The weight on his shoulders felt heavier than it had way back when he was scrounging up chicken eggs. He was damn near as afraid to walk back up those stairs and into his apartment as he'd been to sneak inside those coops full of hens.

Flustered that he'd let it come to this, he spun around and started up the steps. He was no longer a kid wet behind the ears. He was a grown man and could handle anything thrown at him. Had for years and years and would continue to.

Helen was in the living room when he opened the door.

"Is everything all right?" she asked.

"Yes." The sight of her kicked the desires already alive in him up a notch. He turned about and shut the door, then pulled the key out of his pocket to secure the lock. "Why?"

"You were gone for so long."

He closed his eyes, pulling up the will to act platonic. Joe was the actor, not him. That had never bothered him, but right now, he wished he'd have gotten a little bit of that ability in the genes that had been passed down to him.

There were no sounds of footsteps, but he felt her approaching, and swung around. Sidestepping around her, he pocketed the key. "I watched until she pulled out of the parking lot." He gestured toward the window, where sounds of horns blowing and vehicles driving by entered the room. "There's plenty of traffic out there tonight."

"That was nice of you."

He didn't want to be nice. Tossing that thought aside, he pulled off his suit coat and hung it on the stand. "Well, it's been a long day."

"Yes, it has." She bit her bottom lip for a moment. "Could I ask you a question?"

He debated his sanity for a moment, but then nodded. "Yes. What do you want to know?"

"That woman, the one named Rita? She's an actress, isn't she?"

Skepticism struck first. That someone didn't know who Rita Wells was. "Yes, Rita Wells." He waited for her reaction. When there wasn't much of one, other than a simple nod, he asked, "You've never heard of her?"

She shook her head.

"She's very popular. She's been in hundreds of movies and has been interviewed in every gossip magazine there is," he explained.

She sighed and then walked over to one of the armchairs flanking the sofa. "I've only seen a couple of movies, and have never read a gossip magazine. I'm not sure what those even are."

He followed and sat in the opposite chair. "You've never read a gossip magazine? They're a dime a dozen. The newsstands are full of them."

She frowned. "You don't like them, do you?"

"As a whole, no, because they have no regard for decency. The stories are as counterfeit as a three-dollar bill. Many of the articles are written by the actors themselves, telling tales of how they went from rags to riches." However, he had to agree with one thing. "But they sell movie tickets and that's their overall goal." During Joe's debacle the Wagner brothers had taken out large ads in most every magazine, and therefore the magazines had put out double-page spreads about Rita. Full of lies about her wonderful marriage to her then husband. If they'd been truthful, it would have mentioned her love of drinking and extramarital affairs.

He hadn't been able to afford to put out that sort of advertising, not even to clear Joe's name. Not that it would have mattered. Joe had already left town by the time the magazines hit the newsstands.

"Rita is very pretty."

"Yes, she is." He'd never protest that, but next to Helen, Rita looked like any other of the million Janes in Hollywood. Wearing that purple dress and perched on the edge of the stool next to the bar, Helen had outshone all the dames that had been at the party. She still did. He still wanted her, too. The desire was growing stronger by the minute.

"Has she ever been in one of your movies?"

He stood and casually shook one leg, attempting to loosen how tight his pants had become. "No. She's the Wagner brother's bread and butter. Has been for a long time." Gesturing toward the darkness outside of the window with one hand, he said, "It's late."

"I'm sorry," she said while rising off the chair.

"There's nothing to be sorry about."

A hint of a smile crept across her face as she smoothed back the hair at one temple. "I didn't mean to keep you up so late. I just…" She shrugged.

"Just what?"

"Wanted to say thank you for this evening. It was fun."

"It was." He told his feet to stay put. To not take a step closer to her. That would be trouble. But she was looking at him and he couldn't pull his eyes away. His hands itched to caress the side of her face. Her shoulder. Her side. Feel the curves of her beneath the dress as he had earlier, while dancing.

"Well, um, good night, Jack."

She hadn't taken a step, nor had she pulled her eyes off him. It was a struggle, but he finally managed to look the other way. "Good night, Helen."

Chapter Thirteen

Helen couldn't sleep. Her mind wouldn't shut down. Images of dancing with Jack played over and over again. She'd never felt as alive as she had while dancing with him. She kept trying to think logically. To tell herself that she'd been careless going out like she had, and enjoying herself. Someone could have seen her. Logic, however, couldn't be found. Not tonight.

Tonight, she didn't care if her family was the mob, or if they were looking for her. All she could think about was how it had felt to laugh, to dance, to be a normal person. Or as close to normal as she could imagine. That was hard because she'd never been normal. She'd been secluded, either in her parents' house or the private school they'd sent her to, where she'd also been taught to speak only when spoken to, seen only when requested.

That angered her in ways it never had before. Yet, it shouldn't, for in a way it had prepared her for the last two years. Of living in hiding. Not being seen or heard.

Tonight showed her how much she'd been missing. She'd never have discovered that if not for Jack. He was the reason she went out tonight. Beverly had said he needed to be at that party and people there had been genuinely happy to see him, some had even acted surprised. She'd seen how hard he was working to make this movie, get it finished by the deadline. He tried to hide it. Never said a word about the issues he'd faced during the day, but she'd seen the weariness on his face when he came home each night, and inside knew how much this movie meant to him. She'd had to put her fears aside to make sure he went tonight, and in the process, found out she was tired too, so very tired of the life she'd always known.

When Grace stirred, Helen climbed out of bed, certain she hadn't slept a wink, yet must have because daylight was shining outside the window.

She quickly put on one of her brown dresses and changed Grace before picking her up and carrying her to the door.

Heat filled her cheeks at the sight of Jack standing near the sofa wearing only his pants and holding a cup of coffee. His bare chest was defined, so sculpted by the muscles beneath his golden skin. Warmth pooled inside her, much like it had in the car last night when she'd thought he was going to kiss her.

"Morning," he said brightly. "Coffee is done and I put a bottle from the fridge in a pot of warm water for Grace."

"Th-thank you." She bit her lips at how her words stumbled. Her feet might too. She'd recognized how handsome he was before, but this morning, it was all she could think about. That and how he was looking at her, like he couldn't pull his eyes off her any more than she could take hers from him. She'd felt that before, the pull that drew them together when he watched her, especially when he thought she wasn't looking. It affected her in mysterious ways. Ways she couldn't explain.

"I have to get ready to head to the studio." He set his cup on the table. "And I'm sure Grace will want to drink that bottle."

Once he was out of sight, Helen found the ability to walk into the kitchen and feed Grace. Afterward, she was even able to fry Jack some eggs and wish him a good day. But as soon as he walked out the door, she plopped down on the sofa, nearly exhausted. Why did just looking at him leave her breathless? What was wrong with her? More apt, what had she gotten herself into?

She glanced at Grace, lying on a blanket on the floor and playing with her toes. He had been so good to both of them these past weeks. Had provided everything, and more, that they needed. It was only right that she should care about him, want him to succeed, but deep inside, she knew it had become more than that.

That alone should be enough to make her want to get away. Need to get away. But it didn't. This time, she wanted to stay and help. She'd never felt that way before.

She shot to her feet as the doorknob turned.

Jack opened the door and stepped in.

Once again, the sight of him had her heart racing.

"I walked over to the newsstand and picked these up for you."

She carefully stepped around Grace and took the magazines from his hand.

His grin showed his dimple. "You might recognize a few people from the party last night." He then winked and turned about. "See you tonight."

"See you tonight," she repeated, and then, "Thank you."

"You're welcome."

He shut the door and she glanced down at the magazines. They were all about movies, and movie stars. She carried them to the couch and read all three of them from cover to cover, recognizing several people she'd seen last night.

The articles were interesting. She liked the ones about filmmaking more than the ones about movie stars. However, the ads in the back of the magazine were what really caught her attention and sent her mind spinning. She had no idea so many people needed typists. One of the addresses of those seeking help was on the same street as the apartment building, only a few blocks away.

She let several thoughts ferment while getting the house in order and changing her clothes, putting on another new dress Beverly had purchased for her. A light blue one, with polka dots and matching hat.

Pressing a hand to the butterflies in her stomach, she turned away from the mirror. Jack needed help, and this was a way she could provide it.

Even though her mind was made up, she was still nervous and scared, but also determined not to let that rule her, or stop her.

She carried the buggy down the stairway and then hurried back up and collected Grace from the crib. After tucking the magazine next to the baby inside the buggy, she left the apartment building.

Her legs trembled as she walked the first block and she couldn't stop herself from sneaking peeks around her, making sure she wasn't being followed. The number of people was a bit overwhelming, not only in cars driving by, but also in how many walked along the street, in and out of the many buildings.

It would be nearly impossible to recognize anyone. There was too much hustle and bustle. That eased her nerves and she focused on the addresses, searching for the one listed.

She found it in the middle of the fifth block down from Jack's apartment building. Pushing open the tall glass door with her backside, she tugged the buggy inside, and then twisted about.

"May I help you?" a woman behind a tall counter asked.

Helen pushed the buggy closer and then lifted out the magazine. Pointing to the ad, she said, "I'd like to speak with someone concerning this typist job."

The woman's dark black hair was cut short, and her beaded earrings softly clinked as she leaned over the counter to look at the ad. "That is the third floor, suite ten. The elevator is down this first hall."

"Thank you." Helen tucked the magazine back in the buggy and followed the hallway to the elevator.

A man helped her maneuver the buggy into the small area and then stepped in beside them and pulled a cage shut. "What floor?"

"Three, please." Helen held her breath as the elevator shook and creaked before it carried them upward. She'd never liked riding in them whenever she'd gone shopping with her mother. A knot unfurled inside her chest, spewing a sense of warmth. That was the first time that had happened when she'd thought of her mother, of any of her family, in a long time. Other than the elevator rides, she'd enjoyed the shopping trips with Mother. In fact, there had been many things that she'd enjoyed doing with her family. It hadn't all been bad. Why hadn't she remembered that before now?

"What suite?" the man asked.

"Ten," Helen responded.

"Just down the hall on the left," he said, while opening the cage door. He then helped her get the buggy out of the elevator.

"Thank you," Helen said, checking on Grace, who was still sleeping soundly.

He nodded and stepped back into the elevator.

Helen pushed the buggy past several doors until arriving at the one she sought. She took a deep breath, and then pushed open the door.

The posters on the wall had her pausing even before the door was all the way open. They were smaller versions of the ones in the magazines, of movies, actors and actresses.

"May I help you?"

Another woman, this one with short blond hair, smiled at her from behind a desk.

Helen maneuvered the buggy through the door and then lifted out the magazine. "I'm here about the typist job in this ad."

The woman glanced at the buggy. "You brought your baby to a job interview?"

She'd thought about that, but hadn't had a choice. Lifting her head, determined nothing was going to prevent her from helping Jack, Helen said, "Yes."

The woman grinned slightly. "I see, well, Mr. Alfords isn't available right now, but I can take your information and have him contact you."

"I'd appreciate that." Helen reached into her purse

and pulled out the certificate she'd been so excited about earning years ago. "I have completed a secretarial course."

Jack pinched both temples with one hand. Just one day without any issues. Just one. Would that be too much to ask? To expect?

"How much did you get on film?"

Ace Wilson shook his head. "None."

Jack clenched his back teeth, giving himself a moment to control his response. "None?"

"No, sir, not sure what happened. I'm sorry."

Three hours of filming gone. Gone. "It wasn't your fault." Jack nodded at Newton. "We'll have to start over."

"All right." Newton spun around and shouted, "Bring back the other backdrop! Get rid of this one!"

"We still have to film three other scenes today," Jack said. "You know the schedule we're on."

"I do," Newton said. "We all do. We'll film all night if needed."

If there was a silver lining in this movie, it was his crew. They were all willing to do whatever it took to get the job done. He slapped Newton's back. "Thanks." Then he hurried over to help move out the backdrop and bring in the other one.

The cameras worked this round, and other than a few small prop issues, they were able to complete shooting on all of the scenes scheduled for the day.

"That's a wrap!" Newton shouted. "Go home folks, and be back here bright and early tomorrow morning!"

Jack checked his watch. It was almost ten. He'd asked Beverly to stop by and let Helen know he would be late getting home tonight. He'd never done that before, but she'd been on his mind all day. That wasn't unusual, either.

However, it would be later than usual by the time he got home. There was still at least an hour's worth of work he had to complete before he could leave.

He was deep into the midst of getting everything done, when he sensed someone in the hallway outside his door. Lifting his head, he waited for them to walk in. The door was open.

The hair on the back of his neck stood. Newton, who had also stayed late, had already stuck his head in and said good-night.

Jack waited, staring at the door for a few seconds, and then pushed away from the desk. "Who's there?"

Two men, first one and then the other, big and bulky, both strangers, stepped around the doorframe and into his office. Dressed completely in black, including their fedora hats, they scanned the room before moving closer.

"Who are you?" That was a foolish question. He'd never dealt with a mobster before, there had never been a need, but he recognized that's what these two men were. The Broadbents liked to believe they were mobsters, but they were wannabes. These two were the real McCoys.

"The boss is in town from Chicago," the front man said. The taller of the two. "He wants to know that you'll be at the party tomorrow night."

The money behind the new studio was from the Chicago Outfit, so he assumed that's who these men were with as well. So far, he'd met only those running the operation here in California. They weren't gangsters, they were movie men who had needed backing to start their new venture. "I've been told about the party, and plan on attending."

"You had a woman with you last night, wearing a purple dress."

Jack's spine stiffened. "So what if I did?"

"Bring her with you."

Helen had already agreed to go with him, now he was having second thoughts. "Why? She doesn't have anything to do with this movie." He needed this movie, but didn't need to drag Helen into something sinister.

"Bring her." They both turned, headed for the door.

"No." There wasn't a movie on earth worth Helen.

The tallest one pivoted on his heel, leveled a steely stare. "You won't want to disappoint the boss, Mr. McCarney. He won't like that."

Jack wanted to say he didn't care, but the truth was, if they knew Helen had been with him at the party, they also knew where she was right now. And where she'd be tomorrow night. Still, he couldn't let them think he'd bow to their antics. "You can tell *the boss* that this isn't Chicago."

"You can tell him yourself." The man turned and walked to the door. There, he looked over his shoulder. "Tomorrow night."

Jack followed them out the door and down the hall. There wasn't anything he could say, or do. Nothing that he could think of at the moment anyway. But he would.

The two men exited the building. Jack pushed the door open, and his spine quivered as if someone had just walked over his grave. The street and sidewalk were empty. It was as if the men had disappeared into the night.

Not caring about the lights being left on, he locked the door and jogged to the parking lot, looking for any trace of the men the entire way. There wasn't any. Not a single sign.

He jumped in his Chrysler and started the engine. The tires squealed as he shot out of the lot. He planted his foot on the gas pedal, pressed it to the floor and he didn't let it up until he pulled into the parking lot of the apartment building.

Every thud of his heart sent another surge of dread through him. He cut the engine, jumped out of the car and ran for the apartment building.

He threw open the door and flew up the steps two at a time. At the landing, he stumbled. At the landing, both his feet and his mind stumbled. He couldn't go running in there, that would scare the bejesus out of her for no real reason. If there was money in it, the mob was involved. He'd known that from the beginning. Every studio had backers of that sort. It was a given. He just hadn't expected it to hit home this hard.

What he needed to do was keep protecting Helen and Grace. Keep them close so he could keep an eye on them. There was no reason for Helen to know who owned the new theater because it didn't matter. It was all just business as usual. The movie business was cutthroat, with or without mob backing.

It wasn't in the same league as bootlegging or dope dealing. There weren't raids on theaters or studios because the gangsters were behind the scenes, gathering up the money they made. They doled it out too, doubled what they'd made by investing it in the next movie.

It had been that way for years, and would continue to be that way.

His hand shook as he inserted the key in the lock, but his troubles seem to fly away as he opened the door. As his chest filled with warmth.

Helen was on the sofa, curled in one corner, her head on the arm, asleep.

He eased the door shut and inserted the key in the lock.

"You're home."

The sound of her voice stirred the warmth inside him, making it hotter and sending it to every part of his body. He locked the door and pulled out the key before turning around.

She stretched her arms over her head as she sat up. He flattened his hand on the table beside the door at the way his insides reacted to watching her arch her back.

"I saved your supper." She ran a hand over her hair and then stood up. "I just have to heat it up."

He was hot enough already. "I'll eat it cold."

"Nonsense." She walked toward the kitchen. "It will only take me a minute."

A haze hovered around Jack. That's what happened. The ability to focus disappeared whenever she was around. How the hell had it come to this point?

"Beverly said she can watch Grace tomorrow night," she said. "I asked her when she stopped by to say you'd be late."

He nodded. Idiotically. She was in the kitchen and couldn't see him. His stomach sank as a quiver of fear coiled around his spine. Tomorrow night. He'd known she'd catch eyes at the party last night, but he hadn't thought any of those eyes would have belonged to the likes of those who had visited him tonight.

"Are you all right?"

He glanced toward the doorway, where she stood wiping her hands on a towel. Her smile was soft, so was the frown between her eyes. "Yes, I'm fine."

"You've had a long day." She held out a hand. "Come and eat."

Against his better judgment, he stepped forward and took ahold of her hand. Their eyes met, and the desire to pull her close, to kiss her, struck hard and fast. He could imagine how sweet her lips would taste. How soft they'd be beneath his. He almost gave in, but stopped before his lips could touch hers.

Needing something to pacify the urges raging inside him, he softly ran the back of a knuckle down her cheek. Her eyes never wavered, never left his. She was so different from any other woman he'd known. A mixture of sweet innocence and bold determination.

"Jack?"

Like most things in his life, he owed Joe for her being here right now. And like most things with Joe, it was more complicated than necessary. He dropped his hand and walked into the kitchen. "You and Grace will come with me to the studio tomorrow."

"Why?"

Putting his acting heritage to use, he shrugged his shoulders nonchalantly. "You can watch the filming again." He arrived at the stove, where a pot of stew simmered. "You can go to bed, I'll clean this up after eating. We'll leave early."

She nudged him aside. "I'll go to bed after I clean up the kitchen." She ladled stew into a bowl. "And I'll do that after you eat."

That is exactly what happened, and while lying on the sofa after she'd gone into the bedroom, he once again admitted he didn't get any acting genes from either of his parents. Joe got all of those. He got the looks too, and right now, Jack was wondering if Joe got all the brains, as well.

He didn't seem to have a lick right now. He had a woman and baby living with him, both of whom he cared more about each day, and he had the mob breathing down his neck. Of all the pickles Joe had gotten him into, he'd never ended up with anything close to this.

His night was restless, and the following day wasn't any calmer. Another camera problem, this time a film break that required two scenes to be reshot. Then a cloudburst, which never happened this time of year, delaying the shoot until it passed, and to wrap up the day, the Broadbents made a visit, Fred and Cliff, claiming with all the hype of his latest movie, their shares should be worth more.

Dealing with them had not only been the easiest issue to solve, it had been the most satisfying. Jack had grabbed them both by the back of the collars and marched them down the hallway, telling them they didn't own any shares. They'd provided Joe a loan, which was almost paid off, and they wouldn't get any more money once that was done.

He finalized it by shoving them both out the door, one after the other. Cliff got a swift kick in the butt since he was the second one out the door.

His satisfaction waned slightly by the look in Helen's eyes. Since it was time for them to leave in order to get ready for the party, which irritated him because Newton was still filming, he grabbed his coat and escorted her to the door.

"Who were those men?" she asked once they were in the car, and Grace settled on her lap.

He could lie, but there was no reason to. "Some men Joe borrowed money from."

"Are they gangsters? Belong to a mob?"

"No. They are the Broadbent brothers. They'd like to belong to a mob, and pretend they do, but they are too slimy for even the worst of the gangsters."

"What do you mean by that?"

He shifted the car in gear and pulled out of his parking space. "There's a code of honor amongst gangsters."

"There's no honor in killing people."

The iciness of her tone sent a shiver up his spine. Newspapers across the nation hosted stories on how Chicago, Detroit, New York were the birthplaces of major organized crime families. He had no idea what she may have experienced living in Chicago her entire life, and didn't want to frighten her. Didn't want to tell her it was here, too. Just as it was in every major city, and smaller ones alike.

Choosing his words carefully, he agreed, "No, there's not. And there is plenty of that happening. It's in all the newspapers, but the majority of the violence is between outfits. There is competition between them just like there is competition in every other business, but the average palooka in America doesn't have anything to fear from gangsters." He wasn't trying to sugarcoat it, for there was plenty of danger being associated with any gang. On the inside and the outside.

It had always been his job to be the voice of reason, and this was no different. "Where there's money, there is corruption. From our government right down to the newspaper boy peddling his papers on the corner. It's not only his job to sell papers, but to make sure some other boy, selling another paper, doesn't come along and impede upon his turf."

A frown marred her face, yet there was thought in her eyes. So was skepticism.

He shrugged and pulled up one more explanation that might help her understand. "Although it passed, a large majority of people don't like prohibition. They don't like the government telling them what they can and can't consume and many applaud the gangsters for finding a way to provide a product that had been available for centuries. Yes, bootleggers are making a lot of money. It's how supply and demand works, but they are also spending a lot of money. The automobile industry loves them, so do clothes manufacturers, jewelers, home builders, city municipalities. Police precincts can't afford cars powerful enough to chase down the one's gangsters have, so they've sold out to other gangs, ones offering to donate even more powerful cars—to chase down others of course—giving themselves immunity."

"Are you part of a gang?" she asked.

"No, I'm not part of a gang." That wasn't a lie. He wasn't part of one, even though the studio was now deeply involved, financially, with one.

She shook her head. "You sound as if you are. As if you believe in what they are doing."

"I'm not, won't ever be. I don't believe in their tactics or their antics, but I do believe in free enterprise. That businesses have a right to operate and succeed without governmental control."

"Gangsters don't have anything to do with that."

"Yes, they do. Good or bad, without the success they are having right now, without the money they are pouring back into the economy, I wouldn't have a business. The jobs their spending creates is how people can afford to go see the movies." It may not be legitimate, but it was what it was, and that was the truth. The other truth was it would only continue to grow. There was nothing to stop it.

He pulled the car into the apartment building parking lot and cut the engine. "I can't say I like it, in fact, I don't, and I don't see it changing, not for a long, long time."

Her face was scrunched into a frown.

"But, I like making movies," he said honestly. "And I'm good at it." He opened his door, but turned to her before climbing out. "There's good and bad in everything, but we all have the choice to look at things from different angles, find what affects us and those we care about. That's when we have to decide what we want to focus on. The good, or the bad. Long ago, I chose to focus on the good."

Helen's mind was swirling so fast and hard, it made her head hurt. Was there really good and bad in everything as he said? Her family, especially Mother, had tried to shield her from the bad, up until the North End Gang had attacked her cousin, and it could no longer be hidden. After the raid on the restaurant, full of grief, all she'd been able to see, to focus on, was the bad. The corruption of her family ties. But, since coming here, she'd remembered there had been good in the past, in her family. Good times, happy times. But she still couldn't ignore the bad. Things she'd never forget. Things no matter how far she ran, she'd never be released from.

How could she focus on the good?

She glanced down at Grace, and her heart tumbled at the happy little face smiling back up at her. Drawing a deep breath, she kissed the baby's forehead. From the moment Grace had entered her life, she'd been the sunshine in an otherwise dark world.

The car door opened and she glanced up at Jack.

"Beverly said she'd be here within the hour," he said. "Does that give you enough time?"

"Yes," she answered, her mind still swimming in a never-ending sea of questions. Grace was the good in her world. So was Jack, but was she the good in their world? No. If the Outfit found her, they'd drag her back into the family. She'd never be able to escape the binds that tied her to violence and death. There was no good in that, and she certainly didn't want Grace or Jack exposed to any of it.

She climbed out of the car and crossed the parking lot. "Have you heard from Joe?"

Jack pulled open the door of the apartment building before answering, "No."

Helen entered the building and climbed the steps. Beverly had readily agreed to watch Grace again this evening, said she would anytime. That she enjoyed it. Others probably would too. Did that mean Jack didn't really need her to take care of Grace for him? That he was saying that he did only because he knew she had nowhere else to go?

He unlocked the apartment door and held it open for her to cross the threshold. The jumbled mess inside her mind was making her stomach churn, her heart ache.

Unable to look at him, she walked straight to the sofa and propped Grace in the corner with a couple of pillows. "If you don't hear from Joe by the time the movie is done, what will you do with Grace?"

"Do with Grace? I won't do anything with her. I mean, I'll keep her with me, for as long as it takes. She's my niece."

"I know, but—" His hands settled on her shoulders, stealing her thoughts.

"Hey," he whispered, forcing her to turn around. "I didn't mean for all that talk about gangsters to upset you." His arms folded around her shoulders. "You don't have anything to worry about."

But she did. She had a lot to worry about. She planted her hands on the lapels of his jacket to push him away, but the solidness of his chest made her look up instead. The sincerity in his eyes made the air catch in her throat.

"No one will hurt you, or Grace," he said. "I promise."

That was not something he could promise, no matter how much she wished it to be true. He didn't know who she was. What she was. A member of the mob. By way of birth. That couldn't change. Not ever. Closing her eyes at the dread rising inside her, she shook her head.

"Look at me."

She bit her lips together and fought at the sting in her eyes.

"Helen, look at me."

His command was soft, gentle, but also serious.

Lifting her chin, she blinked at the moisture on her lashes, and swallowed against the compassion in his dark eyes. "We can't change the world, but we can change the way we look at it."

"The good," she said. He believed that. If only she could.

"Yes," he whispered. "The good."

His hands grasped the sides of her face, and softly, the heat of his mouth covered hers. His lips touched her so gently, her heart seemed to grow in size, filling her entire chest.

He tilted her head slightly, slanting his lips over hers more completely. He kissed her several times, tenderly. Her lips quivered, and moved toward his, meeting each of his delicate kisses.

An awareness arose inside her. Sent her heart thudding harder with each soft merger of their lips. Her fingers curled around the lapels of his jacket, and she held on tighter as the pressure of his mouth grew.

She'd never experienced the things stirring inside her right now. She'd thought about kissing him many times, but had never imagined it would be this all-consuming.

It was good. So very good.

Heat filled her as everything about her tingled and a craving for more made thinking impossible.

The tip of his tongue touched her lips and she gasped slightly at the thrill it caused. His tongue slipped between her parted lips, entered her mouth. She clutched on to his jacket harder and stretched onto her toes, knowing on some primal level that *this* was the more she'd craved.

The kiss seemed to last forever, but at the same time it seemed to end sooner than she was ready for. His arms tightened around her, held her firmly against him. They were both breathing hard and her heart was thudding so fast, she wasn't sure if she'd ever catch her breath.

Once again, he forced her to look at him, this time with the pressure of a single knuckle beneath her chin. His eyes were sparkling, and the dimple was in his cheek. "The good," he said, with a nod.

Helen couldn't have bit back her own smile if her life depended on it.

"I've wanted to do that for a long time," he said.

She had no choice but to be completely honest. "I've wanted you to do that for a long time."

"You have?"

Heat flushed into her cheeks, but it wasn't embarrassment. It was excitement. "Yes. I have."

His lips landed on hers again. Thrilled, she buried her hands in his hair, and pressed her hips against his, her breasts against his solid, firm chest.

Focusing on the good, she parted her lips, welcoming him completely. He tasted wonderful. Like the sticks of peppermint gum she found in the pockets of his suit jacket before brushing the jacket off and hanging it in the closet.

Her heart couldn't possibly beat any harder, any faster. If it did, it would fly right out of her body.

Just when she thought that might happen, his tongue slid out of her mouth and he kissed her lips, then the tip of her nose, and then her forehead before tucking her head beneath his chin.

She stood there, knees weak and aching in unique ways and places. He rocked her slightly, back and forth, for some time, before he leaned back and looked down at her.

"Beverly will be here soon. You go get ready. I'll see to Grace."

Too lightheaded to think, she let her arms slip away from him, and then turned around and made her way into the bedroom on legs that could barely carry her. Closing the door behind her, she leaned back, and let the door hold her up.

It was a moment, or more, before she had the wherewithal to comprehend what had happened, and another moment for her to fully understand how wonderful, how alive, his kisses had left her.

The good. She could focus on the good.

Happiness nearly exploded inside her as she shot away from the door and hurried to the closet. She chose to wear the green dress he'd bought her. It had several layers of silk thread fringes that started at the neckline and ended just below her knees.

A euphoric, almost dreamlike, sense swirled around her, filled her, as she changed her clothes and settled the matching headband around her forehead. An ostrich feather was attached to the side of the band, and she twisted it, positioning the feather directly above one ear.

There were things she could be thinking about, things that she'd have to face soon, but she refused to let them in. Right now, today, tonight, she was going to do what Jack said he did. Focus on the good. The good things she was experiencing right now.

That proved to be so easy. Mainly because of Jack. From the moment she stepped out of the bedroom, his manner kept her thoughts from going in any other direction. He was so jubilant, she couldn't help but feel that way, too.

The party was once again downtown, in a beautifully decorated private club that was at the very top of a building so tall they could see the ocean outside the window.

"Seriously, this is the first time you've seen the ocean?" Jack tugged her a little closer to his side as they stood near the window, looking at the setting sun cast a rainbow of colors across the water. "We'll drive down there, to the beach, you, me and Grace. Tomorrow."

If he said he would, he would, which is why she shook her head. "You will be too busy filming tomorrow, but another day, when you have time, going to the beach would be nice."

"I'll find the time. We'll have Julia pack us a picnic lunch and go to the beach to eat it. Sit in the sunshine and watch the waves."

Helen took a moment for the beauty outside the window to form a lasting memory in her mind before she turned and smiled up at him. "All right."

His smile grew. "Good."

She bit her bottom lip as his gaze settled on her mouth. Kissing him had done several things to her. Number one being the desire to experience it again. She drew in a deep breath and glanced over his shoulder. At one of the huge sparkling glass chandeliers that hung from the ceiling. There was a dozen or more of them, and more people than she could count mingling beneath those lights. Once again, dressed in flashy outfits, sparkling jewelry, they were carrying drinks, puffing on cigarettes and laughing. Filling the room with a joviality that grew with each new couple or group that sashayed through the huge double doors.

Behind her, people were dancing to music that was provided by a band wearing black tuxedos. As she watched, the roaring, swift beats of the music seemed to enter her, fill her with a sense of excitement. Her life had certainly changed the past few weeks. All because of Jack. He filled her with that same sense of excitement.

"Want to dance?" he asked.

"If you do."

He chuckled and then whispered close to her ear, "I'll always want to dance with you."

Her insides melted, even as her mind forced her to remember that her life may have changed, but she hadn't. There were dozens upon dozens of beautiful women in the room, several of whom were casting glances their way. He didn't seem to notice them, but she did, and she knew why. Jack McCarney was a sought-after man. He could make any one of them a star, but they wanted more. They wanted him.

Maybe she had changed, because she wanted him, too. Or maybe she'd just become an actress, like the others. This couldn't last forever. But it could last for the night. And tomorrow. And every day thereafter until it was time for her to leave.

She'd never wanted to be an actress, but that's what she'd become. For now at least.

A shiver tickled her spine. She stiffened, ignoring it, and smiled up at Jack. "Let's cut a rug."

He laughed. "You are one amazing doll. One amazing doll."

They danced several times, ate from the platters of fancy foods on tables with more ice sculptures, and visited with a variety of jovial people throughout the evening, including the actors from the movie Jack was making. When Jack introduced her, she made a point of remembering names and faces. These were his friends, and she was happy to meet them. Happy to be here with him.

Simply happy. In and out.

Later on, after using the powder room, Helen made her way back down the hallway to the set of double doors leading into the room and nodded at Malcolm Boyd standing just inside the doorway, while scanning the crowd for Jack.

Malcolm handed her a glass. "Here's your noodle juice."

She took the glass of iced tea, having no desire to drink anything stronger. "Thank you, very much, but why aren't you on the dance floor?" For most of the evening he'd had nearly everyone in laughter and awe with his dancing.

Malcolm nodded toward the side of the room. "Because I told Jack I'd watch for you, let you know where he is."

"That was very gallant of you." Her heart flipped a tiny and excited somersault as she caught sight of Jack near the bar. He was so handsome. So amazingly handsome.

Jack turned just then, and the scowl on his face made her stomach sink. "Who is Jack talking to?"

"Roy Alfrods, and it looks like he must have ticked Jack off."

Helen agreed with a nod even as concern made her frown. Jack looked very mad, was marching toward them like he was on his way to a battle.

"I gotta see a man about a dog," Malcom said, shooting into the crowd.

Jack arrived a moment later and took ahold of her arm. "It's time to leave."

Helen didn't even have the chance to put her glass down until they arrived at the elevator. She set it on a table there before stepping into the cage. "What's wrong? Who were you talking to?"

He shot her an angry glare. "Don't pretend you don't know." Nodding at the elevator attendant, he snapped, "Ground floor."

Chapter Fourteen

Jack had been pissed before, numerous times, but he'd never been this downright angry. He'd had only half a mind on what Alfrods had been saying, because he'd caught sight of one of the men that had demanded Helen attend the party that night. But his concern about that had quickly been cut through when Alfrods's words had fully registered. Then, all he could think about was getting Helen out of there to find out exactly what she'd been thinking. The ride to the ground floor had to have been the slowest elevator ride on earth. When the attendant finally slid back the cage door, Jack grabbed Helen's arm and pulled her out.

"Why the hell would you go to Alfrods for a job?" he hissed while pulling her toward the lobby door.

"Who is Alfrods?"

His anger had every muscle tight, and her denial made it worse. "Don't lie to me, Helen. He told me you were at the magazine office yesterday, looking for a job."

"Oh."

"Oh?" He pulled her into one stall of the revolving

door with one hand and shoved the door around with his other. "Is that all you have to say? Oh?"

Squished up against his side, she didn't respond until the door revolved to the outside of the building.

Fury snapped in her eyes as she pulled her arm out of his hold once they both stepped outside. "They are hiring typists."

Momentarily speechless, he stared at her, then grabbed her arm and walked toward the car. He'd wanted to punch Alfrods in the nose when the man had said Helen had been at his office yesterday. Still wanted to punch him.

"I have a secretarial certificate."

"Alfrods told me, that, too."

"He wasn't there yesterday. I only spoke to his secretary. She said she'd contact me—"

"At my address. Alfrods told me all about it, and how he recognized you from the party the night before." Of all the people he knew, he hadn't expected her to be the one to ridicule him. "Everyone who is anyone is at these parties. And they talk to each other. Were you trying to make me the laughingstock of the town?"

"No!" She dug her heels into the pavement like the old mule that used to pull his parents' wagon. "I only wanted to help."

"Help?" He drew in a breath, withholding the anger that wanted to spew out.

"Yes, help. You said this movie was taking all your money. If I had a job, I could pay for anything Grace needs and—"

"You have a job! Taking care of Grace is your job!"

Chin up, she took off toward the car. "A job I get paid for."

"I offered to pay you." He pulled out his billfold. "How much do you want?"

"I don't want your money!"

"You'd rather have everyone thinking I'm so broke I can't provide for my family?"

She wrenched open the car door, and shot him a nasty glare as she plopped onto the seat. "We aren't your family."

He caught the door as she tried to pull it shut. "Yes, you are. Grace is my niece."

"But she's not your responsibility, and neither am I." She released the door handle and stared at the windshield.

He slammed the door shut and stormed around the car. Damn it. She was right. She wasn't his family. But she was his responsibility and he sure as hell didn't need the entire town thinking he was so short on cash that he was forcing her to work. Once in the driver's seat, he started the car. "What did you expect to do with Grace while you went to work?"

She stared straight ahead. Didn't so much as blink.

He bit back another internal curse. They'd been having such a good time he'd even forgotten about the two thugs from last night. He didn't claim to know everyone in LA, but ninety percent of the people at the party had been familiar. The Wagner brothers had been there, and may very well have sent those two men to his office as a scare tactic. He wouldn't put anything past them.

Nothing they did would surprise him. What Alfrods had said had though. It had damn near knocked him off his feet.

He was still flustered, but his flat-out anger was dissolving more and more, especially when he saw her swipe at her cheeks. At the tears that trickled out of her eyes.

She didn't say a word all the way home. Neither did he.

The way Helen greeted Beverly as if nothing was wrong was almost believable, except for the fact that Beverly saw through it and eyed him curiously.

"I'll walk you to your car," he said.

"No," Beverly answered, watching Helen walk into the bedroom where Grace was asleep. "You need to stay here. Clear up whatever went wrong."

"Nothing went wrong," he said.

"Tell it to Sweeney." Beverly opened the door. "I know tear-stained cheeks when I see them." She walked out and shut the door with a solid thud.

Sweeney wouldn't believe him, either. He locked the door and removed his jacket. After clicking off the lights, he walked to the sofa, sat down and removed his shoes and socks, then flipped down his suspenders and took off his shirt.

Not a sound came from the bedroom.

He knew tear-stained cheeks too. Real ones. Not fake. Some women could do that. Cry on cue. That wasn't Helen.

She wasn't an actress.

Nor did she know the ins and outs of Hollywood. She wouldn't know the repercussions of looking for a job, and he had told her that he was putting every penny he had into this movie.

He was. To a point. Having grown up hungry more than not, he'd sworn that would never happen again. Therefore, he was putting every penny of the studio's money into this movie, but he still had some of his own.

Would still be able to eat. To live. His savings weren't enough to make another movie, that took thousands, hundreds of thousands, but he had enough to get by for a while. Enough to take care of Helen and Grace.

Guilt swarmed inside him, growing bigger, and getting stronger with every tick of the clock on the wall. He pushed off the sofa and walked to the bedroom door. As he grasped the knob, he changed his mind, and walked to the kitchen.

"Aw, hell," he muttered, and turned back around, crossed the living room again.

This time he didn't pause at the door. He turned the knob and opened it. Moonlight filled the room, showed him how Helen was lying on her side, her face buried in the pillow.

He walked around to the other side of the bed and climbed on top of the covers. Sliding a hand beneath her pillow, he curled his body up against her back and rested his chin atop her head. It wasn't her fault. None of this was her fault.

"I'm sorry," he whispered.

"So am I." She sniffled. "I just wanted to help."

"I understand that, and I appreciate it." He wrapped his other hand around her waist, wishing the blankets weren't between them, but knowing it was a good thing they were. "I should have explained things better. Movies cost hundreds of thousands to make. A few dollars here or there won't make a difference."

"I just… I just wanted to be good for something."

Her words hit home. For most of his life, knowing he couldn't act, not like his parents, not like Joe, he'd felt the same way. "You are good for many things. No one could ever take better care of Grace than you do."

"Yes, they could. Beverly already does."

Like him, Grace, as much as he loved her, as much as Helen loved her, had been thrust upon her. "If you really want a typing job, I'll give you one."

She sniffled again. "You don't need a typist."

"Yes, I do. Ask Beverly if you don't believe me. She's barely keeping up, and once the filming ends, she'll be working nearly around the clock."

Helen shifted, rolled onto her back and looked up at him. "Why?"

The puffiness of her eyes tugged at his heart. "Because there will be letters, advertisements, invitations, playbills, and all sorts of things that need to be typed up. Good typists are hard to come by. They are in high demand."

"You aren't just saying that?"

He pressed his lips to her temple. "No, I'm not just saying that. You can come to the studio tomorrow and I'll show you."

A hint of a smile tugged at her lips as she laid her head against his shoulder. "All right."

He swallowed a growl at the predicament he'd now put himself into. That of lying on the bed next to her, because there was no way that he could make himself leave it now.

She let out a tiny sigh. "I truly am sorry. I didn't know."

"I know you didn't," he said. "And I'm sorry too. Very sorry." It was a twofold statement, and it was going to be a long night.

The next day wasn't a whole lot better. He'd never had a hard time concentrating on work before, but did today. He couldn't take his eyes off Helen. He'd finally found a second desk in storage and had it placed up front, next to Beverly's. His excuse had been so that the two of them could work together on projects, but in truth, it was so he could get some work done. When she was in his office, all he could think about was kissing her. Lying next to her all night long had left a need inside him boiling.

He had limited himself to one good-night kiss in that bed. And to one good-morning kiss this morning. And sincerely wanted more. It was a game of Russian roulette because one wasn't enough. Would never be enough.

Last night had proven exactly what he'd already known. Helen wasn't Hollywood material. She was too innocent, and he didn't want her to ever lose that innocence. It was what made her *her*.

Those thoughts hung with him as the days and nights rolled by. Helen came with him to work every day, and home with him every night. He made the time to take her to the beach, more than once, to Julia's for lunch several times, and there were more parties.

The pride that welled inside him when he walked into one of those parties with her on his arm was like none other. He'd called Alfrods the morning after the party, and they'd come to an agreement. He bought an ad for his movie in the upcoming magazine, in exchange for Alfrods forgetting Helen had ever inquired about a job. That had been no loss for him. He'd budgeted to buy ads long ago.

Joe hadn't called again, but the weeks were still rolling past. His eight-week timeline was almost up. The movie almost done. Soon, the premiere would be over and Helen would need to be released from the commitment she made to him.

"Jack?"

He looked over at Newton.

"What's wrong?" the director asked. "What part didn't you like?"

Jack shook his head. They'd been watching the final product, and truth be, although his eyes had been on the screen, he hadn't seen most of the last reel. "Nothing. No part. You?" He'd depended on the man's opinion in the past, and really was right now.

"I can't think of anything that would make it better." Newton leaned back and crossed his arms. "Slowing down the speed during the snow scene was great thinking on your part. I like it."

"Me, too." His mind had been on Helen, so he hadn't really seen if the slower speed had worked or not, but trusted Newton's judgment. Filming had long ago ended, so had the editing.

This was week eight.

"Then it's a wrap," Newton said, waving a hand over his head so the projector man, Adam, would know to snip the film at the end of the credits. "Is the theater ready to open this weekend?"

Jack nodded. "I talked to Blake Owens yesterday. He said it would be. That they'll have crews working around the clock, putting on the final touches, so it's ready for people to walk through the door on Saturday night."

"Well, then, I'd say my job is done." Newton popped his knuckles. "How's that next script coming along?"

"I have a rough draft penciled out." It was an older script that he'd wanted a shot at putting together, and if all went well, he'd have it. The new script had a few scenes that would need to be shot off site, on the sea, and that would be expensive.

"Whenever it's ready, send it my way." Newton slapped his shoulder as he stood. "Until then, I'm going to get some rest. You should too."

"I will," Jack said. "Right after Saturday night."

"I'll see you there. The missus is looking forward to it."

Jack watched Newton leave the room, and then looked forward again, watching the screen until it went black. Saturday night would be it. The end.

He didn't like the thought of that, yet hadn't figured out how to ask Helen to stay longer. It would be simple enough, and she'd probably say yes, yet he hadn't asked because she didn't want him to.

Despite the fun they had together, the draw he felt every time he looked at her, she was afraid. Afraid he'd ask her to stay.

He saw that in her eyes.

It wasn't there all the time, but at certain moments, almost as if she remembered something, she'd clam up, or change the subject. It was odd because at other times, she was so vibrant, so vivacious. Half the men in town were jealous of him. He didn't mind that. Nor did he let it be known that she belonged to him.

Because she didn't.

He'd thought long and hard about that, about what he could do about it, but ultimately, realized maybe it was because she didn't want to belong to him.

He couldn't blame her for that. This industry, though full of glitz and glamour on the outside, wasn't the friendliest, or safest, on the inside.

Jack let out a long and slow breath before he stood up and left the darkroom.

Helen was in his office, feeding Grace. His heart welled at the sight. These two had become his world. He didn't want to disrupt any moment of it, nor did he want it to end. But he couldn't escape the fact that Grace was his brother's child. That he was only caring for her temporarily. Neither could he escape the feeling that if Grace left his life, so would Helen—and that thought was beginning to hurt.

"And?" she asked, knowing he and Newton had been viewing the final version.

She was wearing that deep purple dress, the one with a thick fringe that ended just below her knees, highlighting her shapely and sleek legs. The desires that had taken up residence just below the surface sprang to life, as they did every time he set eyes on her. He was still limiting himself to one kiss good-night and one kiss good-morning, and it was killing him.

"Jack," she said, putting Grace in the buggy. "Quit teasing and tell me."

He wasn't teasing her, that would be far too dangerous. "It's a wrap."

With a little squeal, she bolted forward and looped both arms around his neck. "Copacetic!"

It was the little things like this, the way she looked at him, the way her eyes sparkled, that tore at his resistance. Unable not to, he hooked her around the waist and before he could stop himself, took her lips in a full, open-mouth kiss. He loved the taste of her, couldn't get enough of it.

When they separated, more than his heart was throbbing. If only everything was copacetic. Was perfect.

His stomach clenched. Not having these two in his life was going to be hell.

"You'll be happy to know we've finished the letters and playbills," she said, stepping out of his arms. "One hundred copies of each one. The letters are on your desk to sign."

He glanced at the pile she referred to sitting in the center of his desk. The invitations had gone out last week. Hundreds of them. "You two must have blisters on your fingers."

She laughed. "No, we don't. The envelopes are done, too." She'd walked over and lifted Grace out of the buggy, and then the bottle off the table. "I'll stuff them while you're signing them. As soon as Grace finishes her bottle."

He'd been racing against the clock to get this film done and ready for Saturday night—now he wanted time to stop. To stand still.

"Let's go across the street and have lunch first." He wanted to escape, to not think about how limited their time left together truly was.

She held up Grace's bottle, showing him that it was empty. "All right."

He collected the buggy they'd brought to the office for Grace to sleep in during nap times and once Grace was happily settled in it, they left his office.

The diner was busy, but he found a table where he could park the buggy near their chairs. Rosie hurried over to wait on them. Actually, she went directly to the buggy.

"Oh, you're awake," Rosie cooed at Grace. "All bright-eyed and bushy tailed. You are so cute in that little bonnet." She shot a glance their way. "Are you two having the special?"

Helen nodded at him.

"Yes," Jack answered. "With ginger ales."

Rosie reached in and scooped Grace out of the buggy. "All righty," she said. "Coming right up. I just have to go show everyone this little doll first."

Helen rose, smiling brightly. "We'll be back."

He nodded, familiar with the routine. Whenever they brought the baby to the diner, Grace got passed around the workers. Not just Rosie, Greta and Julia, but also Alice and Shirley, the two other dames Julia had hauled home after the raid weeks ago. He didn't know them, but Helen had made friends with them.

His eyes followed her, taking note of how the fringe of her dress swished and swayed as she walked around the counter. When she disappeared into the kitchen, there were already squeals of delight emitting because Rosie had entered the room first, carrying Grace.

He couldn't help but grin, and then glanced toward the door when the bell over it dinged. He waved at the man entering. Walter Russell's list of clients was long, and Jack's name was on it, as was most every producer in Hollywood. Walter been deemed the best lawyer in town for several reasons. He was thorough, quick and, most notably, honest. That was getting harder to come by.

"Jack," Walter greeted as he approached the table. "I have your copyright paperwork in my car to drop off to you as soon as I've had lunch."

"Signed, sealed and delivered," Jack said, which is exactly how it happened every time Walter completed a task for him. He considered that for a moment as something else crossed his mind. A possibility he hadn't thought of until this very moment. "Do you have time for a quick meeting when you drop it off?"

"Sure? Anything wrong?" Walter grasped the back of the chair Helen had left vacant.

Jack had no idea if there was anything legal he could do or not, but he knew Joe, and Grace's future needed to have some sort of security. "No, I just have a few legal questions." He glanced toward the kitchen. "Concerning my niece."

He'd told only a select few of exactly who Grace was, and Walter was one of them. It would come out sooner or later, and he needed to know what rights he had. Or Grace had.

Walter nodded. "All right. Everything set for Saturday night? Your new film is the talk of the town."

"All set on our end and the builder says the theater will be ready."

"Blake Owens is always true to his word. If he says it'll be ready, it will be."

"Will you be able to attend?" Jack wasn't sure if he should ask that or not, but knew Walter had received an invite to the premiere. There had been a time when Walter had attended premieres, but Jack couldn't remember seeing him at one since his wife died three years ago.

Walter shot a quick glance toward the kitchen, before he said, "Yes, yes, I think I will."

"Happy to hear it," Jack said as the bell dinged again.

They both looked in the direction of the door. Chest out and nose up like he owned the place, Karl Van Buren walked in. Jack had considered hiring Karl, once. Newton had refused to work with him, and that hadn't hurt Jack's feelings. Karl was too full of himself. Wanted to be waited on hand and foot and thought all he should have to do was walk across the stage shirtless. Other studios paid him to do just that, and Jack didn't feel sorry for them. Not in the least. A tit for a tat was true when it came to Van Buren.

The sneer on Walter's face said he felt the same way about the actor.

Jack waved to the extra chair at his table and asked Walter, "Care to join us?"

"No," Walter said, pulling his glare off Karl. "I'll sit at the counter, but thanks, and I'll be over to your office after lunch."

Walter walked over to the counter and sat on the last stool, near the wall. A wolf whistle snapped Jack's attention to the other end of the counter where Van Buren was rising to his feet as Helen walked out of the kitchen.

Jack's chair nearly toppled as he jumped to his feet and flew across the room. Planting himself between Helen and the edge of the counter, he put an arm around her shoulders and let every ounce of the ire flaring inside him settle on Van Buren.

Karl slowly lowered back onto the stool. "Jack. Good to see you."

"Karl," he sneered, letting the actor know the sentiments were not the same.

"I—I hear you have a premiere this Saturday." Karl shrugged. "My invitation must have been lost in the mail."

Jack had never purposefully set out to create an enemy, but in this situation, didn't give a rat's ass. Nudging Helen forward, he said, "No, it wasn't."

"Who was that?" Helen asked as they walked to their table.

He took Grace and settled her in the buggy and then held the back of Helen's chair while she sat. "An actor."

"Why do so many of them behave like that?"

He sat. "Like what?"

She shrugged. "Like everyone should fawn over them because they are nice to look at."

His ire sparked a few new flairs. "You think he's nice to look at?"

"I didn't say that." She laid a hand on his arm. "I can't say I even noticed what he looked like. It just seems as if that's the attitude of so many actors."

"It is," he agreed. That was just one of the things she probably couldn't wait to get away from.

"Well, they need to learn that being nice will get them a lot further than looking nice."

Her smile was coy and the fringe of her purple headband caught on her lashes as she blinked.

"Oh?" he asked.

"Yes. Take you for instance. I have yet to meet a man as handsome or nice in all of Hollywood."

She was fighting a giggle. The mirth in her eyes said so. "You don't say?"

"Everyone thinks so, even Julia. She's putting a double amount of egg salad on your sandwich."

"She does know I like egg salad."

Her giggle was soft. "Eggs. You like eggs no matter how they are cooked."

"Why not? They taste good and they are easy to cook."

Her eyes were beaming as she leaned closer to him. "And steal," she whispered.

He had a hell of a time fighting the urge to kiss her. Her eyes danced between his and his mouth, making it all the harder. "I should never have told you that," he whispered. Movement behind her had him leaning back so there was room for Rosie to set their food on the table. "But I guess when we have nothing to hide, we have nothing to fear."

He'd meant it to be a joke, but the way all the happiness disappeared from her face said he'd struck a chord.

"Here we are," Rosie said, setting a plate before Helen. "Two specials and ginger ale." Once her tray was empty, she added, "The cucumbers are delicious today. I picked them fresh this morning."

Jack nodded, but kept his eyes on Helen. "Thanks, Rosie. They look good."

"They're soaked in vinegar with sugar and salt. You have to try them." She made a point of tickling Grace before walking away.

"How's Julia, and everyone else today?" he asked after taking a couple of bites of his sandwich. Helen had barely touched hers.

"Fine. Except for Shirley."

"Why?" He'd seen Shirley only a couple of times. She was on the tiny side with thick blond hair, and a Midwestern accent that said she'd come to Hollywood straight out of a cornfield. Which was reason enough for him to steer clear of her.

"She thought she was going to get a typing job, but didn't, so she's back to washing dishes." Helen shot a sideways glance over one shoulder. "That man at the end of the counter, he's the one who didn't give her the job."

"Walter Russell?"

"Yes. Do you know him? Shirley is quite upset with him."

"I know him. He's my lawyer. We have a meeting this afternoon."

"What for?"

"He's dropping off the paperwork for the copyright he filed on *Home Bound.*"

"I'm so glad you didn't change the name. I really like that one."

"I do too," he agreed. More than that, he liked that she was talking, eating.

"Have you tried the cucumbers yet?" she asked. "They are really delicious."

"No, I was waiting for you to try them first."

Mirth once again twinkled in her eyes. "Oh, you."

"That way we both wouldn't have to spit them out." He followed up his statement with a wink.

"Eat your eggs." She tried to sound stern, but he knew she was giggling inside.

He knew people, and knew that many other women in her position would have asked him to talk to Walter about reconsidering hiring Shirley. That's how it was. Not so much what you knew, but who you knew. Back-scratching. That's what it was called and everyone did it. She wasn't like that, even though she did have him tied around her little finger, and if she'd asked, he'd probably have told Walter to hire Shirley.

When we have nothing to hide, we have nothing to fear.

Try as she might, Helen couldn't get that out of her mind. Jack hadn't meant anything by it the other day, but it had resonated with her. The life she'd been living lately had been so perfect, that she'd forgotten who she was.

Not all the time, but often enough so that when she did remember, it nearly gutted her. She had been focusing on the good, but the good was soon to end.

She had to close her eyes against the sting. There were times when she was certain Jack was about to ask her to stay longer, and each time, she'd stopped him. In different ways, but nonetheless, she'd stopped him. Because if he had asked, she'd have said yes, and she couldn't do that. Her life the past eight weeks has been a farce. She was a farce. If Jack ever discovered exactly who she was, what she'd been hiding all this time, he'd hate her. Although he might see the mob as a necessary evil, she knew enough that he didn't like mobsters, didn't agree with the way they did business.

Both he and Grace would be better off once this was over and she left them.

Forever.

Helen drew a deep breath and swallowed at how hotly her throat burned.

The good. That's what she had to focus on right now. The was the last thing she could do for Jack.

She lifted her eyes and settled them on the image reflected in the mirror. The dress was the most beautiful one she'd ever seen, and it seemed unreal that she was the person wearing it.

Shimmering gold, the gown was fitted from the off-the-shoulder sleeves to the hips and then flared out in a layered skirt that went all the way to the floor. She tugged on the top of one matching gold glove, making sure it was secure on her upper arm, and then the other one. Then twisted and checked her hair. She'd fashioned it into a roll below her ears that wrapped around the back of her head. The beaded gold headband went across her forehead. She lifted her chin and stared at her reflection a bit harder.

This was Jack's night, one he'd worked so hard for and she wanted it to be perfect, but still couldn't squelch the fear inside her. She had to do this for him. That's what you did when you loved someone. Despite the fears and worries, you had to do what they wanted. What they needed.

She did love him. That was what made all of this that much harder.

His stories about stealing eggs showed how he'd done whatever he could to take care of his family from a young age. Then after the death of his parents, how he'd moved to Hollywood and created Star's Studio, and kept it going, despite setbacks that were not his fault, proved how seriously he took responsibilities. Right down to letting her live with him. And he would continue to do so too, which was what she couldn't let happen.

The pain in her heart was so raw, it upset her stomach to the point she had to keep swallowing to make sure she didn't throw up.

A knock sounded on the door. "Almost ready in there?"

The sound of his voice made her smile, even as she pressed her hand against the commotion in her stomach so hard she could almost feel her backbone. "Yes." Turning, she faced the door. "You can come in."

Appreciation shone on his face, but it was the rest of him that took her breath away. His tuxedo pants and long-tailed jacket were raven black. His shirt gold, so was the pocket square. The tie around his neck was made of black silk. A more handsome, more perfect man couldn't exist anywhere else in the world.

"You look stunning."

Warmth filled her cheeks. "You do, too."

"Turn around."

Pressing the toes of one heeled shoe into the floor, she performed what she hoped was a perfect pirouette. The back of the dress was low-cut, leaving a large portion of her skin bare, while the front made a straight line from one off-shoulder sleeve to the other.

"Beyond stunning." He'd stepped closer. "But I think something is missing."

She pressed her lips together. The open back made wearing a brassiere, corselet or slip impossible without it showing. In truth, beneath the gown she was wearing only a pair of silk bloomers and stockings.

"I have it right here," he said softly.

There was a jeweler's box in his hand. As he slowly opened it, her heart rose into her throat.

The box held a set of pearls. Real ones. "Oh, Jack. They are beautiful."

He set the box on the vanity table. "Turn around, I'll put them on you."

She turned, faced the mirror and watched his reflection as he lifted the pearls over her head. After he set the clasp, his hands slid around her waist and he kissed the side of her neck.

Leaning back against him, she studied their reflection in the mirror. "I feel like Cinderella."

His arms tightened around her. "Then I'll make sure we are home by midnight."

He would know the entire Cinderella story. The only thing that might make everything more perfect, was if she could tell him how much she cared for him. That she loved him. But she couldn't, because to declare her love, would be the same as declaring herself to him and she couldn't do that. She couldn't tell him she loved him and then leave.

"Knock, knock, anyone home?"

Jack released her and took ahold of her hand. "I hope you're ready for this, Julia."

"For what?" Julia asked from the other room. "Taking care of Grace? The girls are all jealous you asked me and not one of them."

"No," Jack said as they stepped out of the bedroom. "For this."

Helen's cheeks burned as he released her hand and pointed at her as if presenting her to Julia.

"Oh, Helen." Julia patted her chest and then twirled a finger in the air. "Turn around."

As she had done for Jack, Helen slowly spun around.

"Wow, Jack, you look swanky, but no one is even going to notice you with this doll at your side." Sighing, Julia added, "You look amazing, Helen."

Helen's cheeks blazed. "It's the dress," she attempted to justify. "And the pearls, and the gloves and the head—"

"No, it's not."

Jack and Julia had spoken at the same time, and they both laughed, nodding at each other.

Getting down to business, Helen ignored them both. "There are bottles in the refrigerator, and I left a pan of water on the stove to warm them. Grace is asleep right now, but should be waking in half an hour or so. There are diapers and a sleeping gown on the dresser next to the crib, and—"

"I'll figure it all out," Julia said. "Don't worry. You two just go. Go have the night of your lives." Julia waved a hand at both of them. "I wish I had a camera."

"There will be plenty of those at the premiere," Jack said.

Helen pressed a hand against her stomach, once again telling herself she could not be sick. Would not. "There will be?"

"Yes. Newspaper reporters will be lining the side-walk. They always are."

"Newspaper reporters?"

Jack nodded.

Even his happiness couldn't stop the eruption of her stomach. "Excuse me," she said, dashing into the bathroom.

Chapter Fifteen

Jack had been right. The flashes of miniature light bulbs nearly blinded her as they made their way into the building with huge lit-up letters across the very top that spelled STATE. There were just as many people inside with cameras. The building was huge, with marble walls and dark red velvet curtains stitched with gold thread, and packed full of people. Marble wall to marble wall.

Every person in attendance wanted to talk to Jack, hailed from left and right, front and back. Like he had at all the other parties they'd attended, he held her close to his side. That made her forget everything else.

She was very proud of him. He deserved all of this and more. He hadn't taken a day off, not even a Sunday since she'd met him.

Servers brought around trays of champagne and hors d'oeuvres. There were so many people gathered around them, neither she nor Jack had a chance to sample either, not until they were escorted up a flight of steps and into an elaborately decorated balcony suite. The soft cushions were upholstered with velvet, so were the armrests. She and Jack were given the center front seats, flanked by some of the actors and crew members. Others filled in the rows behind them. Once everyone was seated, waiters in red-and-gold uniforms served them more champagne and set platters of delicious bites of food on small tables near the walls that were covered with heavy red drapes.

"Here's to Jack," Malcolm Boyd said, standing up and lifting his glass of champagne in the air.

"Here, here!" everyone shouted.

Jack touched his glass to hers before he clinked it against other people's. Helen was thirsty, and drank the entire glass. It was tasty, and sweet, but also sent bubbles up her nose, almost making her sneeze.

"Do you want more?" Jack asked.

"No, I'm fine." She grabbed his arm then, because a pipe organ started playing. "I'm so excited to see the movie," she whispered as a hush fell over the entire crowd.

"Thank you for being here."

He made her feel so special, it was indescribable. "I still feel like Cinderella."

"Cinderella was never as beautiful as you," he whispered in her ear.

"There's not an empty seat to be found," Newton, sitting on her other side, whispered at the same time.

Helen peered over the rail, at the rows and rows of seats beneath them. There truly wasn't an empty seat. "How many seats are there?"

"Nine hundred," Jack whispered as the lights slowly faded.

Darkness shrouded the room. Helen wrapped her arm around Jack's and leaned her head against his shoulder. When the film started to roll, and people saw how large the screen was, there were oohs and aahs, but silenced ensued as the pipe organ changed tempo and the words *Star's Studio presents Home Bound* filled the screen.

Helen was as glued to her seat now as she had been that first day at the studio, taking in every scene. Laughter filled the air at times, gasps at others.

By the time the snow scene rolled on the screen, she had both hands wrapped around Jack's arms, rooting for the men to find their way home more than before, having now seen all they'd gone through on their journey. She was holding her breath when the final scene appeared, and shed a tear when it ended. Both of the men's families were at the house. The final scene, before the screen went black, was of the men and their families, singing carols around a Christmas tree.

The applause that broke out was deafening.

The lights were turned on. Everyone below them was standing, looking up at the balcony and clapping.

Jack stood and gestured for everyone else to join him, including her. She couldn't hear what he said due to the clapping, but bowed when he tugged on her arm.

"Bravo! Bravo!" people shouted over and over again. "Bravo!"

When they descended the stairway a short time later, even more people crowded around them than before the showing. They congratulated Jack over and over, saying it was the best movie they'd ever seen. She agreed wholeheartedly.

Helen was surprised when Shirley made her way through the crowd, wearing a beautiful dark blue gown and looking absolutely gorgeous.

"That was amazing!" Shirley said hugging her. "I laughed and I cried. Then laughed and cried again."

"Me, too," Helen admitted.

"How did you do that snow scene, Jack? That was remarkable."

As Jack explained the feathers and fans, Helen realized he was talking to his lawyer, Walter Russell, who had ahold of Shirley's hand. She'd known the other woman only a short time, but Helen admired Shirley. The courage she displayed by coming to California for no other reason than because she wanted to come here, and wished she could be more like that. Courageous.

Helen was about to ask if Shirley had gotten a secretary job with the lawyer after all, but the two were pushed aside by others, including Dr. Baine.

She completely lost sight of Shirley in the crowd as a steady stream of people continued to make their way up to them, congratulating Jack.

There was still a large number of people, snapping pictures and asking for autographs when Jack took ahold of her hand. "Come on, let's make a break for it."

"Where to?" The place was still crowded.

"We have a dinner party, now."

He led her down a long corridor, stopping to shake hands and talk to people along the way, and then into a huge ballroom that was as gorgeous as the rest of the building and set up with more tables and chairs than she could count. A huge bouquet of flowers was in the center of every table, a man played music at a grand piano and people cheered as she and Jack entered the room.

She caught sight of Shirley again, but never got a chance to talk to her because she and Jack were seated at a different table. They were served lobster and steak as well as a variety of other foods and champagne. Every time she set her glass down, someone refilled it.

By the time they took their leave, she was a bit dizzy, wobbly on her feet and overwhelmingly happy.

"You doing all right?" Jack asked as she missed a step and stumbled against him.

"Yes, I guess I was sitting too long."

He wrapped an arm around her. "The champagne might have something to do with that."

The corridor was empty and she leaned against him. "I've never had champagne before."

"I know, that's why I thought I'd better get you home."

For some reason, that was so funny she just couldn't help but laugh. And laugh some more. It felt so good. She felt so good. So carefree and joyful. Remembering something he'd said once, she took off running. "Last one home's a rotten egg." Laughing again at the thought of how much Jack liked eggs, she repeated, "Egg!"

He'd caught up with her, took her hand, and side by side, they ran down the corridor, through the carpeted foyer and out the double glass doors, into the night air.

The marquee lights were flashing above them and she stopped to stare at them. It was magical. Everything. The lights. The night sky. Even the traffic rolling by. And him. Most certainly him.

Head back, she spun in a circle. "Oh, Jack, this has to be what Cinderella felt like."

Smiling, he grabbed her hand and led her along the sidewalk. "Then let's go before your chariot turns into a pumpkin."

She laughed again. "It wasn't a chariot, it was a carriage."

"That's good, because I have a Chrysler."

"Oh, you are so funny!" He was, and that made her so happy. "And handsome. And wonderful."

He opened the car door for her and she climbed in, leaning back, knowing she'd never been so content in her life. Or full of wonder. "Did you see that woman in the pink dress?"

"Which one?"

"The one with the pink ostrich plume. I think I'll buy a pink dress someday."

"And you'll look beautiful in it."

"I've never had a pink dress. Not that I can remember." She tried, but memories didn't want to come forward. "Nope. Must not have. Or silver. There were some pretty silver dresses there tonight, too. Not as pretty as my gold one though. I definitely like my gold one better."

She couldn't seem to stop chattering. They talked all the way home, about the movie, the people, the applause, the food, everything. By the time she got to the top of the stairway of the apartment building, she had to stop in order to catch her breath.

"You all right?" Jack asked.

She glanced down the flight of steps, they'd never made her breathless before.

"You didn't lose a shoe, did you, Cinderella?"

"No." She wiggled her toes to make sure. "If I had, would you come looking for me?"

"From here to eternity," he said. "I wouldn't stop until I found you again."

There was only one thing that could make this night better, and the way he was looking at her right now said he knew what it was. She looped her arms around his neck and stretched onto the tips of her toes so their lips were aligned.

His kisses, even the tiniest ones, filled her with all sorts of warm and wonderful sensations. The one he gave her right then was even more spectacular. He tasted sweet and minty, and she could have gone on kissing him forever.

She loved the feel of his palms on her bare back, the firmness of his chest pressed against her breasts, the silkiness of his hair between her fingers.

He kissed her several times before wrapping her in an extra tight hug. "Time to go inside, Cinderella. It's late, and Julia will want to get home."

Knowing he'd kiss her again, because he always kissed her and Grace good-night, she agreed. "All right, Prince Charming."

They were both laughing when they opened the door, but their laughter stopped abruptly.

The apartment was dark.

"Julia?" He closed the door and flipped on the light. "She must be in the bedroom."

The euphoria filling Helen faded quickly and she held tight to his hand as they walked to the bedroom.

"Julia?" Jack said again.

Helen reached in and flipped the light switch, too full of concern to worry about waking Grace. The bed was empty. So was the crib.

"Jack!"

"Julia!" he shouted, running toward the kitchen.

Helen's entire body trembled as fear clutched her. "Jack, where are they? Where's Grace?"

He ran to the bathroom and threw open the door. "Don't panic. Something must have come up. At the diner. Julia must have taken Grace with her."

Struggling to breathe, Helen grabbed the back of the chair as fear fully engulfed her. "Her purse, Jack. Julia's purse. It's on the floor by the couch. She wouldn't have left without her purse." Her worst fears had come to life. She fell against the chair, her legs unable to hold her up as the terror became too great to combat. "They found me. They found me and they have Grace."

Jack caught her before she completely crumpled onto the floor. "Helen, honey, what are you talking about? No one has Grace. She's with Julia. Someone must have come and got them."

She pushed him away and stumbled backward, up against the chair. Then shot forward and paced the floor. "Someone got them all right. The Outfit. The Outfit has them."

He reached out to take ahold of her, but she batted his hands away. "The Outfit?"

"Yes, the Outfit. The mob. Gangsters. The reason my family was killed back in Chicago."

The concern that had overcome him upon finding the apartment dark turned into cold dread. "The Chicago Outfit killed your family? I thought your family died in a fire?"

"There was no fire." She stormed past him, then spun around. "There were tommy guns. I ran and hid. Stayed hidden. But then I had to bring Grace here. To her father. She wasn't safe with me. They wouldn't stop until they found me. No matter where I went." Tears streamed down her face. "They have Grace, Jack! I know they do."

He grabbed her and pulled her against him. "Hush, now. We'll find her." She had to be imagining things. Had to have drunk too much champagne. "We'll find her."

"Where? How?"

He wasn't sure where or how, but he would find

Grace. Releasing his arms from around her, he grabbed her hand. "Come on."

She didn't ask where, just ran beside him out of the apartment, down the stairs and to the car. Once there, he started the car.

"I knew they'd find me." Her voice was shaky and tears trickled down her cheeks.

"Honey," he said softly. "The mob isn't looking for you."

"Yes, they are. They are!"

He held his silence. There would be no convincing her, but the Outfit wouldn't have taken Grace, there was no money in that, and that's what they were after. That's why they'd opened the theater.

It had to be someone else. He knew Julia. She'd have put up a fight against a stranger entering the apartment. Whoever it had been, she'd known them.

He backed up the car and then swung it around, headed out of the parking lot.

Helen grabbed his arm. "We can't go to the police. They'll be in on it."

He hadn't been planning on going to the police. There was no need. He had a gut feeling of who had been here, who Julia had left with.

"Where are we going?"

"The studio."

"The studio? The Outfit wouldn't go there."

"The Outfit doesn't have Grace."

"Yes, they do! They are after me, Jack. I'm not lying."

A shiver rippled his spine. "The Chicago Outfit?"

"Yes!" She grabbed her forehead. "Oh… Why did I let it come to this? They have her. They have Grace."

* * *

"No," he said. "*They* don't. But you are right, about not going to the police, because there's no law against taking your own child."

"What?"

"It's Joe," he said. Had to be. Suddenly, as if Helen's fear was contagious, his own spiked, and he realized just how much Grace and Helen had come to mean to him. How he didn't want to live without them. How, right now, he hated the idea that Grace belonged to Joe. He'd never been torn like this before. Torn between loving his brother, and Helen and Grace.

"Joe? Why would you say that? He doesn't even know about Grace."

"Yes, he does. He called. I told him."

"When?"

Remorse coated everything else churning inside him. "A while ago."

"A while?" she snapped. "How long is *a while*? Days? Weeks?" She slapped his arm. "When were you going to tell me?"

She was mad. He didn't blame her, but he wasn't the only one who'd kept secrets. "I don't know. When were you going to tell me about the Outfit?"

"That's different. I couldn't tell you. If your brother had been here when I arrived, I would already be gone."

"To where?"

"I don't know. Anywhere." She slapped her thighs with both hands. "I should never have stayed here. Should have—"

"Should have what?" The tires of the car squealed as he steered into the corner. Faster than he should have because he was angry. This was just like Joe. Showing up out of the blue, just like everything else. It was always on his time. What he needed and when with no thought to anyone else.

She grabbed the dashboard, holding on as the car fishtailed while making the corner. "It doesn't matter. But you should have told me about Joe."

He stomped on the gas and kept his eyes on the road. The empty road. The street lights shone, but only on empty spaces. "There's nothing you can do about Joe. Nothing either of us can do."

"You're sure it's him? That he has Grace?"

"Yes, I'm sure." He pushed a heavy sigh out of his lungs. Her family may have been murdered by the mob, that happened to innocent bystanders, and his heart ached for her loss, but the mob had nothing to do with this. "Joe said he was going to get things together and come home. To California."

She didn't say anything more. But he could hear her breathing. Or feel it maybe. Damn it. The best night of his life was just like all the other performances he'd experienced. Outshone by his brother. He hated feeling this way, but couldn't help it. He'd wanted this one. Wanted it to be his. In fact, he wanted it all. Everything he'd had the past few weeks, including her and Grace.

Like everything else, for as long as he could remember, Joe had stepped in and ruined it for him.

The studio was only a block away, and just as he expected, the lights were on. Big ones. The enclosed lot's floodlights. No one would have accidently left those on.

That was Joe's favorite place. The outdoor lot. He'd slept out there. More than once. In a prop bed or on the ground, Joe didn't care. Said it reminded him of the old days, traveling from town to town, and that he loved waking up there, looking at all he'd accomplished since then.

Jack pulled into the lot and cut the car engine. They both threw open their doors and jumped out. Julia's diner was dark, and just as he'd expected, the studio door was unlocked.

He held the door handle, but didn't push it open. Letting go, he turned, faced her. They'd shared so much lately, so many wonderful things, he wanted the air clean between them when she met Joe.

He took ahold of her hand, and was relieved that she didn't pull it way. "I have no idea what Joe's plans are, what his thoughts are, but you, and Grace, are my first concern. I'll always be here for you, and her, in whatever capacity you want that to be. We can look into your family, find out what happened."

Her fingers folded around his, held on tighter as she shook her head. "I know what happened. The restaurant we were at was raided. Tommy guns blasted bullets in every direction."

The honesty, and pain, in her eyes had him pulling her close. Hugging her tightly. Her trauma was real, he fully believed what she said, and could understand her fear and her pain. It angered him that she'd endured so much. He didn't have the heart to tell her that a random raid in Chicago didn't have anything to do with this situation. "I'm sorry, honey, so very sorry."

She leaned back, looked up at him. "They must have followed me here."

She was convinced of that, despite all he'd already said. "No, Helen, they didn't. Joe is here. Here to collect Grace. This is how he works. Knowing that, I spoke with Walter Russell to see if there is anything legal I can do in order for you to keep Grace. I know how much you love her. How well you've cared for her." The truth tore at him. "But there's not. Joe is Grace's father, and there is nothing that can be done. He's the only one who can legally put her in someone else's custody."

She looked away and blinked several times before turning back to him. "I know that, Jack." She swallowed and pinched her lips together as a single tear trickled down her cheek. "I never even dared hope that I could stay with Grace forever. What I told you is true. The Outfit is looking for me, and won't stop until they find me. Grace would never be safe. You will never be safe as long as I'm around."

She buried her face in his chest. "I thought I could escape, but I can't. It's who I am."

He was torn in two, needing to find Grace and Joe, yet wanting to push that aside so he could make her understand she was wrong. That what had happened in Chicago no longer affected her. He kissed the top of her head. "We'll figure it out. Figure something out." The Outfit couldn't be after her. Not her. Someone who wouldn't hurt a flea.

He'd just have to prove that to her, and had the connections to do so. The Outfit members here would be able to confirm he was right. He'd contact them once they found Grace.

Damn it, Joe. Once again, his timing was impeccable when it came to ruining everything.

Jack pushed out another sigh, and dropped one arm. With the other one still around her, he pushed open the door.

Chapter Sixteen

Without switching on a light, Jack led her down the hallway, past his office. He knew the way. Had walked it a million times. This time, the wood beneath his feet felt like a plank, the door ahead a whitecapped rolling ocean. She believed what she'd told him, but he didn't. The part about her not being able to stay with Grace forever. She'd taken care of her since she'd been born, and loved her as if Grace was her own child.

That's also what angered him the most right now. There was nothing he could do about it. Joe couldn't stay in California. The sockdolager of his affair had calmed down, but letting him come back would never happen. The Wagner brothers would never stand for that.

They reached the door to the lot. He gave Helen's shoulder a tight squeeze before opening the door, and stepping through it.

The lot had been cleaned up and put in order the day after filming had ended, and it took him a moment to see what was out of place.

His chair. It was in the center of the lot. A man was

sitting in it, but it wasn't Joe. This guy was older with black-and-gray hair.

Helen gasped and then shot past him. Storming toward the man.

"Where is she, Uncle Vinnie? Where's Grace?"

Jack leaped forward. "Uncle Vinnie?" he asked, nearly jogging to keep up with her.

"I told you it was the Outfit. And that they wouldn't quit looking until they found me."

It wasn't that he hadn't believed her, he just hadn't thought it possible. Or that he'd heard correctly. "He's your uncle?"

"Yes," she hissed.

"Grace is fine." Julia, pushing the buggy, walked out from under the awning. She waved a hand toward two men following her. "These torpedoes stormed into your apartment before I could stop them, but I haven't let Grace out of my sight. Haven't let anyone touch her."

The men were big, burly and beefy. At this moment, Jack wished he was bigger, stronger or had a gun or knife, something he could use to protect his family. His thoughts shifted as a shiver rippled his spine when the two men emerged fully into the light. They were the same two that had visited him in his office, telling him to bring Helen to the party.

"What the hell is going on here?" he asked.

"They have nothing to do with this!" Helen shouted at the man in his chair. "None of them. Let them go. It's only me you want."

Jack grabbed her arm, forcing her to stop moving toward the man while he shot glances at the torpedoes and then the top dog. "She's not going anywhere." He might not be the strongest man on earth, but would fight to the death to keep her from being hurt, from being taken.

"Hello, Mr. McCarney," the top dog said. "I really enjoyed your movie at our new theater this evening. Got a real hit on your hands. Our hands."

Helen stiffened and then shook her head. "You own the new theater?"

"Ask Jack," the gangster said. "He knows."

It nearly gutted him, having her think he'd kept another secret from her. Jack nodded. "The Outfit—the Chicago Outfit—owns the State theater."

"When were you going to tell me that?"

"I didn't think it mattered." Because why would it have? He hadn't known about her connection with the Outfit, hadn't known his connection to them could affect her. Now he could, and feared they could take her away from him. "You can have the film," he told the gangster. He'd not only fight to the death, he'd give up all he had for her. For Grace. "I'll sign over the copyrights. In exchange for Helen."

"No," Helen said, pulling her arm out of his. "He won't. I won't let him."

"You've changed, Helen," the gangster said, looking directly at her. "I noticed that a few weeks ago, when I saw you dancing with Jack. Your father would be proud, he was always afraid you weren't tough enough. I told him you were, right from the night you were born. So tiny none of us thought you'd live to see the light of day. But you did. Surprised us all."

"Tough enough for what?" she asked, her voice icy. "To watch them die?"

"No," the man said. "You should know that the

North End Gang paid for that raid. Paid for killing your brother, your father, your mother—my sister."

The gangster's tone filled Jack with ice, and he wrapped an arm around Helen.

She stiffened and glared straight ahead, at the gangster. Her uncle.

"Happy to know my family is full of bootleggers, thugs and murderers?" She let out a guttural sound. "Well, I'm not. I never wanted to be a part of it and I still don't."

"I know that, and I blame my sister for that, for keeping you sheltered away." The gangster climbed off the chair. "That's why I let you live above Amery's Grocery, because being locked away is all you'd ever known."

"You knew where I was the entire time?" Her voice was laced with scorn.

"Of course I did. You're my niece."

She shook her head. "And then you followed me. Followed me here."

He shook his head. "I didn't, but my men did. It's my job to protect you. Protect every member of my family."

"Like you did my mother, my father, my brother?" She shook her head. "I don't want your protection."

"Want it or not, you have it. You've always had it. You're a member of the family."

Jack stepped forward, in front of Helen. "I'll give you the studio, all the movies, everything. Just let her be." Nothing. No movies, no studios, no money, was worth more than her. "Right now. I'll turn it all over to you."

Helen tried to push him aside. "No, he won't. You've found me. Leave Jack out of this."

The gangster shook his head again. "I can't do that, Helen. He's now as much a part of this as you are."

Helen felt as if she was being ripped apart. She'd known this day would happen, that Uncle Vinnie would find her. Wouldn't stop until he did. That's how the family was. Relentless. There was no escaping them. But she couldn't let them get their claws into Jack. Wouldn't let them.

"Yes, you can," she argued. "I'll go back to Chicago. Do whatever you want."

"Leave Jack and that little baby?"

She kept her head up, her eyes forward. If she looked at Jack her resolve would disappear. "Yes."

Pain clutched her heart as Uncle Vinnie nodded, yet she forced herself not to react outwardly. Inside, the agony was like none other.

Uncle Vinnie took a step closer. She forced her feet to remain still and her expression stoic. She wasn't afraid of him. All that mattered was that he let Jack and Grace go. "I could make you come back, Helen, just like I could have made you move out of that apartment above the grocer. And now that I can see how strong you've become, I know just how much of an asset you would be to the family."

Jack pulled her against him. "Why are you doing this to her? I told you I'd give you everything I have, what more do you want?"

She was spent, worn out, but wouldn't let Uncle Vinnie ruin Jack's life. She pushed at his chest, separated herself from him and stepped toward her uncle. "If I'm part of this—" Her lips burned as she spit out, "*family*, then I should have some say in what happens."

Uncle Vinnie lifted a brow. "I'm listening," he said.

"The Outfit leaves Jack out of this. Leaves him alone, and Grace."

"We can't, Helen. Jack signed a contract with the theater before you ever left Chicago." Uncle Vinnie looked at Jack. "A contract he won't want to break. It would be the end of his studio."

She knew the truth of that even before she glanced toward Jack.

"It doesn't matter," Jack said. "I'll break it."

This was worse than her worst nightmare. Tears once again burned her cheeks. "I can't let you do that, Jack. I can't."

"Yes, you can."

"No, she can't," Uncle Vinnie said. "I won't let her."

Something snapped inside her. Helen took a step forward. "I don't take orders from you."

The hint of a smile that appeared on Uncle Vinnie's face surprised her. It wasn't menacing.

"I was going to do that, force you to obey, to come back to Chicago with me, but I discovered something I hadn't expected to."

He glanced down at the floor, and shook his head, before looking at her again. "No matter how much you hate me, I still love you. Still love the little girl who used to sit on my lap and dig peppermint candies out of my shirt pocket."

Helen's insides jolted. She shook her head, not wanting to remember that, but she did. Her throat burned and her eyes stung as memories of how at one time in her life, she had loved him.

"You remember that, don't you?"

She shook her head again, but couldn't find her voice to deny it.

"When I saw you on the dance floor with Jack, I saw that little girl again. With her eyes all lit up and her smile so big and bright." He took a step closer. "I saw your mother, too. She was my only sister. We crossed the ocean together. As children. Landed in New York with nothing but the clothes on our backs. Our parents died on that voyage to America, and as soon as we stepped foot on solid ground, I swore that I'd protect her with my every being, and I failed."

She didn't want to hear any of this. To know any of this. Tears burned her cheeks as a sob wracked her insides.

"What I saw also made me realize that she wouldn't have wanted, *didn't* want, this life for you. She only ever wanted you to be happy. And so do I."

He looked around, pausing at every person before looking back at her. "The only people who know you are my niece and are alive are Karen and the people right here. You, Jack, Miss Shaw, Dicer-Dan and Bronco. And me. If that changes, I'll know someone in this room talked."

Her insides shook, but she kept her eyes on him and her chin up.

"The North End Gang believes you died, that you were injured in the raid and died later, as do most of the family. I've let them believe that, because they also believe if you hadn't died, I would have found you, brought you home." His round chest heaved as he took in air. "I should, but I won't. There's only one thing I can do now."

Jack's arm was around her and Helen wanted to

lean into his strength, but refused. She was done being afraid. Done being intimidated.

Uncle Vinnie gave her a slight nod, as if recognizing her inner thoughts.

"From this day forward, you will forget I'm your uncle. That we ever knew each other. You will forget what happened in Chicago. Never speak a word of any of it, of your family, ever again."

Helen's spine tingled as confusion worked its way through her. She opened her mouth, but Uncle Vinnie held up his hand.

"And you, Jack, will also forget you ever met me. Never speak of it. You will go on working with the theater, showing your films, knowing your connection to Helen will provide no special benefits." He shifted his stance slightly, glanced toward Julia. "Miss Shaw, I believe we already have an understanding."

"We do," Julia replied.

Turning back to her, Uncle Vinnie gestured toward his men. "Dan and Bronco will go to their graves with deeper secrets than this." He stepped forward. "So will I."

Helen braced herself, not sure if what she thought was happening, was happening. It seemed so surreal. Unbelievable. He couldn't be releasing her from having any connections to the Outfit. That never happened. Never.

He grasped her shoulders and then kissed her cheek. "Godspeed, Helen."

She couldn't move, could barely breathe or comprehend all that had happened, was happening, even as Uncle Vinnie gestured for his men to follow him out the door.

Jack pulled her closer to him. She glanced up at him, but didn't say a word. She was afraid to. Afraid she was dreaming. That this wasn't real. If she spoke, moved, she'd wake up and be living in a nightmare all over again.

It was Julia that broke the silence. "I'd appreciate a ride back to your place so I can get my purse and car."

Something awakened inside Helen and she hurried toward the buggy Julia pushed forward. Grace was asleep but Helen still picked her up, held her close. Jack wrapped his arms around her and they stood there for a moment. She didn't know what to think, but was overly grateful Grace was fine. They were all fine. On the outside. Inside, she was confused, and suspicious.

"I'm so sorry," she whispered.

"For what?" Julia asked. "This hasn't been anything but a quiet Saturday night for me. How about you, Jack?"

Helen felt the air he drew in before he released her.

"It wasn't a quiet Saturday night for me," he said.

A tremble raced over Helen.

"It was the best night of my life." His hand settled on her back. "And I'm ready to go home."

"The premiere was a hit?" Julia asked as she started pushing the buggy toward the door.

"A sensational hit," Jack said. "Better than I'd hoped."

The warmth of his palm penetrated Helen's bare skin of her back as the pressure of his hand encouraged her to follow Julia.

"I'm excited to see the theater. Plan on going tomorrow night with the tickets you gave me and the girls," Julia said.

"Shirley was there," Jack said, "with Walter…"

The two of them continued talking as if nothing other than the premiere had happened tonight. Helen held her silence. Her thoughts were too thick to speak over. It couldn't end this way. Years of hiding, of running. She couldn't forget. Pretend she wasn't who she was.

She stopped in the hallway, watching as Jack turned on the light and Julia pushed the buggy into his office. But she had already been pretending. For weeks. For years.

"Want me to carry Grace?" Jack asked.

Hugging the baby closer, she shook her head. "No. No." She'd never be able to forget tonight. Forget the terror of thinking something had happened to Grace.

Jack and Julia couldn't forget, either. They were pretending. Talking about the premiere as if nothing had happened in the hours between then and now. But things had happened.

At the apartment, Julia collected her purse, and then crossed the room to where Helen stood, Grace still sleeping in her arms.

"I'll watch her anytime," Julia said. Then leaning closer, she kissed Grace before whispering, "You have an amazing man who loves you. That's all you need to think about."

Helen turned, watching Julia walk to the door. Jack stood there, looking at her.

"I'll walk Julia down to her car. You'll be all right?"

"I'll be fine." Oddly enough, she was fine. Helen carried Grace into the bedroom and laid her in the crib. Jack couldn't love her, but she did love him. And they both loved Grace.

A heaviness settled in her chest as she stood there. She tried to push it out in a sigh, but it wouldn't leave. She'd thought her worse fears had come to light tonight, but in truth, they hadn't. It could have been Joe who had taken Grace tonight. She'd rather face Uncle Vinnie a hundred times over than facing that.

"Is she still sleeping?"

"Yes." She drew in a deep breath before turning around.

Jack stood in the doorway, one hand on the frame.

"How are you doing?"

Looking at him, still dressed in his tuxedo, a warmth spread inside her. There was one thing she hadn't been pretending. Him. She loved him. Loved him in a way she'd never imagined. Deeply. Wholly. Completely. "I'm fine."

He lifted a brow.

She took a step forward. Then another. And another. Didn't stop until they were face-to-face. "Is it past midnight?"

He frowned slightly. "Yes."

She'd known that, but was testing the waters. She was going to forget about Uncle Vinnie. Forget about Joe. Jack had just released a movie that was going to take the world by storm. She was going to take the world too in this moment. The one she wanted.

Jack trailed a knuckle over her cheek. "Why?"

She looped her arms around his neck. "Because I still feel like Cinderella."

His smile was all she needed. She pressed her lips against his.

Within seconds, she knew this kiss was different than all their others. There was an immediate desperation to it, a need neither of them had let be released before. They kissed several times, long ones, short ones, as if neither of them could get enough.

His hands roamed her back, her sides, all the while keeping her pressed tightly against him. Her breasts tingled and an amazing heat pooled deep inside her.

Jack was still smiling when he broke the kiss. "I've fallen in love with you." He sounded breathless, and happy.

She believed him. Truly believed him. "I've fallen in love with you, too."

His eyes never left hers. "I don't want to live without you, not even for a day."

"I feel the same way."

He glanced toward Grace's crib. She knew what he was thinking and grasped the back of his neck, pulled his head downward. "We'll cross that bridge when it happens." Sliding her other hand inside his coat, she added, "And not think about it until then."

She kissed him long and slow, drawing it out until she had to break for air.

"I want you, Helen."

"I want you, Jack."

"I mean—"

"I know what you mean." She stepped back, letting her fingers trail along his jawline. "And I know what I mean."

He released her and shrugged out of his tuxedo jacket, eyes locked on her. "You do?" He tossed the coat aside, with no regard as to how it crumpled on the floor.

She pulled the fingers of one glove loose, then tugged it down her arm, loving the way he watched her. The excitement in his eyes doubled that inside her. Finally, when the glove was free, she dropped it onto the floor. "Yes, I do."

Restraint wasn't an option right then. Not for either of them. Clothes were discarded, flung in all directions. Shortly, winded from kissing and undressing, all that was left was her dress, and his pants.

He'd already removed her headband was plucking out the pins from her hair. "Are you afraid?"

"Should I be?"

He ran his fingers through her and then framed her face with both hands. "No."

"Then, I'm not," she answered in all honesty. "I've never been afraid when I'm with you."

"I'll never hurt you, not intentionally."

"I already know that, Jack." To prove her point, she reached up and pulled the off-the-shoulder sleeves down, letting the dress fall along with it. She suddenly felt a bit unsure of what to do next. He took her hand, helped her step over the mass of gold material tangled around her feet.

He pulled her close then, kissing her. Kissing him was even better with their skin touching, her breasts against his chest. She could feel other things too, the hard bulge inside his pants, pressing against her bare stomach.

She grew clumsy when he spun around and pulled her toward the bed. Their legs tangled, and by the time they landed on the bed, their arms and legs were entwined.

"Well, that didn't go as planned," he said, laughing.

"Good thing the bed is as big as it is," she giggled, scooting up to rest her head on a pillow.

He placed a hand on each side of her and slowly made his way upward, kissing her stomach, her breasts, her neck. By the time his lips found hers, she was throbbing in places she didn't know could throb.

She should have known Jack would be as thorough in this as he was in everything else. He didn't miss a detail. There wasn't a part of her that he left untouched. She explored him too, all over. Enthralled by how muscular he was, how sleek his skin felt beneath her hands.

When he positioned himself over her, and the tip of his erection rubbed against her entrance, she sucked in a breath and planted a hand on his chest.

"Are you sure?" he asked, leaning down to kiss her forehead.

"Yes." She was ready, more than sure. "Are you?"

"I've been dreaming about this for weeks."

She lifted her hips, pressing herself harder against him. "Me, too." She'd never have admitted that to anyone else, how she'd thought about doing this with him, but she had. Numerous times.

He used a hand to slowly inch his way inside her, then out again, several times. Each time she wanted more. When that happened, when he slid deep inside her, she gasped, not sure if it was caused by the quick snap of pain or the pleasure that instantly followed.

"Does it hurt?" he asked, stock still.

"No, yes, it did for a second, but not now." She hooked her heels behind his legs. "Don't stop. Not now. Not ever."

From that point on, it was as if he transported her to some magical world, much like the characters in his films. They were on a journey together, each time he thrust inside her, each time she rose up to meet him, they reached another milestone.

The intense cravings inside her were partially satisfied at the same time they kept growing and growing. Pressure built inside her, like a bag stuffed too full. Something would have to give and she had no idea what that might be.

"Are you feeling that, Helen?"

"Yes, yes." She was glad he'd asked. "I don't know what to do."

"You're doing it darling."

He sounded out of breath, yet kept going, kept the pleasure in her building and building.

"But what do I do next?"

"Let it go."

"Let what—" An explosion happened, like a dam bursting, a big one, that released all the pressure and filled her with more euphoria than imaginable.

Jack had gone rigid, and she held on to him, sensing he was experiencing the same thing as her. She clung to him as several miniature little explosions let loose inside her and continued until they slowly, sweetly dissolved. Sinking deep into the mattress, she let her arms fall to her sides, feeling completely spent. And happy.

Oh, so happy.

Jack untangled himself from her and rolled onto his side. Trailing a hand over her ribcage, he kissed the side of one of her perfect and pert breasts. "How are you doing?"

"Wonderful."

He could say the same. Petting, lovemaking, had never been so intense. It was as if her flesh was magical, had put him under a spell that made him feel everything deeper, stronger, longer. The aftermath of his climax was still living inside him, spreading pleasure all the way to his toes.

"And you?" she asked.

"Sorry."

She shot up.

He laughed. Teasing her was nearly as pleasurable as lovemaking. He licked one of her nipples. "Sorry that we hadn't done this long before now."

She fell back down on the bed. "There's a time for teasing, Jack McCarney, and for not teasing."

"I did not know that." He licked her nipple again and then took it between his thumb and finger, rolling it. Could it be possible for him to want her all over again, this soon?

"Yes, you did." She gave out a little moan and then looked at his hand, how he was touching her. "What are you doing?"

It was possible all right. He wanted her all over again. "Teasing you." He pinched her gently. "But can stop if you want."

Her eyes were smoldering when she brought them up to look at him. "No, don't stop. I like your teasing."

Chapter Seventeen

Jack took the steps up to the apartment two at a time. Not even in his wildest dreams could he have imagined the movie would have been this successful. The money had started coming in practically the day after the premiere, and continued to flow, in large amounts. The Broadbents were completely paid off, every one of his crew members, staff and actors, received bonuses they continued to gush about, and he still had more money than he knew what to do with. No, that wasn't true. He knew what to do with it. Had already sent out casting calls for his next movie. The State theater had offered him a contract to host exclusive premieres for his next four films, with an amendment to include the next four after those. Even though the theater was owned by the Outfit, he trusted Helen's uncle enough to take him at his word. Yes, financially they were involved, but Jack knew that would never touch Helen or Grace ever again.

Helen had told him about Chicago, how the North End Gang had been a rival of the Outfit and murdered her family in a raid at a restaurant while the Outfit had been celebrating Vinnie's birthday. True to his word, her uncle hadn't contacted Helen or him again, and Jack hoped it stayed that way. Although Helen acted happy, he could tell her past still bothered her. He was at a loss as to what to do about that, and hoped today's news would give her something else to focus on.

He opened the apartment door, and grinned at the sight of Grace sitting on a blanket in the center of the living room. She'd started sitting up last week, and like everything else, had mastered it almost immediately.

"You're home early today," Helen said, walking out of the kitchen.

She was wearing a blue polka dot dress with an apron tied around her waist, and looked more fetching than any woman on or off screen.

"I haven't even started supper yet," she said, stepping closer.

He hooked her around the waist. "Good, because we have some place to go."

"We do?"

Not only beautiful, she was the best necker on the planet, and he couldn't wait a moment longer to taste her lips. Her response made it hard for him to not carry her into the bedroom. He managed. Somehow.

"We do," he answered as he ended the kiss.

Her hands slipped off his neck. "Where?"

"Get ready and I'll show you."

He loved this about her too, that she was always up for an adventure. Within minutes, they were in the car and driving up the boulevard that was familiar to both of them.

"Are we going to the studio?"

Excitement nearly had him telling her, but he refrained. "You'll see."

"Sometimes you drive me crazy."

"In or out of the bedroom?"

She laughed. "Both."

Unable not to, he reached down and felt his pocket, made sure the little box was still there. He'd carried it around for almost a week now, waiting for the right moment. There had been one thing that kept that moment from happening.

Joe.

There still hadn't been any word from him. His brother could show up at any time and say he was taking Grace to Florida with him, or anywhere else. That would break Helen's heart. Taking Grace away from her.

It hadn't been until this morning, after yet another sleepless night that Jack had decided he was done. Done waiting for Joe to return. Done concentrating on the past, done living his life fulfilling dreams others had started. This was his dream. Helen. Grace. And no one was going to take it away from him.

It felt good to take a stand. Good to focus on what he wanted.

He prayed it was what she wanted, too.

"Where are we going?" Helen asked, twisting to peer out his window of the car as they rolled past the studio.

He shot a glance her way, and lifted a brow.

Pointing out the windshield, she said, "There's nothing out this way except Hollywoodland."

She was right. Nothing but acres and acres up for sale, to those who had enough money. The land wasn't cheap and houses had to be built to specific standards to keep the entire development area riff-raff-free.

He downshifted the Chrysler as he started driving up one of the many hills in the area. The lot he'd picked out was on top of a hill, with mature trees. One of which he'd already picked out a branch of to hang a swing on for Grace.

"What aren't you telling me?"

"You'll see." A couple turns later, he was on the last stretch. "It's right up here."

"What is? There aren't even any houses up here."

"No, there's not. Some of those we just drove by are nice, though, don't you think?"

She shifted Grace onto her other knee. "Nice? They are gorgeous. Especially that white brick one. Did you notice the arched porch over the front door?"

"Blake Owens built it. He built the State theater."

"I recall that. He does fantastic work."

His smile grew. Blake had already agreed to build their house. The plans were in the backseat. She hadn't noticed that, probably because there was a large stack of papers back there. Copies of his next script. She'd typed them for him.

He slowed and pulled off the road, onto the grass he hired someone to have mowed yesterday. "We're here."

She scanned the area out her window before turning to him. "And where is *here*?"

Giving her a wink, he opened his door. He walked around the car, opened her door and took Grace so she could climb out. "I just bought this lot. Blake Owens is going to build a house on it." He probably should ask her to marry him first, but was saving that for this evening. Julia had agreed to be at the apartment in an hour, to watch Grace, and he was going to take Helen out to dinner downtown. Now that he'd made up his mind that today was the day, the ring was burning a hole in his pocket.

"A house?" Her eyes sparked as she laid her hand on his.

"Yes, a house. The plans are on the backseat. I'll show you them, but first, come take a walk with me. Let me show you it."

They walked the entire perimeter of the lot. He showed her the tree that would be perfect for a swing, and told her how the driveway would make a horseshoe in front of the house.

She was quiet, solemn, when they arrived back at the car.

"You don't like it?" he asked.

She shook her head. "No, it's beautiful. I can imagine the house just as you described it."

"Then what's wrong?"

"Nothing's wrong." She stretched on her toes and kissed his cheek.

The smile on her lips was strained, and there was no shine in her eyes. He considered asking her to marry him then instead of later, but sensed that wouldn't solve what bothered her. He lifted her chin. "I can tell something is."

Helen had to swallow against the burning in the back of her throat. The land he'd purchased was lovely, and she could imagine a house there just like he described, right down to the swing in the backyard. The past few weeks of falling to sleep in his arms, and waking to the feel of his hands roaming over her had been so wonderful. Waking up to that delight had set the tone for every day that followed, and the nights.

Even now, the simplest touch of his finger beneath her chin thrilled her, and she hated the idea that she had to end it.

She'd tried. Tried harder than she'd ever tried before, but even though Uncle Vinnie hadn't contacted her, she knew he was out there. Despite what he said, she was still his niece. Would always be his niece, and at some point, that was going to affect Jack.

"Tell me what it is," he said.

Helen pushed out the air burning her lungs. Forgetting who she was, who she'd been born as, wasn't possible. She'd tried but finally had to admit that was as bad as hiding. More so because this time, she was hiding inside herself. "It's nothing, really." She forced her smile to be brighter and kissed his cheek again. "Other than Grace is going to need a bottle soon."

She did that more often than not lately, used Grace as an excuse. Especially to herself. Actually, she'd been doing that since the baby had been born. She loved her, truly, truly did, just as she loved him. That was what made this so hard. Had made it all so hard from the beginning.

History, the past she couldn't forget, couldn't erase, was a heavy burden, but it was her burden. Not his, and not Grace's. Uncle Vinnie might have released her from the family, but if anyone ever found out her connections to them, the North End Gang, or some other family competing with the Outfit could and would use that to their advantage. And she couldn't risk that involving Grace or Jack. She wouldn't.

Jack opened the car door, and she climbed in, settling Grace on her lap. She tried to sound happy on the ride home, talked about the house he would have built, but her acting ability failed her today.

Jack remained unusually quiet all the way home, and the heavy sigh he let out as they arrived at their apartment door caused a solid knot of guilt to form in her stomach.

She needed to tell him the truth. That she couldn't pretend that the past wouldn't catch up with her. At some point. At some time. "Jack, I—"

He shook his head. "I gave Julia a key." He nodded his head toward the door. "She's inside waiting."

"Why?" Concern flashed inside her. "Is something wrong?"

"No." He grew serious, perhaps even a bit unsure. "I asked her to watch Grace so I could take you out for dinner. Just the two of us. We have some things we need to discuss."

They did. Whether she was ready for it to happen or not. "All right."

He gave a slight nod, then twisted the doorknob.

She walked in first, and her feet slid to a stop, gluing themselves to the floor. Julia was there. So was a man. Even if she hadn't seen pictures of him, Helen would have known it was Joe. She tightened her hold on Grace and willed herself not to turn around and run back out the door.

"Jack!" Joe had stood and walked around the coffee table. Coming toward them. "It's good to see you, little brother. So good."

Jack walked around her and the brothers hugged, slapped each other on the back.

"This must be my daughter, Grace," Joe said.

"Yes, this is Grace," Jack said. "And Helen."

Helen held her breath as a newfound fear filled her. This was the bridge she'd never wanted to cross, but had to, despite the fast-flowing water beneath. Rapids. White-water rapids. And rocks. Cliffs. Huge cliffs.

"Helen?"

She looked up at Jack.

"Joe asked if he could hold Grace."

No. Wishing she could, but knowing she couldn't deny Joe anything when it came to Grace, she handed Grace to Joe.

"She looks like me, don't you think?" Joe was holding Grace at arm's length, both hands around her waist. "You too, little brother, she looks like you did when you were little."

"I wouldn't remember that," Jack said. "Careful, she might think you're going to drop her, holding her out like that."

"Oh." Joe brought Grace up against his chest, and stiffly patted her back while turning his head far to the side. "I'm not very good at this. Never held a baby before."

"Just imagine you're acting." There wasn't necessarily scorn in Julia's voice, more like disappointment. Same with the look she cast toward Jack. "I'm assuming you don't need me to watch her this evening."

"No." There was serious disappointment in his tone.

"I'll be going then." She lifted her purse off the floor before rising from the chair. "Guess I'll be seeing you around, Joe."

"No, you won't. My train ticket is round-trip. California is no longer for me." Joe sat in an armchair and bounced Grace on his knee. "But it was good seeing you, Julia."

"You, too." Julia stopped near Jack on her way to the door. "I'll see you two later."

Jack nodded.

When Julia's eyes settled on her, Helen almost burst into tears. There were no words needed. None that could be said, either. Julia shook her head then gave her a tight hug before she walked out the door.

Helen couldn't stand still any longer. It wasn't doing her any good. "I—I have a meatloaf ready to go in the oven."

Jack took ahold of her arm.

She shook her head and walked into the kitchen. There, she grasped ahold of the back of one chair and took a few moments to breathe. Just breathe. She was so sick and tired of this life she'd been given.

"How long are you staying?" she heard Jack ask Joe.

"Don't know. Not long," Joe replied. "Heard about your latest movie. A real hit. Starring Boyd."

"And Wes Jenkins."

"Wes. How's he doing? I always liked him."

"Good. He's doing good."

Helen released the chair and lit the oven before going to the refrigerator for the meatloaf she'd assembled that afternoon. The potatoes were ready to bake too, and the cucumber salad was in a bowl, chilling. If she hadn't been so efficient earlier, she'd have more to do right now. She liked having everything ready when Jack got home, but right now, something to occupy her would be heaven sent.

"Newton still directing for you?" Joe asked.

"Yes."

While they talked about a few other crew members, she took a bottle of milk out of the refrigerator and put it in a pan of boiling water to warm. Grace would be getting hungry soon, and would need to be changed.

She was checking the milk temperature by dribbling some on her wrist when Jack said something that stopped her in her tracks. Holding her breath, she waited for Joe's answer. Waited until her ears started ringing.

"Joe, I said I don't think Grace should go to South Carolina with you," Jack repeated.

"I heard what you said, Jack," Joe answered. "And I can't say I disagree with you."

Helen's heart did a somersault. She spun around and hurried to the doorway, not wanting to miss a word.

Grace might have noticed her or the bottle, either way, she began to whimper and squirm.

Joe glanced her way, then held Grace up.

Helen collected Grace and kissed her before sitting down on the couch to feed her.

"You've been taking care of her since she was born?" Joe asked.

He looked a lot like his picture, except thinner, his cheeks more prominent. Far thinner than Jack, that was for sure, and not nearly as handsome.

"Yes," she said. "I met Vera shortly before Grace was born."

Joe nodded and planted his elbows on his knees. "Looks like you've done a good job with her."

"Helen's done an excellent job of taking care of Grace," Jack said, leveling a serious stare at his brother. "She couldn't have better care. Not from anyone."

"Jack's done a lot for her, too," Helen said. "He's provided everything Grace has needed. Food, clothes, furniture, toys, everything."

"I knew you would," Joe said. "That's why I didn't

rush right out here. You were the youngest, yet the one everyone else depended on." He huffed out a chuckle. "Remember how you used to steal eggs?"

"We used to steal eggs," Jack corrected.

"Yes, I was along many times, but there were others, when the folks and I would be practicing our lines and you'd be nowhere in sight. Later, we'd discover it was because you'd been out finding supper so we could eat after performing that night."

"You were the star of the family. Not me."

There was no animosity in Jack's tone, or on his face. Helen glanced at Joe, who was looking down at the floor.

Jack leaned back in his chair. "I need you to think about what I'm about to say, Joe. Think long and hard because I'm being dead serious."

Joe didn't look up, but nodded, and Helen held her breath. She had no idea what Jack was about to say, but had never seen him so stone-faced. "Grace is a baby, and babies need constant care. I can say that from experience, having lived with one for well over two months. Don't get me wrong, Grace is a good baby, but I believe most of that is because of the care Helen gives her."

Helen wanted to add *and you*, but because she wasn't sure what Jack would say next, she held her silence.

"It's not just care," he said. "It's love. Babies need to be loved. Not just to fix bottles and change diapers, but in the middle of the night when they are fussy, teething or just being cranky. That's when they need someone who loves them the most. Some who will walk the floor all night long, no matter how tired they are, and never lose their patience."

Jack's gaze had settled on her, and Helen pressed

her lips together to keep from saying that even those things were a pleasure. He already knew she felt that way. He was trying to make his brother understand all it was going to take in order for him to care for Grace.

"Providing for a child is one thing. Buying them things. Making sure they have clothes and milk." Jack had settled his gaze back on Joe. "If you can't tell me you have that for Grace, right now, today, then I can't let you take her. Won't let you take her."

Helen's heart leaped into her throat. She knew Jack loved Grace, but hadn't expected him to say that. Joe was Grace's father.

"It's for her own good, Joe. Grace's own good," Jack said. "You think about that. Not yourself. Not what you want. But her. What she needs, and will need for years to come."

Joe lifted his head slowly, cautiously. "You'd be willing to keep her?"

Helen bit down on her bottom lip so hard she tasted blood.

"Yes." Jack reached over and laid a hand on her knee. "I am, but not just until you find someone to care for her. It will be forever. When she's old enough, I'll make sure she knows you're her real father, but she'll live with me, because you'll have to consent to me legally adopting her."

Joe rose and walked across the room to the table by the door, and stood there with his back to them for some time.

Helen looked at Jack, and though his smile was meant to reassure her, there was worry in his eyes. Inside her, too. If Joe said no, there was nothing anyone could do.

"I didn't want to have to ask you that, Jack. Didn't want to saddle you with one more of my mistakes. I've done that to you my entire life." Joe turned around and tears glistened in his eyes. "Truth is, I had to get clearance to come here. From a doctor at the sanitarium. I have TB. Almost everyone that worked at the circus did. Living the way we did. In tents. Cold, damp, tents." He shook his head. "I left as soon as I discovered I had it, hoping Vera didn't. She was so healthy then. Full of life."

Helen set the bottle down and clutched Grace close. She'd thought the TB scare was over.

Joe looked at her. "I made sure I didn't breathe on her and I haven't had a coughing spell for over three weeks. The spores live in the lungs and are expelled into the air by coughs. I took the time to learn everything I could about how it's spread before coming here." He turned to Jack. "In truth, I considered not coming, but I had to. I couldn't leave this all on your shoulders, Jack. I've done that too often. Far too often. But you're right about Grace, about caring for her. I don't have what she needs. I'll never have that. I'm told that I'll be able to live outside of a sanitarium someday, but I can't say when, and it wouldn't be fair for me to make promises that I can't keep. Not to Grace, or you."

Jack stood up, and walked to Joe.

Helen could see the concern on his face. Feel it in her heart.

He laid a hand on Joe's shoulder. "Are you getting good care there? Dr. Baine said the best sanitarium in the world is right here, in California."

"I can't live in California, remember?" Joe wiped at his eyes and grinned. "I'm getting good care. It's a good place. Been there over a year now. Actually, I'm a star again. There. I do my juggling shows and magic tricks. Sing and dance when I can. Mainly I teach others. How to act. How to pretend to be strong and brave even when you aren't."

"I bet they love you as much as all your other audiences did," Jack said.

Helen had to wipe her eyes, had to stop the tears from falling, but it was no use, when Jack was hurting, she was hurting.

That pain increased as the brothers hugged. She glanced down at Grace, and then at the brothers again. Jack had overcome so much in his life, yet didn't let it define him. Didn't let it rule him.

It was one of the many things she loved about him.

A tingle made the hair on her arms stand up. Perhaps it was time that she didn't let her past define her, either.

Chapter Eighteen

"**Y**ou did what?" Over the past couple of months, Jack had been flustered by Helen, frustrated, worried, frightened for her safety, but he'd never been mad at something she'd done. Until this moment. He was beyond mad. Furious. So furious he couldn't think straight. "What the hell were you thinking?" He pushed away from his office desk and shot to his feet. "You weren't thinking. Obviously. Because only a dumb Dora—"

"Stop shouting!" She slammed her hand on his desk.

"—would do what you just did!" he finished his statement at the top of his lungs.

"You're going to wake—"

A wail like he'd never heard before emitted from the buggy by the sofa, interrupting Helen.

"Grace!" Glaring at him, she spun around and marched to the buggy, and promptly picked up Grace.

Guilt struck him as the baby, eyes scrunched, sobbed out another wail.

"Are you happy now?" Helen asked, bouncing Grace with one hand while digging a bottle out of her purse with her other. "Waking her? Making her cry?"

Still mad, he waved a hand. "She's probably scared to death over what you did. She was there that night, too." He stormed around the edge of desk. "So was I, and I heard every word!"

"Quit yelling!" Helen shouted over Grace's wails, who wanted nothing to do with the bottle. "Do you want everyone in the studio to hear?"

"I want *you* to hear! Evidently you didn't that night!" Exasperated, he threw his arms in the air. "Are you trying to get yourself bumped off?"

"Of course not!"

"It doesn't sound that way to me!"

In the split second of silence between his shout and another wail from Grace, a knock sounded on the door.

His anger peaked. "Go away!"

Helen glared at him, then shouted, "Come in!"

Grace wailed.

The door opened and Beverly walked in. Holding a single finger in the air and not saying a word, she crossed the room, took Grace and the bottle from Helen, and walked back to the door, out it, closed it behind her.

"Now there's a smart woman!"

If Helen's eyes could have held bullets, he'd be dead right now. Probably would be in a few days after what she'd done.

As if reading his mind, Helen stomped forward. "I did it for you! For Joe!"

He squeezed his temples with one hand. It didn't help collect his mind, but he did lower his voice so no one outside the door could hear. "Did you forget what your uncle said that night? I didn't. Why would you contact him?"

"No, I didn't forget, and I just told you." She heaved out a sigh. "For you and your brother."

"Neither of us need you talking to a mob boss."

She rolled her eyes and then settled a stare on him. "I didn't just go knock on his door."

"I'd hope not." He couldn't believe this. Couldn't believe she'd contacted her uncle. For any reason. In any way. "What did you do? Pick up the phone?"

"No." She crossed her arms.

He tried not to notice how her breasts rose and fell, or how the sparkling blue dress hugged her curves. He should be too mad for that.

"I know how to get a message to someone when I need to."

Her saucy attitude did not impress him. "Oh, you know how, do you?"

"Yes, I do, but I won't tell you, so don't ask."

"I don't want to know!" Frustrated, he grabbed her by both arms. "Damn it, Helen. He wasn't blowing smoke."

"No, he wasn't, but I still had to contact him."

Jack was still mad, so was she, but the sincerity in her tone swirled around his heart. He loved her so much, and the danger she'd just put herself in petrified him. That's why he was so mad. He was about to have everything. Her, Grace. They were everything to him. "No, you didn't, honey. You didn't have to do anything."

She broke away from him and spun around. "Yes, I did."

He drew in a deep breath and tried to get his head around the fact she'd contacted her uncle, and what they could do about it. Not much until he knew more details. "Exactly what do you expect him to do?"

She walked over and sat down on the sofa. "Exactly what I asked him to do. You just have to make sure Joe doesn't leave town."

Not understanding why she'd want that, he walked to the sofa and knelt down in front of her. "Joe and I went to see Walter this morning. He's drawing up custody papers for Grace. Forever. Joe can't care for her, but we can. That's what's best for Grace. Isn't that what you want?"

"Yes, it is, and I also want what is best for you. That's why I contacted Uncle Vinnie."

There was so much emotion in her face, in her voice, his heart ached for her. He laid a hand on her cheek. "You are what's best for me. I love you, Helen."

She closed her eyes and leaned against his palm. "I love you too, Jack. So very, very much."

He had to let her know they'd get through this, somehow, together. The ring was still in his pocket. A pale blue sapphire surrounded by diamonds. He'd wanted it to be romantic, which this wasn't, considering they were still in the middle of an argument, but they were no longer shouting at each other. He stuck his hand in his pocket and wrapped his fingers around the jeweler's box.

"I not only love you, Helen, I need you. Grace needs you."

She opened her eyes, looked at him with such sweet sorrow, his insides sank. All the times he'd blamed Joe for being selfish were nothing compared to what he was doing right now. She'd contacted her uncle because of him. The dangers of that were real, but that hadn't stopped her. All because she loved him. Loved him beyond all else.

Something dawned on him them. He loved her just as much. Had anyone else delivered Grace to his office, he'd have kept the baby and sent them on their way. He hadn't, because from the moment he'd laid eyes on her, he'd known she was different. Special. Unique.

"I want you to know that Grace isn't the reason I love you, Helen. The reason I need you." Keeping the box enclosed in his palm, he pulled his hand out of his pocket. "I love you for who you are. The most beautiful, the most amazing woman I'll ever meet. My life was empty until you came along. I didn't know what was missing until you filled a void deep inside me. An emptiness I didn't know existed. I used to resent the responsibilities I felt toward Joe, and then I met you. And saw how you cared for Grace. A baby you weren't responsible for. One you didn't have to love. But you did. Did wholeheartedly. Through you, I've learned what love truly is, and that all the sacrifices we make are based on that love. Until you, I didn't understand that. I wasn't complete. But I am now."

He lifted the box before her, and opened the lid. Never taking his eyes off hers, he asked, "Helen Hathaway, will you marry me? Make me the happiest man on earth for the rest of my life?"

She pressed the back of one hand over her mouth, covering a half gasp, half sob, sound. Then, with a single tear slipping out of one eye, she grasped both of his wrists.

"I want to marry you, Jack, very much, but…"

"But what? I swear to you, Helen, I will forever

strive to give you the best life possible. Everything you want. Everything you need."

"You already have, Jack." Her eyes glistened as she looked up at him. "You've already given me more than I'll ever want. More than I'll ever need. That's why I contacted Uncle Vinnie. Because you've already given me so much, I wanted to give you something in return."

He still didn't know exactly what she'd asked of her uncle, but had to make her understand. "There is nothing I need Helen."

"Yes, there is. I watched you and Joe last night. You love him." She brushed the pad of her thumb over his lips. "You want what's best for him as much as you want that for Grace. And me."

After the conversation concerning Grace last night, he and Joe had visited for hours, talking about old times. Trials and errors, good times and bad. He'd missed that. Missed Joe. His brother had been all he'd had for years.

"I thought about that all night," she continued. "How the two of you had laughed, how much pride you had in your eyes when you talked about Joe's acting, how famous he'd become. And I saw the sorrow, the frustration when you spoke about him being blackballed."

They had talked about that too, he and Joe, with regrets, but also acceptance. "That's behind us, Helen. Both Joe and I have moved on."

"It's time everyone else does, too." Her chin was up, her eyes serious. "That's why I asked Uncle Vinnie to have Joe's name removed from the blackball list."

An icy shiver rippled through him. He could understand why she would do that. She had a heart of gold, but there were consequences. Major consequences.

"The Outfit can do that. Easily."

His nerves were jittery, his insides swirling. Still holding her wrists, he stood, bringing her off the couch at the same time. "I'm sure they can do that, but your uncle specifically said that I wasn't to expect special treatment. And I don't want special treatment. Not of any kind."

"I know you don't." She dropped her hands to her sides. "But I can't change who I am."

Confused, he shook his head. "Change who you are? What are you talking about?"

Helen drew in a deep breath. It was hard to explain, but inside she fully understood. This was the life she'd been given, and she refused to run from it any longer. Instead, she was going to live despite it. Perhaps even embrace it at times. "You taught me things too, Jack. How truly wonderful life can be. That there are things I can't change, but that I can change the way I looked at them."

He frowned.

She bit her lip. The desire to simply say yes, yes, she would marry him was so strong, but she couldn't do that until he knew what marrying her meant.

After sending a message to Uncle Vinnie, she'd waited for the car she'd known would arrive. A taxi, so it looked like she was merely getting a ride to the studio, which is where she had been dropped off. After speaking with her uncle.

It hadn't been a regular taxi, one that would pick up anyone looking for a ride, and she hadn't been driven directly to the studio.

Uncle Vinnie had been in the backseat of the car.

There had been an inkling of fear inside her, but it had been overshadowed by determination. For Jack, she'd do anything. Including crossing a line she'd never crossed before. This was her life. His life. Their life. And nothing would stop her from making it the best one ever.

Lifting her chin, she nodded. "I'm a member of the Outfit, Jack. The daughter of a gangster. The niece of a mob boss. That will never change. I can't pretend it will or act like it doesn't matter."

He grasped her shoulders. "It doesn't matter."

"Yes, it does," she said honestly. Accepting that had been what she'd struggled with for years. She glanced to the sofa, to the ring box he'd set down. "It's who I am. If you can live with that, I'll marry you."

"Live with that? How?"

"I'm not going to start carrying a tommy gun, or spout my heritage from the rooftops, but I'm not going to ignore it, or forget it, either. We can keep it just between us, and Uncle Vinnie, but if you, or Grace, or anyone else that I love needs protection, they are going to have it. It's like what you said about there being good and bad in everything. It's how we look at it. Well, I'm going to look at the good in my connection with the Outfit. I'm going to *do* good with who I am. I want to do good with it." She laid a hand on his arm. "Not all gangsters are bad. In fact, plenty are rather normal people."

Jack rubbed his chin, then reached down to picked up the ring box.

Her heart shot into her throat, hoping he understood. Hoping he could accept her for who she was, because deep down, she knew she couldn't change. It would be like hiding her entire life, and she wanted to be done with that. Had to be done with that so she could focus on loving him for the rest of her life.

Once again, he held the ring box out in front of her.

"So you will marry me?" she asked.

He laughed. "I thought I was the one doing the asking." The ring he pulled out of box was gorgeous. A pale blue sapphire surrounded by diamonds. As he slid it on her finger, he said, "I don't care who your uncle is. I don't even care if you do shout your heritage from the rooftop or carry a tommy gun, because I love you. Every part of you. Your past, your present and your future. The only thing I do care about, is that I'm your husband."

Stretching on her toes, she brought her lips next to his, where his breath mingled with hers. "I love you, Jack McCarney."

"I love you, too. Now and forever."

"I won't—"

His kiss prevented her from vowing that she wouldn't carry around a tommy gun, and by the time their lips parted, her thoughts had shifted to other things.

His had too. "Did you know that my office door locks?"

Perplexed, she asked, "Why would I need to know that?"

"Because since the moment you walked into this room, I've been thinking about one thing."

The teasing glint in his eyes had grown into a shimmer, one she was very familiar with, but only at night, in their bedroom. A thrill shot clear to her toes, and up again. She bit into her bottom lip as the sensations erupted inside her. "What one thing might that be?"

He kissed the side of her neck, just below her ear. "How about I show you?"

She tilted her head, giving him access to trail kisses along her neckline. "Right now?"

"Yes." He kissed his way up her neck, to her chin. "Unless you're afraid."

He was looking at her now. His eyes glowing. She lifted her chin, looked him straight in the eye. "I'm not afraid of anything."

She wasn't, would never be again, and was more than willing to show him that, over and over again.

Epilogue

"It's a good thing we don't have neighbors yet. They'd turn us in for disturbing the peace."

Helen laughed, and leaned back against Jack, loving the feel of his arms around her. The backyard was full of people, eating, laughing, celebrating. "Julia outdid herself, the food is fabulous."

"If I recall," he said, kissing the top of her shoulder, right where it met her neck, "my wife had a lot to do with all this. Not only the food."

Helen glanced down at the double-tier cake she'd spent most of yesterday baking and frosting, and had just topped off with a single candle. "Grace will only turn one once."

Jack laughed. "From the looks of it, we'll need a bigger house by the time she turns two."

He was referring to the large pile of gaily wrapped presents in the center of the large tent that had been erected and which took up a large portion of the backyard.

"We have six bedrooms," she needlessly reminded him.

He caressed her stomach. "I know. Two down and three to go."

Only the two of them knew that in about seven months they'd once again have a baby in the house. Dr. Baine had confirmed it last week, and Jack hadn't stopped grinning since. She either. It felt so good to think about the future, and know it would be every bit as wonderful as the present.

She rubbed her hands along his arms. Everything about her life was so wonderful. She was not only Jack's wife, and would soon be the mother of his child, she was also his assistant. Had her own office at the studio and worked along with him on every aspect of making movies. Especially the special effects. She was become renowned for them. Jack claimed that all of the praise for a shipwreck scene in their latest movie was because of her work, that she was invaluable to the studio. She was proud of that, but was more proud of being invaluable to him.

"There is only one gift that I'm wondering about." Looking past the tent, to where Joe was holding Grace and showing her what he'd bought her, she asked, "Where on earth are we going to keep a pony?"

"Don't worry about that. Joe already talked to Sherman Majors. You know Sherman, we used stock from his stables in that scene a couple of days ago. He has plenty of room for a pony." Jack twirled her around to face him. "And if the time comes that he doesn't, we'll build a new house, with a stable and even more bedrooms." He kissed the tip of her nose. "Every little girl needs a pony."

The teasing glint in his eyes had her shaking her head. "Joe didn't buy that pony. You did."

He shrugged.

"When were you going to tell me that?"

"No one said Joe bought the pony, he just delivered it."

"Jack McCarney." She playfully slapped his chest. "We will need a bigger house, because I have a feeling every child we have is going to have a pony."

She couldn't resist looking over at where Joe was currently holding Grace in his arms. So much had happened in the last few months. True to his word, Uncle Vinnie had cleared Joe's name and he was no longer blackballed from Hollywood. Joe had even received a job offer from the Wagner brothers, but he had turned them down, saying he'd only ever work for Star's Studios...for his brother. Joe had needed to return to South Carolina for a while, saying that he'd made promises he had to keep. Insisting that he'd broken too many in the past, and wouldn't break any more. But he'd returned in time to be the best man at their wedding.

Looking back up at Jack, Helen grinned as he brought his lips down to meet hers. Jack didn't care who might be looking. She didn't care, either, and returned his kiss with one that promised more to come, later, when they were alone.

A bit breathless afterward, she held on to his hand with both of hers as he led her around the table and into the center of the tent.

"Joe, bring Grace over here to open her other presents!" he shouted.

Others gathered close, stars, crew members, the girls from Julia's diner and many others who were friends of Jack's, and hers, as Joe carried Grace over and set her down near the large pile of presents.

"Oh, ducky!" Beverly exclaimed as Grace toddled toward her presents. "When did she start walking?"

"Last week," Helen answered proudly.

Both she and Jack moved closer to their daughter, just in case she needed them.

Grace stopped near a big present.

"Looks like this is the one she wants to open first," Jack said, poking a hole in the paper so Grace could rip it away.

With giggles of delight, Grace tore away all the colorful paper. Jack opened up the box and lifted out a shiny red pedal car.

"Who is that from?" Joe asked as Jack settled Grace on the seat of her new car.

Helen looked at Jack, and sharing a secret, they both smiled.

"The State theater," Jack answered.

Both of them knew that this, like their wedding present and Christmas presents that had arrived several months ago, were from Uncle Vinnie. No one else would ever know, but they did.

They knew.

* * * * *

*Whilst you're waiting for the next book in the
Brides of the Roaring Twenties miniseries
be sure to find these other great reads
by Lauri Robinson*

Winning the Mail-Order Bride
Married to Claim the Rancher's Heir
In the Sheriff's Protection
Diary of a War Bride